Taming D'Ar

By

Fi Whyms

Copyright © 2022 Fiona Whyms

ISBN: 9798364071323

All rights reserved, including the right to reproduce this book, or portions thereof in any form. No part of this text may be reproduced, transmitted, downloaded, decompiled, reverse engineered, or stored, in any form or introduced into any information storage and retrieval system, in any form or by any means, whether electronic or mechanical without the express written permission of the author.

This is a work of fiction. Names and characters are the product of the author's imagination and any resemblance to actual persons, living or dead, is entirely coincidental.

The views expressed in this work are solely those of the author and do not necessarily reflect the views of the publisher, and the publisher hereby disclaims any responsibility for them.

Chapter One

It is, I think, a fairly common fantasy to imagine living in a French château. For those fortunate or intrepid enough to be able to do so, it is often the realisation of a dream that has been many years in the planning. Then there are others who have done no planning at all, have never dreamed of or fantasised about living in one, but one day, out of the blue, find they are doing just that.

I fall into the latter category. I married a French man, and he inherited a château. When Guy (or D'Artagnan as he is known to me) first swaggered into my life, he trained the crosshairs of his hunting rifle and fired the tranquilising dart with such perfect precision, that I still felt sedated when we were married five months later in Chelsea registry office.

It thereafter quickly became apparent that he did not intend to consume the flesh of his tranquilised prey in London. Oh no: we were going to live in the château he was about to inherit in rural South-West France. Gazing into his dark, liquid eyes as we exchanged our marriage vows, I was blissfully unaware that I would shortly find myself imprisoned in his ancient, dynastic family home.

Because this is the thing: a château will take you prisoner without your knowledge. One minute you are popping out of your chic 95m^2 apartment to dine in a cool new restaurant off the Brompton Road; the next you are trying desperately to convince yourself that yes, you can contemplate leaving this enormous, ancient house with floors of smooth, cool stone, where the limestone walls constantly shed a fine white dust, the plumbing is capricious on a good day, and ninety per cent of the time you only live in fifty of the 600m^2 floor space. You fantasise about living somewhere normal, in a house where you are not constantly worrying about what's going to go wrong next; a house with only one fuse box, for example – that is your current fantasy. Because you have recently discovered the *sixth* fuse box, this one hidden in a small, cobweb-infested cupboard at the very far end of the third cobweb-infested series of adjoining rooms on the second floor of the château. And you have absolutely NO idea what those ten little fuses in the sixth fuse box are connected to, or what electrical malfunction they might be responsible for because, let's face it, unexplained electrical malfunctions have become a daily part of your life.

But when you are honest with yourself, you know your heart has been captured. The thought of waking elsewhere, in a room without four-metre-high ceilings, not opening the thick, rose-gold jacquard curtains, and not seeing the graceful screen of poplar trees across the lawn, verdant in spring and summer, gold and red in autumn, stark in winter; that thought makes you feel melancholy. Not to walk barefoot across the silky, oak floorboards, not to wash your sleepy face in the marble bathroom with the Bisazza mosaiced wall, and then not to wander into the sanctity of your luxuriously carpeted dressing room is inconceivable. The realisation that you cannot conceive of leaving your prison is bittersweet.

Our château has a lot of character; I secretly refer to her as the Duchess. Technically, this is incorrect as a château in French is masculine, but it is unthinkable to me that the she is not feminine. The Duchess positively screams femininity. The transient human form that she occasionally assumes, that I sometimes glimpse fleetingly out of the corner of my eye, is slightly tattered around the edges. The skirts of her antique ballgown are frayed at the edges, strands of hair from the elaborate, coiffured confection on her head have come loose and trail across her creamy breasts that bulge from her tightly laced, lightly stained silk bodice.

The Duchess dates from the early seventeenth century and has been in Guy's family since then. Over the centuries she has endured some modernisation, but at the time D'Artagnan became the latest in the long, unbroken line of the Du Beauchamp dynasty to inherit her, she had avoided any exposure to the new millennium.

We are very new to each other, she and I, and I know that she considers me an unworthy, peasant-class harlot. She adores D'Artagnan, however; I swear I can hear her purring contentedly when he is in the midst of one of his complicated culinary experiments in the kitchen.

Being a tenacious ex-colonial *arriviste*, I have insisted nonetheless that she is coaxed into the twenty-first century, and I am aware that she is pretty furious about it. On one occasion, she took spectacular revenge at my unashamed coercion of her beloved D'Artagnan, as well as at my foolhardy decision to mess about with her innards...

It was a gloriously sunny day in late September, shortly after Gabriela and Camille had finished the renovation of our luxurious bedroom suite. Guy had left early that morning for a meeting in Bordeaux and would not be back until the evening, and I had a hair appointment. If I had listened carefully, I might have heard the Duchess rubbing her slightly gnarled hands together as she plotted.

I put lippy on in the bathroom mirror then stepped into Heaven, my purpose-built dressing room, to view my latest acquisition in the floor-to-ceiling mirrored doors: a pale blue Chloé dress that had arrived a week earlier from Paris, nestling among layers of ivory tissue paper in an ivory box tied with blue ribbon.

It looked stunning against my suntan. I smiled happily and twirled away from the mirror – not too shabby looking for thirty-seven! I glanced at my watch and realised I was going to be late if I didn't get a move on. Just time for a quick pee.

I reached behind the toilet seat and pressed the electric flush on the macerator. Water trickled in to fill the bowl, the bowl filled, then came the normal grinding noise and the contents of the bowl were sucked away at high speed.

The Duchess muttered something evil under her breath.

I washed my hands.

More insistent muttering.

I ignored her, dried my newly manicured nails on the thick white towel and admired them; so pretty!

The mutterings became more audible; insults were discernible.

'No,' I said. 'Not now. I don't care. I have a rendezvous. Goodbye.'

The Duchess growled, an awful, tormented, metallic growl, followed by another, deeper and angrier.

I did not pause, I walked swiftly from the bathroom, around the corner into the bedroom and...
WHOOOOOOOSHHHHHHHHIIIIIIITTTTTALLOVERTHEBATHROOMCEILLINGANDWALLS.
I smiled brightly at my elegant image in the hallway mirror. Not my problem, I said cheerfully to myself. I had repeatedly told D'Artagnan not to shit in that loo; I had told him that I thought that there was a problem with it, and that Gabriela was coming tomorrow to look at it. I had told him to use the loo in the old bathroom, but would he listen? Oh no, would he fuck! He goes *'Bah, ouais ouais.* I know, Nicole, you are always telling me, but it is a new toilet, it is only just installed. How can it be a toilet that we can only pee-pee in, *putain*...?!'

I was most of the way down the stairs, still desperately trying to tell myself that it wasn't up to me to deal with it, that it was up to him to clean the shit off our beautiful – my beautiful – white marble bathroom, before I got to the bottom of the staircase and accepted that the Duchess had won again. Tears pricking my eyes, I phoned and cancelled my hair appointment, apologising profusely for the late notice without going into the gory detail.

I found the Marigolds and a large bottle of bleach under the sink. Very reluctantly, and with a blackened heart, I climbed the staircase again to clean human shit off the walls of our bathroom. I really, really wanted to leave it exactly as it was for all sorts of reasons (starting with the gag reflex), but I knew that if I left it as it was, the grout in the mosaic – and certainly the satin-effect white walls – might be indelibly stained. The whole bathroom would have to be repainted, or worse, regrouted and repainted.

First, I took off the lovely dress.

For those uninitiated in the surprisingly synergistic art of château restoration and sewage management, sometimes a macerator toilet is the only option if you don't want to deface the façade of your fairy-tale residence with a bloody great waste pipe. The list of options for sewage evacuation in the Duchess's case had been short: rip up half her interior to connect the new bathroom to the existing waste pipe, or install a macerator toilet. A macerator toilet evacuates waste at high speed down a narrow pipe, which can be disguised on the façade of your fairy-tale château. Unfortunately, macerators are also the prima ballerinas of the plumbing world; any blockage, and they spew forth their harvest from the nearest and weakest point: in this case, the exquisitely elegant twin-basin unit, imported directly from Bisazza in Italy. Twin fountains of Italian-styled shit. Truly worthy of Fellini.

I met Guy while I was working for a sociopath in London. The sociopath worked in the sociopath-heavy world of investment banking, the dense epicentre of pure, unadulterated narcissism in the City of London. He was VP of an American bank, and I had been employed as his personal assistant for a couple of years before D'Artagnan appeared on the scene.

The sociopath was your common-or-garden type: inbred and public-school educated. His family owned half of England, and he was pretty much born to be an investment banker (that, or a member of the royal family). He could seem exhausting to the outsider, but once you knew how to handle him (he had nanny issues, so it really was textbook stuff) it was pretty straightforward. He paid me exceptionally well, didn't try to sexually harass me (inconceivable to harass Nanny!) and although the hours could sometimes be long, it wasn't stressful work.

He had a fetish for high-end designer fashion, and I was pretty certain he was a closet transvestite. On my third and, I hoped, final interview, after the HR bod had left and it was just the two of us in his office, he made an odd, but in retrospect unsurprising, proposal. He would provide me with a platinum Amex card which I was to use to purchase my work wardrobe of exclusively high-end designer labels. The clothes would belong to me; I was simply required to wear them at work.

He suggested a monthly limit of around £5,000, and explained that it was important to project an image of expensive perfection, that it would be instrumental in ensuring his promotion within the bank. But deep down I knew that it was just a way to vicariously scratch that transvestite itch.

I left the interview and spent the weekend thinking over his proposition, finally accepting it with the caveat that if he ever so much as hinted at any sort of favour owing as a result of the clothing allowance, I would hand in my notice and immediately bring a case against him for sexual harassment. I made him put the conditions in writing. He accepted without batting an eyelid and was true to his word.

But, as we all know, there really isn't such a thing as a free lunch, and there was a sexual undertone to my role. The problem is, I also have an itch. It is my vice, my last, real, remaining one: beautiful clothes.

I love them. I love to shop for them. I love to take them home and unfold the layers of soft tissue paper. I love to bathe in the thrill of possessing things of such beauty. I take exquisite care of them once they are mine. My apartment is crammed with them.

I spent ten years on the catwalk and in front of the camera, so being objectively sexualised for the sake of fashion wasn't anything new to me. I examined the sociopath's proposal very carefully and concluded that this time things were different: I was in control of my body, and I was in control of what I chose to wear, even if someone else was paying for the clothes.

In any event, the sexual aspect of my role was negligible. Whenever a new client or professional colleague came into the office for the first time, the sociopath would make a point of introducing me, always in the same way. 'Oh, and this is Nicole, my wonderful personal assistant. I don't know what I would do without her to keep me on the straight and narrow! Nicole, this is X or Y from Z bank/company.'

Small pause.

'Oh God. [Looks shocked.] Nicole, are you really wearing [Chanel/Dior/Gucci, etc] again?!' [Turning to new client:] 'I pay her FAR too much. She used to be on the catwalk, and you know what they say – you can take the girl off the catwalk but…' [Tuts, rolls eyes, etcetera.]

This didn't always go down particularly well with new female clients, but he was far too narcissistic to realise it.

Cue for me to stand up, smile ever so slightly coquettishly, greet and shake the new client's hand. The subtext was undeniable: 'I am fucking my secretary, who used to be a model, *BY THE WAY*. Aren´t I the *STUD*?!'

The routine with D'Artagnan, however, didn't follow the script. I stood and extended my hand. 'So pleased to meet you, Guy.' Flutter eyelashes.

He stepped forward, took my hand firmly and fixed me directly with his dark-brown eyes, a smile playing around the edge of his full-lipped mouth. '*Trés enchanté*, Nicole.' Pause. Sultry eyes. A suggestive eyebrow. 'But you are not wearing Dior.'

WOW. That accent. Those eyes.

D'Artagnan turned to glance at the sociopath. He still hadn't let go of my hand.

Awkward pause. The sociopath baulked. 'Well, yes. It is Dior, I think, isn't it, Nicole?'

Once you have tamed your sociopath, never show him up in front of a new client or colleague. It takes weeks to dust off the toys.

I was wearing Chanel. I opted for ditzy. 'Um, I think it is, Stephen. I'm sure I went to take the grey Dior out of the wardrobe today, but I'm not absolutely certain because I was so tired this morning.' Little giggle, more fluttering eyelashes. 'It was a really late night and...'

'Oh!' D'Artagnan dropped my hand suddenly, slapped his forehead in an exaggerated manner, followed swiftly by pantomime Gallic contrition: eyes rolled in mock horror, hands raised, an almost imperceptible shudder. '*Mon dieu*! I am so sorry, lovely Nicole, but I am an idiot!' (He pronounced this *id-e-otte*, which caused a little part of me to melt as it was exactly what Juliette's dad used to say.)

'It is, of course, Dior – but it is the new designer. I did not see it at first! What a fool I am! Please forgive me!'

Which had two (calculated) purposes: the sociopath got a massive hard-on for having proved the Frenchman wrong (submission, you understand), and at the same time he fell a little bit in love with Guy for giving him the hard-on (submission, you understand).

D'Artagnan didn't really need to give me the sexy smile and the wink as he followed the sociopath into his office.

He became a regular feature in our lives after that. He worked for one of the big French banks; both his and our bank had been mandated by an American client in a messy bidding war for a European-based engineering firm. There were lots of meetings in our offices, which the sociopath adored as it meant he could be REALLY IMPORTANT, strut around looking dynamic and shouting at his underlings, and occasionally even at Guy's underlings, or the various law firm's lawyers, or the law firm's lawyers' underlings. In brief, he could do lots of dick waving about how brilliant and dominant he was in front of his suave new best friend Guy.

D'Artagnan, on the other hand, spent a lot of time sitting in one of the smart guest chairs outside the sociopath's office. He pulled it over to the side of my desk and set about charming me. Occasionally, he would wander back into the meeting room to titillate or soothe the sociopath as the mood required, but there wasn't a day when he didn't manage to spend some time chatting to me.

Our bank's associate wannabe sociopaths, and even some of the fully qualified senior ones, began muttering darkly under their breath about lazy Frogs doing fuck-all except trying to shag the secretary, which D'Artagnan was well aware of and chose to ignore.

He had a sharp, wicked sense of humour and I found him delightful. At first, I didn't take him seriously. He was quite a bit older than me and I assumed he spent most of his time chatting up all the young women, or at least younger women, that he encountered. He had the louche air of an accomplished seducer, and I was absolutely certain that he wasn't going to be nailing my knickers to his bedpost anytime soon.

But I had to admit that he was attractive. His salt-and-pepper beard was carefully kept, as was his dark, slightly-too-long-to-be-English hair. He had a strong aquiline nose, and those deep, deep brown eyes (when one allowed oneself to gaze into them) could cause an occasional skipped heartbeat. He was tall, athletic looking and solidly built. And of course, there was that accent.

Aside from the more obvious seductive chatter, he was interesting to talk to, interested in art, in music, in travel, world politics. He spent time quizzing me about what it was like growing up in South Africa, whether I felt it had finally escaped its colonial, apartheid past, how long I'd lived in the UK and whether I missed home. He contrasted it with France's Algerian history and colonial past, which he seemed to know a lot about.

He was curious about my ex-modelling career, but there was nothing leery in his interest; the few dates I'd had before I'd given up on the dating game had all become a bit creepy when they'd found out I was once a model. D'Artagnan certainly didn't ask if I'd ever done Victoria's Secret, which is the point at which I leave and go far, far away, as far away as I can from whichever sad little pervert has asked the question.

He was delighted when I admitted that I spoke some French and immediately switched to that language whenever he had an observation that wasn't appropriate to be overheard. He referred to the sociopath as *le petit prince*.

He established pretty quickly that I was not married or in a relationship. I made it very clear that I had no desire to be in one either. 'Sore 'eart?' he enquired, putting his hand over his chest.

'Not anymore!' I smiled. 'Perfectly fine, happy, healthy heart, thank you.'

'For 'ow long 'as it been sore?'

'It's not sore.'

He nodded sagely. 'Mine 'as been sore for nearly two years. But it feels better now.' He gave me the lazy, sexy smile. 'Now that I 'ave met *le petit prince*, I am *très, très heureux* again.'

I involuntarily started choking on the water I had just sipped. Alarmed, he jumped up, came around behind my desk and thumped me hard on the back several times. 'Ow, that hurt!' I pushed him away, still spluttering.

'Oh, I am sorry, I didn't mean to – I overreact. It's because my wife, she did the same thing once but she nearly died. I had to do that manoeuvre, you know that one where you...' He went to put his arms around me from behind.

'Don't you dare touch me!' I croaked angrily.

He looked genuinely upset, went back to the other side of the desk and sat down again.

I glared at him, still coughing. 'Anyway, why are you spending so much time chatting me up when you're married?'

He gazed at me steadily. 'I am not married. Not anymore. I am divorced, two years now.'

I didn't even bother to conceal the eye roll. 'For fuck's sake...' I muttered to myself, then to him, 'Well, you need to go now. I'm busy and I must do some work.'

He didn't move. 'You don't believe me?'

I moved some papers around, tapped them sharply on the desk to get them into a neat pile, pressed a key on the keyboard to bring the screen back up; in short, I ignored him.

He sighed. 'Tomorrow, I bring the divorce papers to show you.' Then he got up and left, leaving me feeling angry and a bit bereft, inwardly shouting at myself, 'Oh my *GOD*, I can't believe you're falling for an ageing, philandering, French gigolo! Haven't you learned *anything*?!'

Chapter Two

It took another couple of weeks before I finally agreed to go for a drink with him. I spent some time discussing whether this was a good idea with the Muffins, but neither of them seemed to have a strong opinion on the subject. Mrs Muffin rolled languorously onto her back and purred while I tickled her tummy, and as usual Mr Muffin tried repeatedly to bite me when I stroked him.

It had been a big step for me to agree to adopt them from my elderly neighbour, Mrs Robertson, when she'd had to go into a retirement home the year before and couldn't take them with her. It was the first time in my life I'd ever taken responsibility for another living creature but, given my decision to embrace spinsterhood wholeheartedly after the last cherry-on-the-cake of online dating, Creepy Yoga Guy, they fitted the narrative rather well. Crazy Cat Lady was a natural, almost obligatory stop on the way to full-blown, weekend-onesie singledom.

The Muffins had been happy to accept my offer to come and live in my apartment and be their slave, and Mrs Robertson enjoyed hearing about them when I visited her in the retirement home.

By the time we went for a drink, D'Artagnan was skating on pretty thin ice as far as the investment deal that he was ostensibly working on was concerned. The sociopath was starting to get antsy about his hanging around my desk; he had even dared to snap at Nanny once or twice.

'One drink,' I told the Muffins. 'It's mostly just to get him off my case because he's starting to jeopardise my job,' I told them. Perhaps he *might* not be an arsehole like all the other men I'd dated.

'ONE drink,' I told him, as I climbed into the waiting taxi.

'*Bah*, of course!' He sounded a bit annoyed as he got in behind me. 'You can leave at any time. I'm not going to kidnap you and drag you into my dungeon, you know.'

'Why are we talking about dungeons all of a sudden?'

He ignored me and told the cabby the name of a restaurant. It was a French restaurant in a cobbled street near Covent Garden; underneath it was a French wine bar. It was clearly his local as the barman glanced up and greeted him warmly by name when we descended the staircase, and a large, Gaulish-looking rugby-player type at the far end of the bar raised his glass of *rouge* at him and grunted.

'A French bar. How terribly exotic,' I murmured, as D'Artagnan motioned me forward towards a quiet booth at the rear of the busy bar. There was a reserved sign on the table.

'You are very cynical, Nicole.'

'Is this your local? Is it so that you can pretend you are in Paris?'

He rolled his eyes, sighed and made a signal to the barman. 'I have told you already, my family is not from Paris. My family is from Bordeaux. I come here because the wine is good, and the cheese is good. Sometimes I just want to drink some good wine and eat some good cheese. If that is a stereotype ... *bah*, well, I am a stereotype.' Followed by the Gallic shrug, which goes something like this:

1. Raise one (or, if you are going for extra emphasis, two) eyebrow/s.
2. Raise your shoulders slightly to indicate thoughtfulness/dismissiveness/indecision/scepticism; raise them higher to indicate any of the above profoundly.
3. Optional wiggle of upper body (a little like a cockatoo on its perch) if you are particularly undecided.
4. Purse your lips, preferably with added pout.
5. For greater thoughtfulness/dismissiveness/indecision/scepticism, expel a little air through aforementioned pursed lips.

Voilà: the Gallic shrug.

A bottle of white wine and two glasses arrived at our table. The waiter uncorked the bottle, the cork was sniffed, a little was poured in D'Artagnan's glass. He lifted it and inhaled deeply, smiled and nodded at the waiter. A third of a glass of wine was poured into each glass.

'Do I not get a choice?' I asked. 'A look at a wine list, perhaps?'

'Do you like wine?'

'Well yes, but white wine isn't necessarily my favourite.'

He shrugged. 'Okay. But try this wine. You have not tasted this wine.'

I stared at him. The arrogance! I remember I was quite cross at that point. I remember thinking quite clearly, 'Fuck me, I can't believe I'm going to waste a whole evening with an arsehole who's going to mansplain my preferences.'

'I've drunk white wine in America, Australia, Japan, California, Chile and pretty much every country in Europe. It's kind of helped me to realise that I prefer red wine. Actually.'

'Yes, but have you tasted *this* one? It is from the Bordeaux region. It is quite hard to find here and in other countries.'

Astounding persistence.

I glared at the label on the bottle: *Pessac-Léognan, Cru Classé de Graves*. 'I'm not an expert on French wine regions. Is it Chardonnay? I hate Chardonnay.'

He made an exasperated noise.

I made as if to gather my coat.

'*Merde*, Nicole! Is it so difficult for you to just take a sip of the wine?'

Suffice to say that white wine from the Pessac-Léognan region of Bordeaux is now my favourite. It transpired that the wine we were drinking was produced by D'Artagnan's sister and her three daughters, who were all either qualified vignerons or in the process of becoming so. It was elegant, smooth and fruity, leaving a long luxurious aftertaste.

That is the entire wine-appreciation content in this story.

'Why didn't you just tell me at the outset that it was made by your sister? It would have saved a lot of aggro.'

'Then I would not have known if you really appreciated it, or if you were just saying that you do to be polite.' He shot me a sidelong glance. 'But I am actually not sure you would have bothered to be polite, since you are not often polite to me.'

'I am perfectly polite to you and to everyone, when it's merited.' I smiled sweetly at him.

He took the bottle out of the cooling bucket and motioned toward my glass. 'Would you like some more wine? Or is that more than one drink?' A coyly raised eyebrow.

'No, it's the same glass, so it's still one drink.'

'Just so long as you're sure that it is, that I'm not trying to get you drunk and take you away to my dungeon...' A big, sly grin.

'Less talk of dungeons, please.'

Halfway through the bottle, he motioned to the barman and a short while later a plate of excellent French cheeses arrived accompanied by fresh bread. Yes, it's true – IMO, in any event: contrary to received wisdom, cheese does indeed go very well with white wine; in fact, I would argue that it goes better than red wine.

I made an exception to the no-carb rule on the grounds that I was feeling a little drunk already, having only had a couple of rice crackers and a handful of nuts for lunch. The wine made it easier to talk, to let my guard down a little. He told me how old he was (forty-eight) and asked how old I was; he told me about Isabelle, his ex-wife, a commercial lawyer who had now moved back to Paris, that they had met at Sciences Po in Paris when he was studying economics and she law. He spoke proudly of her, her achievements and how she had been made partner at an international law firm; how they had raised 'two great kids, a boy and a girl', and then about how their marriage had begun to falter when she had accepted the offer of partnership in Paris despite his misgivings about a long-distance marriage. It had ended a while later when it became clear that his misgivings were justified.

'And I haven't been dating anyone since I was divorced, you know.' He stared at me hard.

'Okay.' I could not resist another nibble of the delicious Camembert.

'You don't believe me!'

I looked him steadily in the eyes. 'No. At least yes, you're right, I don't believe you.'

Exasperated shrug. 'Well, I can't prove something to you that doesn't exist. Why do you think I am lying to you?'

I took another sip of wine and adopted a philosophical air. 'I can't pinpoint it exactly, but I will say that your world-class seduction technique has all the alarm bells clanging like fuckery. I mean, c'mon, Guy. You're like every woman's French fantasy shag, but on steroids! I worked with a lovely girl for a while. She was very pretty but also very naive, and she was always being hit on by men like ... well, men like you. Italian men, Swiss men, French men. They were pretty much all married. She fell for it every time, and they all shagged her, dumped her and went off after the next conquest! She was constantly in tears. It was irritating to watch.'

He didn't seem perturbed by what I'd just said about him. 'And you, Nicole? You always know who is an asshole? You can always avoid the bad ones so that you don't get hurt? But you did get hurt, didn't you? Who broke your heart?'

I looked away, annoyed. 'Never mind. It's nothing to do with you. My heart is just fine. Stop obsessing about it.'

'So you have decided all men are assholes, you are not going to be hurt again.' He nodded thoughtfully, sagely. 'It is not an unusual way to cope with a broken—' He caught my eye, paused. 'Well, it is not unusual. But thirty-six is very young to stop living all of life, all of the passion and the pleasure and yes, sometimes the pain. A real life.' And then, out of the blue, 'What do you do for sex?'

'Excuse me?!'

'It's a serious question. We all, us humans, we need to have sex, we need to have a release from this existence, this cruel, short life that we live, where we pretend to ourselves all the time that we are not going to get old, that we are not going to die.'

'It's really absolutely none of your business what I do for sex!'

He paused, took a sip of wine. 'I masturbate,' he said frankly. 'Oh, and I don't make babies. I 'ave a vasectomy some years ago.'

I started laughing, amazed at the turn of the conversation. 'Please, that's way more information than I need!'

He put down his glass, leaned closer across the table, chin on hand. His gaze was very direct, very intent. 'No, it is not. I want you to know it. I don't have casual sex. I never cheated on my wife all of the time we were married, even when she was back in Paris, and I knew she was having an affair with someone else. I don't chat up girls in bars or nightclubs or on my mobile phone, and I don't see prostitutes. I cannot have sex with someone I don't care about deeply, very deeply. And until I came to Stephen's office, I was not interested in anyone. And then I saw you, and in one second looking in your beautiful green eyes I saw all this passion – this beautiful, passionate, clever woman – and—' He paused, and his fingers grazed the back of my hand. 'And now I am interested in you. Not anyone else. It's you I want, Nicole. I am not a cheater or a liar. I am very serious.'

The room seemed to be fizzing around the edges of him as we continued to gaze at each other, and the hubbub in the bar had become strangely quiet and far away.

I finally managed to drag my gaze away. 'Well. Okay. Good to know.' But my heart was hammering, and my mouth was suddenly dry.

He touched my hand again. 'It's okay, I don't want to frighten you. I just think it is important to be honest, that you know some things about me. Real things.'

I reached for my glass; it was almost empty, as was the bottle.

D'Artagnan reached forward and touched my cheek very lightly with the tips of his fingers. I raised my eyes to his, allowed myself to plunge back into the warm, dark-chocolate depths of his gaze. It felt a bit like drowning, only this time I took a very, very deep breath.

'I think maybe you need to go home now. I will put you in a taxi.' He didn't take his eyes from mine. 'Do not, whatever happens, let me get in the taxi with you, even if I beg you. Because I want very, very much to come home with you, and it is too soon.'

'I'll try not to.' I didn't want to go home; I didn't want to leave him. My hand was damp and sweaty under his warm, dry one. I didn't want not to be mesmerised by those amazing eyes.

STOP!!! my brain screamed from somewhere very far off. I can't believe this is happening, you mad bitch, I can't believe you're falling for this man, of all men!

'But you will have dinner with me tomorrow night?' D'Artagnan asked. 'I have a reservation at the Shard. I don't know if you've been there. The food is not so good I think, but the view is quite *merveilleuse*.'

'You've already made a reservation? When did you do that?'
'Today. When you say you would come for ONE drink.'
'How did you know I would agree to dinner?'
His eyes twinkled. 'Because I knew that if I could take some time to tell you how I feel about you, you would agree to have dinner with me.'

We did indeed have dinner at the Shard the following evening, though for the life of me I have absolutely no recollection of what – or indeed if – we ate. The view was doubtlessly *merveilleuse*, but all I have is a vague memory of some twinkling lights far away.

The only memory that is indelibly printed on my brain was when we got into the elevator after the (alleged) meal. We were at the back as it filled with people. D'Artagnan cradled my head in his hands and kissed me so slowly, so deeply, so sensually all the way down to the ground floor that I could barely walk with desire by the time we arrived.

Chapter Three

At first I tried to resist D'Artagnan, but it was impossible; the sexual chemistry between us was explosive, voracious, utterly compelling, like nothing I had ever experienced. I would find myself in a trance at work, in front of the photocopier, in the sociopath's office taking dictation, at my desk, feeble-minded with lust as a flashback from the night before or the weekend suddenly ignited my consciousness.

D'Artagnan talked to me, watched me, guided me while we had sex, sought my affirmation to his softly spoken questions, murmured instructions, exhalations, exclamations – almost always in French. It was insanely arousing. At the same time, the speed of the intensity between us made me anxious: '*Je t'aime*' quickly became part of the script. I backed off reciprocating in French or in English; it was too fast in either language. But D'Artagnan persisted in being irresistible, and I could feel my resistance weakening.

I lived in Highgate where (mostly) everyone was middle-class, ate organic food and worried about – well, everything sweetie. He lived in South Kensington, where (mostly) everyone was French, ate organic food and worried about whether their children were going to grow up more British than French. I was pleased and relieved that he liked cats. Mr Muffin immediately scratched him when he went to stroke him, and D'Artagnan just laughed, ruffled his head and didn't seem offended. I explained that Mr Muffin had had a difficult kittenhood, and that his social skills were not very well developed.

D'Artagnan had a large circle of French but also Spanish, Italian, mostly European friends, and we occasionally went to dinner parties at their apartments in and around South Ken. They could be exhausting as the conversation was often in French, Spanish or Italian (he spoke excellent Spanish and some Italian; I spoke neither), and invariably became more heated as the wine bottles were depleted. He always kept an eye on how I was doing though, and once swooped in to rescue me from an anorexic blonde who cornered me and in a loud, caustic tone asked, 'A personal assistant? To a banker? Do you mean you are a *secretary*?'

D'Artagnan was suddenly next to me. 'Ah Christelle, *salut*. You know, I saw Jean-François just last week. He was looking great!' That caused her lip to curl even further and, after a truly poisonous glare at him, she stalked off to the other side of the room.

'You didn't need to do that,' I murmured. 'I'm perfectly capable of handling it on my own. I don't find anything shameful in being a secretary. It's a significantly more honourable profession than the last one I had.'

'I know *ma chérie*, but I really detest that woman. She was terrible to my friend Jean-François. I like to remind her how much happier he is without her.' He slipped an arm around my waist and pulled me close against his side, his breath hot against my ear. 'And I had to come over to say that you look so gorgeous tonight. I just want to fuck you so much; shall we go to the bathroom quickly?'

I smiled weakly and pushed him away a little, although now that he'd said it, I had an insatiable urge to do exactly that. We had to leave the dinner party before dessert as the sexual tension became increasingly unbearable each time I caught his dark, liquid eyes across the table. Lust is a relentless master.

Guy did have one English friend, Tim, with whom he played extremely competitive tennis, or squash if the weather was bad, regularly on a Saturday morning. The *entente cordiale* was imperilled on the days D'Artagnan lost. Tim and his uptight wife Caroline, invited us round to dinner one night, and Guy gave such a masterful performance in the art of French charm and seduction that Caroline was practically drooling by the time we left.

I told him off for doing so in the taxi on the way home, and he denied it. 'It is normal to be complimentary to the hostess, Nicole!' Pause. 'Even if that food... My God, such terrible food the Anglo-Saxons eat! How can you eat such terrible food all of your life?'

'I'm hoping that's a rhetorical question as you know perfectly well that I'm not English.'

'I know I know, but you are Anglo-Saxon. You have a British passport.'

'That doesn't make me English, or Anglo-Saxon as you so archaically put it. I'm naturalised British, not born.'

'So you are still South African?'

I had given this some thought in recent years, but whenever I tried to focus on my birth country and how I felt about it, it slid away under my mental probing. A lot of that was to do with my shitty childhood, but I was aware of an underlying sense of shame at the casual racism that continued to be expressed by some of my fellow white South Africans while I lived there, despite the apartheid era having ended when I was a child.

Family holidays and travel around the country were not part of my upbringing; the Durban beachfront and, as I got older the green, sub-tropical city itself, was my playground, but I was aware of the diversity, beauty and vibrancy of the country. I did love it; I just wasn't sure that it loved me – a descendant of white colonials – back.

'No, I don't think so. I had to give up my South African citizenship when I was naturalised. I don't know what I am, really,' I mused. 'I suppose I would like to say I'm a Londoner, if I had to identify as belonging somewhere. I love this city. It's a wonderful place to live. I love how international, multicultural, multiracial it is, even after bloody Brexit. I love that it's full of clever, funny, creative people who are also friendly and often kind, too.'

'British, then!'

'No! It's not the same thing! A Londoner might be British, but they might also be Irish, or Bangladeshi, or Portuguese or South African like me or – imagine – French, like you! There are so many different nationalities here in London. People from all over the world have made their homes here, their lives here, have effectively become Londoners.'

'No, that's not possible.' He shook his head firmly.

I glanced at him, confused. 'It's not whether or not it's possible or impossible Guy, it just *is*. London does exist, you know. We're currently sitting in a taxi stuck in the middle of it, so it absolutely is possible.'

'No, what you said about the French. When you are French you are ALWAYS French. Maybe you live in London, but you are still French. You are never a Londoner.'

I started laughing, shaking my head in slightly bemused wonder. 'Oh my GOD, that's all you took from that whole speech I've just made? That's hilarious! It's so true about you Gauls, you're so arrogant!'

Sulkily: 'It is not arrogant to say that. It is just a fact. And, I am not a fucking Gaul, Nicole.' (He pronounced this 'furking'; even now, it still kills me.) 'The Gaul is from north France. I am from Gascony, the south, the country of D'Artagnan.'

'Well, D'Artagnan, did you perhaps not notice that there were some other nationalities I mentioned there, that I wasn't talking ONLY about French people?'

A small expulsion of air from between pursed lips, a sniff as he turned away and looked out of the window. I leaned over, touched his arm. 'Oh, please don't sulk, Guy. I find the arrogance fascinating, it amuses me. It's one of the things I...' I stopped mid-sentence, sat back. I had been about to say 'love about you'.

'What? It is one of the things you – what?' He turned, fully focused on me now.

'Uh, like about you?'

'*Pfffft*. You are a *couarde* Nicole. Just say it, it is not very frightening. It is one of the things you LOVE about me. You can say this word. It is not a big, scary word that will bite you if you say it.'

I swallowed. It was just a figure of speech after all, and it was a bit pathetic that I couldn't even say it in that context. 'Okay, it's one of the things I love about you.' In a small voice.

'See? It is not so hard!' He touched my face gently, turned my head so that he was looking straight into my eyes. 'Nicole, I love you. I have told you many times already. But I say it in French because it is more real to me. *Je t'aime, mon amour.*' A soft kiss. 'Even if you are always, always mocking me*, merde!*'

I phoned Jules. 'I've met this man. He's French. He's so bloody arrogant, like SUPER-alpha, but incredibly charming. He's too old for me, though. I mean, he's twelve years older than me, Jules – AND he's a bastard investment banker! Did I mention

21

that he's French, from Paris – well, Bordeaux – but anyway, he's a French investment banker? I mean they don't come any more arrogant, Jules. He's just so not my type, exactly the kind I avoid like the plague, but I can't seem to stop seeing him and I don't know how this has happened, but it feels like it's getting serious really quickly and it's scary, Jules. I'm not looking for – I'm not ready for a serious relationship. I feel like I'm going fucking crazy!'

'Oh, that's brilliant! I'm so pleased you've met someone that you like, Nicky. He sounds amazing!'

'Jules – did you not hear what I just said?'

'Of course I did, Nicky. You clearly like him. A lot. Or you wouldn't be telling me about him.' Her voice, soft down the line. 'So, how's the sex?'

'Oh my God,' I groaned. 'It's unbelievable. Fist-gnawingly amazing. Insanely addictive.'

Her rich, warm giggle burbled down the phone; it reminded me of when we were kids, lying side by side on her bed reading her older sister's teen magazines, giggling at the articles about having a boyfriend, about falling in love. In those heady, uncomplicated days when we didn't understand what any of that meant.

'Sounds like it might be a bit late for you to avoid getting involved with him, sweetheart. Besides, Nicky, darling…' She paused. 'It has been over four years since Karl. You need to let go of that. You can't just shut yourself away. I know you think you can, but it's silly to believe that you're never going to have another relationship. You're too young and too gorgeous.'

I didn't say anything, carried on walking towards the gym where my yoga class was starting in twenty minutes.

'Nicky? Are you there?'

'Yeah. Yeah, I heard what you said. It's just – I didn't expect this, Jules, I didn't expect someone like this. He's not … he's not like Karl, like not at ALL! He's kind of blowing my mind. I feel a bit unstable. And you know I'm not very good at instability.'

There is no one else in the world other than Jules who knows how quickly and how badly unstable I can become.

I heard her sigh then take a deep breath. 'I think you're just frightened of falling in love with someone again, Nicky darling.

And to me, it sounds like that's what's happening to you. Tell you what, why don't you bring him down here next weekend? We'll give him the once-over and tell you whether we think he's worth it or not. Mark will make that vegetarian stir-fry that you like, and the kids will be so happy to see you again. The last time they saw you was for Josh's birthday and that was ages ago!'

I had arranged to meet D'Artagnan for lunch in Chelsea after yoga. I searched the crowded restaurant for him and, remembering what Jules had said, felt my heart give a little pulse and my cheeks flush as I spotted him.

Was I really falling in love with him? Surely it was just an obsessive sexual fling? If Karl – slender, sleek, slightly androgynous – was my 'type', then Guy was his alpha opposite; he radiated rude, insouciant, entirely masculine charm.

He stood up as I came over to the table, slipped his arms around me and, smiling lazily murmured, *'Ma belle Nicole, ça va?'* He kissed me softly on the lips once, twice, then a deep breath and a corresponding deep sigh, as if he were unable to contain himself. It was a deep, sensuous, unrestrained kiss, as if we were completely alone, one hand caressing the back of my neck, the other sliding across my hips, holding me tight against the length of his body so that I could feel him hardening against my stomach as we kissed. And even though I was fully aware that it was a busy, crowded restaurant, that we were not alone and that people close to us were staring, I was entirely powerless to resist him.

That night, I dreamt of Karl again. It was a new dream, not one of the recurring ones. We were in Ibiza, in his father's villa, sitting inches apart, face to face on the floor in a pool of moonlight. Silver sparks were flying from his eyes into mine; green sparks from my eyes were flying into his; silver and green sparks were filling the space between us, shimmering, shimmering, a cloud of shimmering green and silver sparks, behind which he was starting to disappear.

I tried desperately to keep sight of him but the shimmering sparks became thicker and thicker until eventually his face, his body, disappeared completely, and I was overcome with the profound, aching sense of loss that every dream about Karl engendered.

I woke, my throat constricted, my cheeks wet with tears.

I knew nothing about love when I fell in love with Karl. I didn't know you were supposed to be careful, that you should take a deep breath before diving in. I just dived in, dived straight in to Karl, and I drowned almost instantly. Sometimes, when I was high, I tried to explain to him how this felt. He always said he felt the same. He said he had drowned in me too.

We were beautiful together in the real world; we were a beautiful couple, everyone said so, and we knew that we were. But that world was irrelevant; in the other world, the deep, rich, depths of the soft, velvety heroin underworld, we were celestial. We existed exclusively for each other; inseparable, we repeatedly drowned together in that world.

But sometimes, when we'd chased the smack with coke, with Champagne, when we were alive, manic, after we'd had sex and were cutting more lines, sometimes we'd talk about the future. We talked about how he would be a wildly successful photographer, how I would be a wildly successful novelist, how we would always be together. We talked about living in Arizona (he was obsessed with Arizona, obsessed with the skies in Arizona, yeah, that song). We talked about the children, the beautiful, celestial, green-eyed, silver-haired children we would have (he wanted two boys and a girl, I wanted two girls and a boy). We planned our future together and it was beautiful, shiny. It shimmered, glowed with the love we had for each other.

But Karl was capable of coming up for air and I wasn't. He came up for air after we'd been together for about two years and it hurt me viciously. But he pleaded, begged, insisted it meant nothing, insisted he could not live without me, and I was powerless to resist him. So, we plunged back into the deep, lush, enthralling world of mutual addiction, lubricated by heroin.

The second time I was a lot more cautious. And the third time was the end.

It still hurt. I curled up in a foetal ball, careful not to disturb Guy who was sleeping soundly next to me. I waited while the dream faded, and I fell asleep again. When I woke the next morning, he was curved around me. His body felt strong, solid; his chest hair was slightly scratchy against my back, his arm was lying heavily across my waist. He felt very real, not ethereal like Karl had always felt somehow. And that was different. I found that I quite liked that.

On the Hyde-side of the all-consuming, passionate Gascon, were the usual, less attractive vices. Control. Jealousy. Possessiveness. On a memorable occasion the following weekend, there was a hat trick.

1. Control.

We were having a rare lazy Saturday morning in bed at my apartment as Tim had cancelled their rendezvous (I later realised it was of course Guy who had cancelled it) and he had persuaded me in a non-verbal manner against going to yoga as I normally did. It was a grizzly morning.

Both cats were snoozing at the bottom of the bed. I was lying across one of Guy's legs, half under the duvet, reading Hilary Mantel's *Bring up the Bodies* (which is astoundingly brilliant on the subject of sociopaths IMO); he was resting against the pillows, scrolling through his phone. He put it down after a while and nodded his head in the direction of the Prada bag on the bedroom chair in the corner. 'Shopping again yesterday, *ma chérie*?'

I nodded absently.

'Maybe, you know, you spend a lot of money on clothes. Maybe you should not spend so much money on clothes. How much did you spend yesterday at Prada?'

I raised my head slowly, warily, and looked at him. 'I think that falls in the category of NOYB, actually.'

He thought for a minute. 'None of your business, right?'

'*Voilà*, Romeo.' I went back to my book.

A pause. 'But how much, seriously? Last week it was something in a big bag from Celine. The bank must be paying you a lot of money.'

I raised my head to look at him again, frowning this time. 'Uh, ditto?'

Another small pause. I returned once again to my book, but a vague sense of foreboding was starting to manifest itself. Why these questions, why now?

It suddenly dawned on me that the sociopath would have got a massive hard-on telling him about the clothing allowance, that he gave me money to buy and wear designer clothes, implying that he owned me in some way. A calculated, mean little triumph over the deceitful Frog who was now shagging his secretary. I wondered how long ago he had told him.

'Is it the bank that is paying you that much money? Or is it someone else?'

'Oh for God's sake, Guy! You know perfectly well that Stephen gives me a clothing allowance.'

He recoiled in mock horror. 'What? I did not know this! Why does he "give" you a clothing allowance?' A pause. 'For Dior? For Prada? Every week? That is a very big clothing allowance! What do you have to do to for this clothing allowance?!'

2. Jealousy

'Do you have to fuck him, Nicole, for the clothing allowance?' Angrily, really angrily. I quickly worked out he had not known for very long because the anger was raw, primal. Come to think of it, the sex that morning had been pretty rough – not really '*je t'aime*' sex. So yesterday, then; had he seen the sociopath yesterday? Yes, of course he had! They had lunch together, meetings in the afternoon. Oh, the sociopath must have been creaming his pants.

'Right, enough. Time for you to go, I think!' I scrambled over him to get off the bed.

He grabbed me tightly by the arms. 'Are you? Is that what you have to do? You must see, Nicole, it is not NORMAL, this giving your assistant money so that you can dress her like a doll, so that you can sit in your office and look at her and masturbate about her getting dressed up in the clothes you have bought for her!'

'It is NOTHING to do with you!' I shouted right into his face because that was how close he had pulled me. He was holding me, hurting my arms. 'How DARE you tell me what I can and can't do? How DARE you tell me how I should live my life? How DARE you make assumptions about me and what I do or don't do with my body?! You can FUCK OFF! LET ME GO, LET GO of me you

ARSEHOLE, you're HURTING ME!' I was surprised at my anger, but I suddenly felt both furious and very afraid.

He was surprised too, and he let go of me immediately. 'I'm sorry, Nicole. I did not mean to hurt you, but it is totally inappropriate. He is exploiting you and you are letting him!'

I scrambled off him, grabbed my kimono from the end of the bed and tied it tightly around me. I stood at the bedroom door, shaking. 'Don't you talk to me about exploitation, you entitled ARSEHOLE!! You know NOTHING about exploitation. If I were to tell you about REAL exploitation, your privileged little mind would IMPLODE!'

I was dismayed to find that I was sobbing. I stood at the bedroom door, pointing toward the front door. 'GO!' I shouted again 'GO! Get out of here! I don't want to see you again, EVER!!' I was shaking and tears were streaming down my face.

He stared at me. 'I just...' He looked a bit panicked.

'GET OUT!!'

He sheepishly got out of bed and began searching for his clothes. I went into the living room, trying hard not to cry but crying uncontrollably all the same.

He came in quietly when he was dressed. 'I am so sorry, Nicole. I really did not mean to hurt you, and I did not mean to frighten you.'

'Just go.'

'I know you are not fucking him. He tell me that you are not fucking him.'

I had a mental image of him holding the sociopath up against the wall by the throat. I hoped it was true.

3. Possessiveness

'It is just very difficult to accept that another man is buying clothes for MY girlfriend, is looking at her all day when she is wearing those clothes. The woman that I love, that I am in love with.' He took a step toward me.

I looked away. 'Please go. I don't want to talk to you anymore.' I wiped at the snot on my face with the back of my hand. Attractive look!

He went. Quietly.

Chapter Four

I phoned Jules and cancelled our plans to go down to Buckinghamshire that evening. 'He's just a controlling ARSEHOLE,' I sobbed down the phone at her.

She made sympathetic noises. 'Why don't you come down anyway, Nicky?'

'No. I'm so sorry, Jules. I'm sorry to let you down so late, but I really don't want to go anywhere. I'm too upset and I can't stop crying. I just want to stay in with the cats. I TOLD you he wasn't my type. He's way too controlling.'

'Oh sweetheart, I'm so sorry. I hate to hear you so unhappy – do you want me to come up to London?'

That just made me cry harder.

I love Jules so much; sometimes I don't think I'd be alive if it weren't for her. She's my best friend – she's been my best friend since we were seven. In the block of flats that my mother, the vile Tiffany, and I lived in, Juliette's family lived two floors down. We were in the same class at school. I would often go back to her family's flat after school to hang out; we would lie side by side on her bed, reading comic books together or flicking through the sublime images in French *Vogue,* which her oldest sister insisted on buying despite the exorbitant cost of imported magazines. That was definitely where my love of clothes was born. Often, if Tiffany wasn't home or if she'd recently acquired a new boyfriend, I stayed for dinner with Juliette's family.

I could usually read the Tiffany-mood pretty well, and there were only a couple of painfully embarrassing occasions on which she descended to reclaim her property in a jealous, drunken rage. She would bang on Jules's parents' door, shout and swear at them, then drag me by the arm back upstairs so that I had bruises the next day. It wasn't because she missed having her daughter around, but because someone was trying to take something away that belonged to her and was possibly deriving pleasure from it. Because Juliette's family cared for me; even as a kid, I knew they did.

My desk at work became festooned with beautiful long-stemmed red roses, delivered daily and accompanied by cards which all read: '*Je suis si désolé, mon amour. Je t'aime*'.

'Lover's tiff?' The sociopath oozed smug malevolence as it slithered past.

I smiled brightly at him. 'Oh no, he's just French. You know how romantic they are.' And rolled my eyes girlishly, while thinking, *Fuck you, odious little slimeball. I'm not going to confirm that your festering hand grenade had exactly the outcome you desired.*

Eventually, I warily agreed to go for a drink with D'Artagnan again. We met, at his suggestion, in the cocktail bar of a super-chic London hotel, and for once he did not try to order for me.

He apologised sincerely and thoughtfully for losing his temper. He reiterated that he had not meant to hurt me, that it had never been his intention to hurt me, to frighten me. He had tears in his eyes as he said it. I had never seen him so contrite, and I believed that he was sincere.

I told him that he had some extremely dated ideas about control. He reluctantly agreed that maybe he had.

'There's no maybe in it, Guy. You really need to change the way you think. You have no right to control me or what I do with my life. It's the twenty-first bloody century. I am perfectly entitled to decide how I live, and what I do or don't do, according to my own agenda, without reference to you and the rest of the sodding patriarchy who still seem to have tremendous difficulty accepting that!'

'Nicole, I have an enormous respect for you, and I was not trying to control you. I was just very angry when I found out about Stephen paying you the clothing allowance. I did not know about that. I have never heard about this happening before.' His gaze was steady, serious.

'But you accept that it's my decision that Stephen pays me a clothing allowance. That I am an adult who chooses what I do with my life, that I know if I'm being exploited, or not as the case may be, and that's for ME to decide, not you?'

Slow blink, eyes fixed on me, slight Gallic shrug. 'Yes, Nicole, I accept that it is your decision. Even if I don't agree with your decision.' A sniff, extra eyebrow, added pout. 'Even if I really don't like this decision.'

I took a sip of my martini and stared at him. 'But you're not going to challenge my right to make this decision, or any other decision that I may believe is best for me, are you?'

Aside from the Gallic shrug, French people do a wide range of expressive things with their mouths, usually with an eyebrow movement for emphasis to indicate disdain, disinterest and most other things beginning with 'dis'. The English do not do this; most non-verbal expression is through the eyes. The 'dis' in French often means 'yeah, whatever'.

He did a little dis. '*Bah*... Nicole, I have said I am sorry. I am very, very, deeply sorry that I hurt you, that I frighten you. I will never do this again. I cannot be more certain, more sincere, about this.'

He reached over, took my hand between his and pressed my fingers gently to his lips. 'Please forgive me, Nicole. I love you so much. I need you in my life – I cannot live without you in my life.' Big, deep brown eyes, like the eyes of drowning puppies.

I sighed deeply, looked away from him. It was starting to dawn on me that he wasn't being deliberately obtuse; he actually was incapable of understanding the point I was trying to make. In his mind, his only wrongdoing had been to lose his temper. The fact that he had lost it because I was doing something he disapproved of, that he believed he had every right to disapprove of, and that I had failed to accept was an erroneous decision on my part – none of this was part of his contrition.

I gazed at him. He held my gaze, my fingers still pressed against his lips, still held between his broad, long-fingered hands. I started to realise that his jealous, controlling, possessive instincts were not going to be easily subdued. I had been lulled by our vertiginous lust into assuming that everything else was going to slot neatly into place like our bodies did; that he just needed a short, sharp, lucid lesson in modern sexual politics, a lesson that would be absorbed, respected and never forgotten. And now it was clear that wasn't the case. D'Artagnan was more complex, his instincts were hard-wired and his understanding of the inevitable boundaries and compromises of relationships was very different to mine.

Either I had to learn to live with that or end the relationship *tout de suite.*

'Nicole,' he said quietly, kissing the tips of my fingers. 'Please will you forgive me, *mon amour?*'

I took a deep breath. I plunged into those mesmerising eyes and said, 'Okay, I forgive you,' even though he didn't understand that what I was actually saying was that I forgave myself. I was in too deep, and I hadn't realised it. I didn't really know what I was doing anymore, but somehow it had become impossible for me to walk away from D'Artagnan.

So, we kissed and made up.

Lubricated with nitro-glycerine. It was a Friday night. He'd booked a suite in the hotel, ordered a bottle of Dom Perignon, which was already on ice in the room. On the bed was an ivory box tied with black ribbon; inside was exquisite lace underwear and a silk negligée from La Perla; on top of the box another smaller, unmistakeable Bordeaux-red, gold-engraved box from Cartier, containing the iconic Love pendant necklace in rose gold with pavé diamonds.

'And I have called the people that you use when we went to Donostia, and they will feed your Muffins tonight and tomorrow morning, *mon amour.*' He fastened the Cartier necklace around my neck carefully, kissed me softly, eyes sultry.

I gazed into those amazing eyes, shaking my head slowly. 'And all this you did because you knew, you just KNEW, that I would forgive you?!'

Slight sexy Gallic shrug.

'I sometimes wonder, darling man, what it must be like to live in your world, this world where everything you want, everything you desire, every wish you've ever expressed is always granted to you. Do you ever stop and think about that, about how fortunate you are?'

'*Bah,* Nicole, you forget it was not easy for me to persuade you that I was the man for you. And I don't get everything that I want. For example, I am very, very unhappy that you are working for that *connard*—'

I put my index finger firmly against his lips. He took it into his mouth, velvety and warm, holding my eyes with his. I was instantly, irrationally, consumed with desire.

We drank the Champagne very slowly over the course of the evening. I wore the ivory silk negligée and the Cartier necklace the first time we fucked; the second time I wore the exquisite underwear (he insisted). The third time, in the very early hours, the dawn hours, naked apart from the necklace, I writhed under his hands, his fingers, his mouth, as he slowly, expertly brought me to the edge of orgasm, both of us glistening with perspiration, his eyes half-closed, watching me all the time. 'You are so incredibly beautiful *mon ange. Mon dieu,* you make me so hard... Tell me, Nicole, do you want me to fuck you now? Do you? Tell me, *mon amour.*'

And I did, I begged him and he did, and my entire being closed tightly around him inside me, arched against him, pulsated in ecstasy so that I cried out, astounded by the intensity of the orgasm.

He lifted my trembling, slippery body off the bed as it finally began to subside, one hand tangled in my hair, his voice hoarse, his mouth against my ear. '*T'appartiens à moi, mon ange, t'es à moi, tu m'appartiens. Mon dieu, je t'aime, je t'aime,*' and then thrust, fully, deeply, hard, three, four, five times. I felt him pulse hotly inside me several times, a great, raw groan, his mouth gasping, beard rough against my throat.

Afterwards, still wrapped around him still inside me, nose to nose, eyes almost closed. 'What does that word mean? That new word, the one that sounds like apartments?'

A lazy little smile. '*Appartenir.* It means to belong. *T'appartiens à moi.* You belong to me.'

I frowned sleepily. 'Do you think that's healthy, given that we've only just been arguing about control and possessiveness?'

The slightest shrug. 'Yes, it's very healthy. I mean in sex, you belong to me. I bring you alive. I know you have never been this alive before, and that makes me feel incredible, so powerful, it makes the sex so, so good. It's why I'm so crazy about you, *mon ange.*' A gentle kiss. 'But I knew this immediately. The first time I saw you, I saw this. I knew it would be like this. So, I have been in love with you all that time, from that first time I ever saw you. I just had to be very careful not to frighten you, not to let you know that I know this, because you are easily frightened. I know this too.'

I felt mildly confused by this – 'frightened' is a strong word. Perhaps something had got lost in translation. And I still wasn't sure that it was entirely healthy to make declarations of possession, even in the heat of the moment. But I was too tired, too satiated, too in love with him just then, so I pressed my lips against his, closed my eyes, and fell into the deepest, most wonderful sleep.

On Monday morning, I was still in a stupefied trance, standing slack-jawed and glazed-eyed on the platform at Highgate station, lost in the replay while three underground trains arrived and departed. Eventually one of the station staff came over to ask if I was okay, which finally snapped me out of it.

The following weekend, we drove out to Buckinghamshire for the postponed weekend with Juliette and her husband, Mark.

'So Nicole, how do I look?' Guy stood up as I walked into the living room, did a little *voilà* with his hands outstretched.

I stopped, frowned at him, trying to fix the other earring in my ear. 'Uh, fine? Great, nice shirt – uh, why? We're only going to their house for dinner, we're not going anywhere fancy.'

'Yes, but I am being presented for approval. I need to make a good impression, *n'est-çe pas?*' He came over to me, brushed my hair away from my neck to help me put the earring in, smiling the lazy smile.

I laughed a little. 'No, you're just meeting my friends, that's all.'

'*Pffft*. This is your best friend. She is going to give her approval of me or not, and she is French, so I know I need to make an effort.'

'Well, in some ways she's more South African than she is French – and yes, before you start again with all that crap about the sanctity of French blood, Jules was born in South Africa, her parents were French and she's French by birth, but she's never actually lived in France.'

Juliette's family were from the French island of Réunion; they had emigrated to South Africa in the mid-eighties just before Juliette, their last and youngest child, was born. She had four elder siblings, two brothers and two sisters, and the whole family lived together in a cramped three-bedroom apartment. Her mother spoke no English, her father only a little, and they survived on her father's salary as a factory worker, which wasn't much. Nevertheless, they always insisted that I ate with them when I was there. I'm pretty sure it's where my love of garlic was born, and it was where I learned to eat *moules marinières*, my only non-vegetarian concession. They spoke French at home, so I spoke French with them; my spongy kid's brain absorbed it as if it were perfectly natural. They looked out for me a lot, more than I was aware at the time.

That is, until around the time my father, Jeff, appeared for the last time; after that, they weren't so keen on me, or on Juliette being friends with me. The feral years had begun: I started hanging with the surfer boys, smoking cigarettes and weed in the stairwells of the apartment block, getting speedy-high on diet pills or cough medicine, drinking in the park and on the beach, getting shagged in the bushes. Y'know, all that healthy teenage stuff, the desperate and dangerous hunt for male validation, male approval, male – or indeed any kind of – love.

Jules and I stayed friends during our teenage years, although she had to hide our friendship from her parents, and she cried and held me tight when I told her I was leaving South Africa. Days after my seventeenth birthday, the ink hardly dry on my brand-new South African passport which my 'boyfriend' Greg had been able to get for me by forging Tiffany's signature, we were on a BA flight to London. He wasted no time in getting one of his seedy East End photographer mates to shoot my portfolio, and then tried to sell the photos to, amongst other dubious publications, the tabloids. They weren't particularly interested as I didn't have big tits, but he did manage to engage the attention of one of the modelling agencies and – hey presto! His airline-fare investment started to pay off.

It was many years later when Jules contacted me out of the blue. She was in London; her father had died the year before, and her mother had moved back to mainland France. She'd seen photos of me in a magazine and contacted the agency, somehow persuading them to give her my details.

I was so thrilled to see her, awed to see her, this person from some other life that seemed like someone else's vague memory. At that time, I'd just met Karl and had started doing smack, was flying way out there on the very edge of the roller-coaster, tethered only by something very tenuous and elastic ... the faintest life force, perhaps. Anyway, I was a bitch to Juliette. I let her down all the time. I never kept to our arrangements, never called her when I said I would. We never did any of the things I would enthuse manically about one minute then completely forget the next. But she hung in there. She took some steps back from me, met Mark, and they fell in love; then she took some steps forward again while I was in rehab, and she's never stepped back again since. I know I owe her my life because I couldn't have gotten through the post-rehab debacle without her.

I had explained some of this to Guy, but I'd glossed over the bit about my own family. I just said we weren't very close; I was an only child, and we weren't really in touch anymore. To have to explain my shameful upbringing to my sophisticated, intelligent and supremely confident (I am trying to limit use of the word 'arrogant') new boyfriend was to be avoided.

Chapter Five

It was a clear, cold winter's afternoon when we arrived at their house just outside Marlow. Josh and Katie came running out when they heard the car tyres on the gravel and threw their arms around me as soon as I got out of the car. I felt a surge of happiness and hugged them tightly, laughing delightedly. 'Oh my, you two! How lovely to see you, my two gorgeous little bears! Gosh, you've both gotten really big, really strong – such strong hugs!!'

They both started talking at once. 'Aunty Nicky, Aunty Nicky, come and see the swings daddy's built in the garden. Aunty Nicky, come and see my rabbit, come, come now, no come with me—' each taking a hand and pulling me in opposite directions.

'Kids, kids, slow down! Let go of Nicky, stop pulling her around.' Jules followed them out the front door, her pretty face lit with a big grin. 'Nicky darling, how wonderful to see you again!' She embraced me warmly.

I hugged her back as hard as I could. There is only one person in the world who can make me feel grounded, feel safe: Jules. I breathed in her Chanel No.5 scent, her long, curly hair soft against my cheek. We finally let go of each other, and I glanced over to where Guy was standing at the front of the car, smiling, watching us.

'Jules, this is Guy. Guy – Jules, my best friend in the whole world! And this is Josh.' I put my hand on his shoulder. 'He's, uh, nine now, I think, aren't you Josh?' He looked up at me and nodded, quieter now that there was a tall, bearded man standing there. 'And Katie, my sweet little Katie, who's five!' I stroked her soft hair with my fingers.

She turned her mother's sapphire-blue, dark-lashed eyes up at me and said solemnly, 'I'm five and a half, Aunty Nicky.'

Guy crouched down so that he was level with them. 'Hello Josh, hello Katie. I am Guy.' He smiled at them, then stopped as if he'd got a shock and recoiled. 'Oh my, but Katie, you have something behind your ear. Here…' He reached behind her ear, pulled out a pound coin and held it out to her. 'Where did that come from? Oh no, look, look! Another one – you are made of gold, Katie! Where are all these coins coming from?'

Katie, mesmerised, gave a big, shy grin as she took the coins. Guy's attention now turned to Josh; another big mock surprise. 'And you, Josh! You have one, too! Oh my, you also have another one!'

They both started giggling, taking the coins, Katie dancing in front of him. 'Do me, do mine again, I have more!' Only this time he pulled out a foil-wrapped chocolate, then the same for Josh who was by now hanging on his shoulder, jumping about excitedly.

Jules and I watched, slightly fascinated. 'A magician, too?' she murmured, grinning.

I widened my eyes at her, shrugged slightly. 'Who knew?'

He stood up again as Josh and Katie started tearing the foil off the chocolates. 'Juliette, *enchanté*. I am Guy.' His most charming smile, kissing her warmly on both cheeks.

'Wow!' she mouthed silently at me from around his shoulder.

I was deeply embarrassed at the stupid, uncontrolled grin that had colonised my face, and I had to bend down to talk to Josh and Katie, their mouths now smeared with chocolate.

I realised later that I had, in fact, been quite anxious about introducing Guy. Much less so about Jules, whom I knew he would charm and be charmed by, and I wasn't wrong; they were flirting with each other within minutes. They chatted easily in French; he knew the company she worked for well (Jules is a very successful business analyst), and after a while he teased her about her incorrect grammar – she'd had no formal French education even though it was her mother tongue. She in turn teased him about being a bourgeois *Académie Française* snob.

I had been more concerned about Mark, mostly because Mark leaned decidedly to the left politically and Guy… Well, I knew he didn't lean to the right (his dislike of the Le Pen dynasty was strong to the point of fanatical), but he was the embodiment of the liberal, free-market capitalist.

Mark taught maths and physics in a private school and had an exceptionally sharp, sardonic sense of humour that often had me aching with laughter, snorting uncontrollably like a stuck pig. His passion was music; he played bass guitar and had an enormous vinyl collection in the basement of their house which he'd converted into a music studio. He spent at least one evening a week practising with his band, and occasionally played gigs in local pubs. Outside of his passion for music, he was easy going and had only one non-negotiable rule: the entire family was obliged, no excuses, to go to Glastonbury every year. I was roped in one year and it was just as gorily, muddily, hilariously awful as Jules had always told me it was. Mark called me a lightweight, mud-fearing malingerer when I refused to go again.

I'd stayed with them for about three months while I reconstructed (or indeed constructed from scratch) a new life for myself in my early thirties, post-rehab, post-Karl, post-Irish exile, and that period remained very special to me. For the first time ever I felt safe, cocooned, loved, and I began to understand what being a family meant. I was grateful that I could be useful, helping them with childcare for Josh, who was five, and Katie, an energetic two-year-old.

Spending time with them both was a bittersweet delight; sometimes I was utterly shattered by the end of the day, but it forced me to stop and really think about whether Karl and I had been ready to be parents. It made me realise that we probably hadn't been. In any event, I told myself this because it helped. Our relationship had been too volatile, would have been an unstable and damaging environment in which to raise a child, would have ended up being a repetition of our own unstable and damaging childhoods.

I liked to think I would never have been as bad a mother as Tiffany, but on the bad days when I hadn't slept well, or when I awoke with the memory of Karl's silver eyes fresh in my mind, when Katie was whiny and tetchy all day and Josh was asking 'But why, Auntie Nicky?' for the seventy-ninth time that afternoon, I was overwhelmed with relief when Juliette or Mark came home and took over. I took some small comfort then, and offset that comfort against the grief that I was physically unable to have children. Aside from – but no, I wouldn't go there. I was not going to gaze into that yawning what-if abyss.

I needn't have worried about Guy and Mark getting on. Mark returned from running an errand shortly after we arrived and within fifteen minutes they were having a surprisingly heated and detailed discussion about music and bands. It was very much news to me that D'Artagnan had spent a large part of his youth going to gigs in Paris and elsewhere in Europe. I struggled to reconcile the image of him in his early twenties at a Nick Cave gig (the only thing he and Mark seemed to agree on was Nick Cave) and the current pastel-coloured-jumper-around-the-shoulders suave Frenchman.

He discussed the French territorial diaspora with Jules while we ate dinner, was genuinely interested in her parents' lives in Réunion, asked about where her family were living in France and whether she had also contemplated returning to live there. I listened closely to this conversation; I knew Jules was concerned about her mother, who was now in her early seventies and not in great health. She was living with Jules' older brother Pascal in south-western France, just outside Biarritz, but Jules seemed to think this was only a temporary situation.

'It's difficult,' she said. 'I mean, my mum really wants us to live in France, she misses her grandchildren so much. But Mark's family is here in England, and they're very close to us too. We did have a serious chat about it when the whole Brexit vote happened. We were both so shocked, and we still are. '

'It's the most ridiculous decision ever, a circular fucking firing squad of stupidity!!' Mark interjected angrily.

'Don't forget the parrots, sweetie' she frowned and motioned her head towards the living room, where the kids were watching something on the TV and dreamily spooning ice cream into their mouths.

'And although I can work from pretty much anywhere, and Mark is happy to try something new, there's the question of language both for him and for the kids. I know it's my fault, that I ought to have spoken French to them more, but neither of them are very fluent. They only speak it a bit when we go to visit my mum because she doesn't really speak English.'

Guy nodded sagely. 'Yes, I can see this could be complicated.'

'What about you? Didn't Brexit make you think about going back? I've heard that loads of the French in London have gone back, that South Kensington is practically a ghost town now!'

Slight Gallic shrug. 'Yes, we were all very surprised at the vote, and quite a lot of my friends have returned to France or Europe, or will go back soon. I feel it has changed – London has changed, and that makes me sad. I don't like it so much now.' He stopped, then gazed at me across the table. 'Before I met Nicole, I was thinking I would go back to France. My children are both in Paris, but my sister and my nieces are in Bordeaux, and I am close to them. It is where I am from. I am talking with a friend now about maybe developing some property together in Bordeaux.' He had mentioned this in passing to me.

'Well, you're not allowed to take Nicky away from us to France, you know!' Jules joked.

He gave her a sly little smile. 'But Juliette, I think Nicole would love to live in France. It is where all the beautiful clothes come from. Nicole belongs in France, I think.' He glanced at me again, a suggestive eyebrow, slight curve at the edge of his mouth.

I glared at him. 'I'm slightly less one-dimensional than that, Guy. And I don't "belong" anywhere, remember?'

'*Bah*, of course I don't mean you are only interested in clothes, *mon amour*, but I know how much you love them, otherwise you would not take the allowance from— *AIIEEE* Nicole!! Why do you do that?!' as I jabbed the heel of my shoe into the toe of his. He frowned and reached down to rub his foot, frowning at me. 'Oh I see, so you don't tell Juliette either about the clothing—'

I made angry, threatening eyes at him. Jules did know about the sociopath's clothing allowance; of course I had discussed it with her. She hadn't been keen, and it was she who had suggested I get an agreement in writing to pre-empt any idea that favours might be owing in exchange. Ultimately, she'd said, 'You're an adult, Nicky. It's your decision.' But Mark didn't know; I'd asked her not to tell him. It felt too difficult to explain to him, too nuanced.

'Oh yes, I know about that.' She smiled at Guy, winked at me and then, as Mark opened his mouth, frowning, to ask what was going on, she said, 'Sweetie, pass the wine, will you? Oh, is it empty? Won't you be a darling and go and get another bottle from the kitchen? And I'll take the kids up. They both look tired; it's been a long day.'

'I'll take them up if you like, Jules,' I offered, knowing that she would quickly and firmly put an end to any further conversations about clothing allowances.

I pulled the children up off the couch, hugged their sleepy bodies against mine and took them upstairs, made sure they brushed their teeth and helped them put on their pyjamas. I read them each a story, Katie first, who was asleep within minutes, then Josh. I kissed them on their soft, perfect little cheeks, swallowed the little lump in my throat, and went back downstairs to chastise D'Artagnan from across the table.

As planned, we stayed over in the guest room to avoid the drive back to London. Next morning, we all went for a wander around the pretty town of Marlow and then had brunch, where D'Artagnan once more delighted Josh and Katie (and us all, a bit) by performing more clever little magic tricks with coins and chocolates, and generally making them giggle until Josh got hiccups.

But in the car on the way back to London that Sunday afternoon, Guy was pensive, subdued. As we slowed to a grinding halt in the car park that is the M40 on a Sunday afternoon, he placed his hand firmly over mine, lifted it off my knee, squeezed it. 'I like your friends very much, Nicole. But I am worried about something. I need to ask you a serious question.'

I glanced at him. He was looking ahead, a frown creasing his forehead.

'Okay, ask away.' But my heart skipped a beat, then was suddenly beating faster. I HATE suspense. Well, non-sexual suspense.

'I am very serious about us, Nicole, and it is clear to me that you are very close to Josh and Katie. You love them very much and they love you. You are still young, you can still have children, and I have already told you that I have a vasectomy. I cannot give you children, and I am very worried that you will want them in the future.'

I breathed out again. He glanced at me.

'Oh, darling man. I probably should have told you.' I took a deep breath. It was easier to talk when I wasn't looking at him, when I didn't have to make eye contact. 'I can't have children, Guy. I tried for about two years but it didn't happen, and it seems that I'm just one of those women who can't. It might be to do with weight issues when I was modelling, or the drug problems, or maybe it was never possible. Whatever the reason, it seems it's impossible.'

Except. But I don't trespass on 'except' territory; it's unexplored, vertiginously unexplorable, there where the what-if abyss lies.

'Oh Nicole, I'm so sorry.' He raised my hand to his lips, kissed the back of it. 'That was very painful for you, I am sure, *mon amour*. Did you see a specialist? Did you get good medical advice?'

I nodded, shrugged, watched the car in front inch forwards. 'Yes, I saw several. I had IVF, it didn't wofk, and it was a difficult time. But it's in the past now. I don't think about it a lot.'

He nodded slowly, thoughtfully. Then, 'So, who was this person you wanted to have a family with? This is the person that broke your heart, yes? Is this why that relationship end, because you couldn't have children and he wanted children?'

I bit my lip and didn't answer. I felt a bit cross, a bit ambushed. I didn't want to talk about Karl, about that agonising, cosmic pile-up.

He glanced at me. 'You don't want to answer this, Nicole? This is still painful for you?'

'No, it's not painful. I just don't want to talk about it, Guy. It's in the past. I don't think about it anymore, and I don't really want to have to drag it all up again.' I realised my voice was quite sharp, took another deep breath and said more gently, 'You're in my life now, my darling. I'm still not quite sure how it happened, but here you are. And even though you're not quite what I expected, it seems I've become kind of addicted to you.'

He smiled the lazy smile at me. 'I am very addicted to you, Nicole. Very, VERY addicted.' Another squeeze of my hand.

'Yes,' I said slowly, frowning. 'And that worries me, a little.' I bit my lip, then plunged on and forced myself to say it aloud. 'I worry that this is all going too fast. We've only been seeing each other just over two months, and sometimes I get the feeling that you think I'm someone other than who I am. I'm not sure you really understood what I was trying to tell you, about the craziness and the drugs and the rehab. I'm concerned that you think I'm this whole, healthy person, a stable person like you, and really, without meaning to sound melodramatic, I'm not. And I think you need to absorb that before this relationship goes any further and you feel that you've been deceived.'

Very early on, possibly even the night after the Shard night, I had forced myself to tell him that I'd been in rehab in my late twenties for heroin and cocaine addiction. Being honest with one's partner, or potential partner, was a fundamental cornerstone of the counselling we'd received, and I was determined that I needed to be clear about it with Guy from the outset. But I hadn't told him that Karl had been my co-addict; I hadn't mentioned Karl at all.

A little shrug. 'Yes, I know this Nicole, you tell me all this in the beginning. Nobody is perfect, we all have some history and some have more pain in it than others, it's true. You are not the first person to have a problem with drugs, whether they are illegal drugs or alcohol or drugs from your doctor. And I know the fashion world has a lot of drugs in it, but so does my world. I have a colleague, he is in rehab since a month ago now – cocaine, I think – I didn't ask, but it happens. And the other drugs, the opioids, heroin, this is not unusual in the financial world. It is not a big deal.' He shrugged again.

I found the notion of a roomful of alpha investment bankers smacked up to the eyeballs faintly hilarious, but then my sense of humour is a bit dark.

'Yes, I know it's not that unusual. But you need to know that there's residual damage from those years. Sometimes something will trigger for no good reason, and I'll have a panic attack. Sometimes it can be really, really bad. And then I have to take diazepam for a while, sometimes for days, and sometimes antidepressants for longer. And I hate it, I hate being so weak. It depresses me, and depression is difficult to manage. I need you to be aware that this can happen – has happened – to me.' I continued staring ahead, didn't make eye contact with him.

I also wanted to say: and sometimes I wake up in the middle of the night with Karl's face etched on the inside of my eyelids, an enormous empty space inside me, like the inverse of a punch in the stomach. And I didn't want to examine why I still had those dreams, didn't want to peel back all the stiff, congealed gauze that I'd packed around the wound four years ago and poke at it to see if it had healed at all. But I couldn't tell Guy that; anyway, what was there to tell? That I didn't know if I was over Karl? Ultimately, that was the issue – I didn't know – so what was the point in torturing him with my own lack of knowledge?

He turned to look at me, smiled gently. 'So, we deal with that when it happens, *mon amour*. You are very hard on yourself, Nicole. You must not be. I understand what you are saying. I can be strong for both of us. It does not make me any less in love with you.' His eyes soft and warm, he put my hand to his lips and kissed it again.

And even if I wasn't over Karl, it felt like Guy and I had crossed another invisible but important line in having that conversation. That Sunday afternoon, as we drove home, I realised that there wasn't just a risk that I was falling in love with D'Artagnan; I might already have fallen in love with him.

Chapter Six

The following week Guy was away in New York, working on a new deal. We spoke in the day, in the evening, in the night, sometimes at 4am in the morning because 'I just want to hear your voice, *mon amour*', which was exhausting after the third night of interrupted sleep.

In the daytime when we talked, he sounded pissed off, would phone me up to rant about '*ces incompétents connards, putain de merde!*' who were working on the deal with him. Sometimes it was just a long stream of invective and swearing in French about the deal and how stupid it was, what a waste of his time, while I held the phone between shoulder and ear and tried to carry on working. In the middle of the night, it was all soft and breathy, all '*je t'aime*' and '*tu me manques, mon ange*', and sometimes it was almost phone sex, but then he'd get miserable and arsey about the fact that he was still in New York and I wasn't.

'Can't you come to New York, Nicole? Please, *mon amour*, I need you here. I can't sleep. I miss you, *tu me manques, mon ange?*'

'No, darling man, I can't. I'm actually really busy at work. I thought you were coming back at the weekend? It's only two days away.'

'*Bah non,* I don't think so. We are going to be working all weekend because these *putain d'enculés* are incapable of doing really simple easy things like making really simple easy fucking decisions so that we can agree this *putain* deal!'

I could hear voices in the background; I felt sorry for any of the *putain d'enculés* that were in the room with him.

'Oh.' I was disappointed. 'I'm sorry, my darling. I thought you'd at least be able to come back at the weekend. I miss you too.'

A long pause, heavy breathing.

'Maybe I can get away on Sunday. Why don't you come to Saint Barts this weekend? I will book you on Virgin Upper and I will take a jet. I will be there on Saturday night, or very early on Sunday. I need you Nicole, and I need some sun. There is a great hotel there, the villas have private pools – we can spend Sunday fucking in the sunshine, yes?'

He might be a complicated man, but he had straightforward, if expensive (and horrifyingly un-eco), taste in holidays: sun, sex, good food, expensive hotels, first-class travel. On rare occasions, private jet if he was particularly determined.

I sighed, then heard him talking to someone else, his voice muffled for a minute. 'Are there other people in the room with you, Guy?'

More muffled talking, then, *'Ouais. Pourquoi?'*

I smiled wryly, embarrassed even at a distance. 'You really shouldn't be saying things like that out loud around other people.'

'*Pfffft*. It is only my staff. So, you take a plane on Friday, yes? I book the ticket and the hotel now.'

'No! I've just told you, I'm busy and I won't be finished work until late on Friday! I'm not flying halfway around the world just for one day, as lovely as it would be to see you. Anyway, I have to be back at work on Monday, so I'd have to leave on Sunday afternoon. And Mr Muffin has a vet's appointment on Saturday morning. He's done something stupid to his paw and he can't walk on it, and it was the first appointment I could get for him. So no, I can't come to St Barts at the weekend, my darling. I'm sorry, but it's just unrealistic. I'm sure you'll be able to come back to London soon. I miss you and I'll be here waiting for you.' And then, really daringly, 'I love you, Guy, please don't be miserable.'

Long pause. More heavy breathing. 'Okay, Nicole. I talk to you later. *Je t'aime.*' End of call.

He was back the following Saturday. He arrived early in the morning at Heathrow and was at my flat at 7.30am; undid the tie on my silk kimono and slid his arms around my naked body at the front door, lifting me up so that my legs wrapped around his hips, kicked the door shut behind him and carried me through to the bedroom without taking his mouth off mine. We resurfaced at about 7.30pm that evening.

But it was clear that ten days in NYC on his own had given him time to contemplate the bigger picture, to plot The Future According to D'Artagnan.

We were in a restaurant just behind Selfridges on the Sunday afternoon. He was not in a good mood, first because he had just found out he had to go back to NYC early on Monday morning, and secondly because he'd had to pretend that he wasn't watching me buy a pair of Givenchy trousers that may or may not have been paid for by the sociopath. The topic was absolutely off-limits, and he knew it abundantly well.

He ate half of his steak and then pushed his plate away. 'The steak in this country is *merde*!'

'The steak in this restaurant comes from Argentina, as it says all over the menu if you had bothered to look.'

He ignored that and picked at his teeth with a toothpick. 'Do you know, Nicole, that the fashion industry is one of the most damaging industries to the environment?'

'That is the *fast*-fashion industry, I think you'll find. The clothes I buy are not fast fashion. I never throw them away. And besides,' I pointed my fork at the half-eaten steak on his plate, 'do you know, Guy, that if all the meat-eaters on the planet ate one less piece of red meat every week, it would have more effect in reducing greenhouse-gas emissions than all of the other greenhouse-gas saving efforts combined? Including all the flying you do?'

Hostile stare across the table. 'So, because you are vegetarian it means you can destroy the environment with fashion instead?' He hears the bits he wants to hear.

'Guy. Don't go there.'

He shot me a look, pursed his lips and looked around the room for a while. Then, out of the blue, 'You know, Nicole, we need to get married.'

I stared at him, frowning.

He sniffed. 'Yes. I think we should talk about it. It is stupid keeping two apartments. It is a long way for me to come to Highgate from Heathrow all the time when I am travelling. I want you to be in South Kensington. It is much closer to Heathrow.'

I sighed, pushed my mostly uneaten salad away. Nervousness instantly kills my appetite, and I was nervous. How the hell were we suddenly talking about marriage?

'That's SO romantic, darling man. How could anyone possibly resist such a romantic proposal?'

Another imperious sniff. 'This is not the proposal. This is the negotiation for the proposal. I know that I have to negotiate everything with you first, so that you are very clear about what I am proposing.' He leaned back in his chair, stretched his arms behind him slowly and languorously, then folded them across his chest and gazed at me neutrally.

I took a sip of water. 'There is the traditional interim stage of living together, you know. One doesn't have to leap into marriage.'

'No.' Firmly. 'That is a bullshit stage. I know how I feel. I want you to be my wife. I want us to live together all of the time.'

'Is this so that you can persuade me to give up my job? Am I sensing an unhealthy desire for control manifesting itself again?'

A very long, cool stare. 'No, Nicole. I will not interfere with your work. I respect your decision to continue to work for that—' he could not resist '—that *connard*, if that's what you want.' *Connard* can mean arsehole or, depending on the strength of feeling, cunt in French. From the intonation, it was clear he meant the latter.

'Thank you.'

A little smile. 'So, is that *oui ou non, ma chérie*?'

'I thought this was the negotiation, not an actual proposal?'

He rolled his eyes exasperatedly, shook his head. '*Merde*, Nicole, you are a difficult woman. Fine, we will talk about it another time.' He picked a chip off his plate, popped it in his mouth. 'Have you finished eating, Nicole? You have not eaten very much; you know this is why you are always cold. I worry about you, you need to eat more. Here, eat some of my *frites*.' He pushed his plate toward me.

'As I have explained, dear heart, every single item of clothing in my extensive, non-throwaway clothing collection is size thirty-six. I eat exactly as much as I need to ensure that never changes, and that has been the case for many, many years, long before I met you. I'm hardly ever ill and generally have excellent health, thank you. So no, I don't want any of your horrible, soggy chips, my darling.'

'*Mon dieu,* Nicole, you are always arguing with me about everything, *merde!*' He stood up abruptly, threw his napkin on the table. 'Come, we must leave, I need to have a *putain de* cigarette to be calm again.'

He had a nicotine habit that involved one cigarette every now and then, sometimes days, sometimes weeks apart. I was deeply jealous of that. When I used to smoke it was forty, sixty a day, a constant craving, a constant need to have a cigarette between my fingers, between my lips, that was never sated. An addict can never do anything by halves.

Another week in NYC. The mood was positively mutinous.

'*Putain de merde,* I can't do this anymore, Nicole. I am too old, too tired of these *putain de connards* that I have to work with!'

The sociopath was standing in front of me, frowning crossly; he had just asked me a question despite it being obvious that I was on the phone. I put it against my shoulder. 'I'm sorry, Stephen, I didn't hear the question?'

'I need the file for Project Mazda, Nicole. I need it now! You brought me the wrong file! What's going on in your head these days? You're not at all focused! And who are you talking to, anyway? Are you talking to that crazy French bastard again?'

The phone on my shoulder positively vibrated with incandescent transatlantic fury. Guy had obviously heard that. I hung up; I knew it wasn't humanly possible for him to get any angrier, so I wasn't risking anything by doing so.

'Stephen, you asked me for the file for Project Marguerite, which is what I gave you. I am perfectly aware of the difference between the two projects, and my head is completely focused, thank you. And, since you ask, I was talking to your mother. She rang asking if it would be possible for you to have a lunch with her sometime in the next month, since you've cancelled the last three lunches that I scheduled for you with her.' All in a very precise, very firm Mary Poppins' tone (and I really did have his mother on the phone that morning). 'However, I do apologise if you're unhappy about my performance for some other reason.

Please go back into your office, and I will bring you the file for Project Mazda immediately.'

I didn't like to think about it, in fact it gave me the creeps to think about it as I went to get the file, but I'm pretty sure that he had a hard-on as he walked back into his office having been so thoroughly and concisely chastised by Nanny.

Guy returned the following Saturday, again at 7.30am. I had not been expecting him until Sunday, was still half asleep as he gathered me up in his arms at the door. This time, a pause in the bedroom.

'I have a present for you, *mon amour*.' He held out the burnt-orange coloured bag he was carrying. It had not gone unnoticed; burnt-orange-coloured bags are some of my favourites. Inside the bag was a rectangular box, and inside the box not one, but two Hermès Kelly bracelets in black leather with rose-gold fasteners, nestling on top of two black, monogrammed silk scarves.

I sat in his lap, his arms around my waist. 'Why two of everything? You know, my angel, you don't need to bring me gifts every time you come back. I'm just happy that you're here.' I kissed him softly.

'Yes, I know this, Nicole. But I have been thinking about you all week. I have been thinking about these gifts all week. I have been imagining giving you these special gifts all week, *mon amour*, and it has been driving me crazy.'

He traced his index finger over my upper lip, then over my lower lip, eyes heavy. 'Now, come, I put them on you. One on this wrist, here.' He wrapped the first bracelet carefully around my left wrist, slipped the first catch and then the second over the lock mechanism, twisted it shut. 'And the other one on this wrist here.' He twisted the lock on the second bracelet shut. I looked at him; his eyes were very dark, a sly smile at the edge of his mouth.

'The first scarf, it goes here.' He folded it carefully, gazed into my eyes, one eyebrow raised slightly in question. I blinked, acquiesced, and he laid it over my eyes, fastened it firmly behind my head. I felt his mouth on mine. '*Mon dieu, Nicole, je t'aime, mon ange,*' his breath warm on my lips.

He lifted me up, laid me down carefully on the bed, slipped the kimono off my arms. 'And the second scarf, it goes here.' I felt him slip the second scarf through the leather bracelets, then he gently raised my arms above my head and tied the scarf to the art-deco metal headboard. Then, his mouth on mine again, strong hands on either side of my ribcage, thumbs gently brushing my nipples so that my body impulsively arched toward him; he groaned a little. 'Fuck, Nicole, this body... *Mon dieu, je t'aime...*'

I heard him get off the bed and undress, his phone beep as he Bluetoothed it to the stereo, the opening chords to Nick Cave's 'Do You Love Me' and then...

But there was also something else on his agenda other than mind-blowing sex. At the point where I could only repeat, like some parched, demented desert survivor finally within reach of the oasis of clear, cool water, 'Please, please, please, oh my God, please, Guy, please,' at that point he asked, his voice ragged, raw, 'Nicole, will you marry me? Say you will marry me, *mon ange*? Tell me, will you?'

Which was grossly coercive and unfair, and I told him so later, because it was completely and utterly beyond my power to answer in the negative. He said it wasn't unfair, wasn't coercive: it still counted.

Chapter Seven

His next trip to NYC was cut short; he was back in London on Wednesday evening. He called me when he landed and said he was coming straight to my flat; he didn't say why. When he arrived, his eyes were red and he looked exhausted, deflated, sad. He hugged me tightly against him after we'd kissed hello, but there was none of the usual passion.

'It's my mother,' he replied bleakly when I asked what was wrong. 'She has died, last night in Paris. I need to go there tomorrow. You must come with me, Nicole, please.'

'Oh my God, I'm so sorry, my darling. Of course I'll come with you.' I hugged him again, hard. 'I'm so, so sorry. Were you very close to her?' He had never mentioned his mother; I had sort of assumed she was no longer alive, given his age and the fact that he was the youngest of four children.

Slight Gallic shrug. 'Not really. But she was my mother, she was a good mother, and she loved her grandchildren very much. They are very sad. We must go tomorrow to Paris even though the funeral is not until Sunday, in Bordeaux. There are things we must organise. My sister is there now.' He touched my cheek. 'And I want you to meet my family, my sister, my children. We are going to have dinner with them tomorrow night, and in Bordeaux you can meet my nieces, too.'

I successfully repressed a shudder of dread. The thought of being presented to his family *en masse* filled me with a special kind of horror. D'Artagnan on his own was one thing, but what if they had all fallen from the same Tree of Arrogance, all been breast-fed at the Imperious Fountain?

At first I only met his sister Françoise, and she had certainly not been. She was slim, elegant, with dark shoulder-length hair and the same beautiful brown eyes as Guy's, but none of the pout, the slight haughtiness that was often her brother's resting expression. She embraced me warmly and without hesitation when we arrived at his mother's apartment the following day.

I had quietly taken five milligrams of diazepam on the Eurostar just before we arrived in Paris, but it didn't seem to have touched sides. I still felt nervous, anxious, my heart fluttering in my ribcage.

'Nicole, how lovely to meet you! I have heard so much about you from Guy!' Her English was slightly more accented than his, but I was grateful to her for the effort. My rusty French had recently and dramatically improved in the rather niche categories of swearing and bedroom talk, but although I understood the gist of most of what was said I was far from fluent in conversation.

'It's lovely to meet you too, Françoise. I'm so very sorry for your loss.' I had been rehearsing stock phrases that I'd Googled on my phone. I had no experience of a parental loss in the family; the closest I'd come was when Juliette told me that her father had died. I'd felt vaguely sad but detached, mostly because Karl and I were in the extremely manic early stages of our relationship, and I was unable to focus on anything other than him.

I still felt bad about that, had apologized to her many years later for not having told her how sorry I was at the time. Her father had been very kind to me when I was a child, and I remembered him and his deep blue eyes with sadness.

Françoise gave a little smile. 'Thank you, Nicole. We are all very sad, but it was not a big surprise. She was eighty-four years old, and she had been very fragile for a long time. For us, it is a relief that she died peacefully when she was sleeping.' Her voice was solemn, resigned. But then her tone lightened. 'But I hear from Guy that *félicitations* are necessary – that you are engaged! How wonderful! I am so pleased for you.'

'Uh, thank you?' I felt my face flush, felt a little panicked. Had he told his whole family already? I wasn't prepared, hadn't known he was going to do that. It had only been the previous weekend that I'd agreed, and I was still turning the idea of getting married over in my mind, examining it from the many different, complex angles that it demanded. All of them were anxiety-inducing.

Guy had wandered off into another room after embracing his sister and introducing us, but now he wandered back. He caught the distraught look on my face and came over, slipped an arm around my waist.

'So, where are you going to get married?' Françoise asked us, smiling at him, at me.

I gave a big shrug. Perhaps he was rubbing off on me more than I realised. 'We haven't really—' I started to say, when he interrupted me.

'Now that I have seen my *archi-pieux* brother and his miserable wife again, not in a *putain d'église catholique*, that is certain!' he said crossly. He turned to me. 'Unless of course that's what you want, Nicole?' as if he'd just realised that I might have an opinion on the subject.

I stared at him. 'No, of course I don't want to get married in a church! I'm not religious.' Thinking: *how can you possibly think that's something I would want? If we'd been together more than three months, you would know this!* And then: *oh fuck! What am I doing, this is crazy, it's only been three months, we know NOTHING about each other and now he's told his whole family and it's a stupid idea, it's too soon, we need more time, why the hell did I say yes, I mean, even after, the next morning, I should have said it's too soon!*

And as I stared at him while my brain raced around like a caged ferret, I felt it: the first, very faint, insidious tingle above my upper lip. I checked my breathing. Yup, there wasn't any. I tried to breathe out, naturally, calmly, but my lungs felt tight, constrained.

My eyes widened. Please, please not now, not an attack now. Not when his mother has just died, when I was being presented to his family for the first time: the new, too young, silly ex-model fiancée who doesn't really speak French, doesn't belong in this culture, is surely just a bit of arm candy and…

'I'm so sorry, Françoise, but I need to use the bathroom. Could you show me where it is please?' I asked faintly, trying hard to not sound breathless. The tingling was getting worse. Why hadn't the five milligrams kicked in?

'I will show you, *mon amour.*' He was still looking at me, but his head was slightly on one side – he was watching me. He took my arm by the elbow, turned and guided me gently back into the corridor where we were alone. 'Are you okay, Nicole?'

'No,' I gasped. 'Need diazepam. Quick. Bathroom.'

54

He took the foil wrapper from me as I tried desperately to liberate a tablet, popped one out and gave it to me. He emptied out the contents of the toothbrush glass and filled it with water, then held it while I drank and swallowed the tablet. I was shaking now from head to toe.

Then he sat next to me on the edge of the bath, put his arm tightly around my shoulders, stroked my hair back from my face with his other hand, all the time making soothing noises. 'It's okay, it's okay, Nicole, it's okay. It's just a lot of people you don't know, and you are tired, you are a bit frightened. Is that enough that you took? Do you need to take more?'

My heart hammered like a pneumatic drill in my chest, and my lungs continued to allow only tiny amounts of air to be inhaled and exhaled. Black dots appeared and disappeared in my vision, but I tried with all my might to focus, focus on the mantra 'The Drugs Will Start Working, The Drugs Will Start Working, The Drugs Will Start Working', until gradually, very gradually, the crushing pain in my chest started to reduce so that I was able to breathe in, breathe out, just a little bit more, then a little bit more until finally, still trembling from head to foot, I could let out a whole, full breath, and breathe in a whole full breath.

The first five milligrams had finally kicked in; it was going to be okay. I wasn't going to die, not this time. Which is the stage at which the tears usually start and, sure enough, no matter how much I tried not to, there they were, relentlessly falling from my eyes and rolling down my cheeks.

'Oh Nicole, I'm so sorry, *mon ange*. Please don't cry, I'm so sorry to bring you here, to make you so scared.' He moved off the edge of the bath to crouch in front of me while I tried to hide my face behind my hands and sobbed uncontrollably. He carried on stroking my thighs, murmuring, 'It's okay, it's okay, I'm so sorry, *mon amour*. I should not have made you come. Please don't cry. It's okay, it's okay,' until finally the sobs began to subside as the diazepam started to dull the edges.

Then, quietly, 'Is it a bit better now?' To which I nodded, unable to make eye contact, deeply embarrassed at what had happened but now slightly detached as well. Guy stood up, found a box of tissues and wet a wad of them under the tap, then handed them to me. They were cool against my hot face.

'I'm so sorry,' I finally whispered.

'It's not you who should be sorry, it is me. I am sorry to bring you here. It is too much emotion. Too much too quickly, too many new people.' He sat next to me on the bath again, his arm around my shoulders.

I made a face. 'So far I've only met your sister, who is lovely, so that's a pretty bloody pathetic excuse.'

'You don't have to meet anyone else. We can stay in the hotel. We will take the train to Bordeaux on Saturday, and afterwards we will go back to London. You don't have to meet any more of my family. Please don't worry, Nicole.'

'No.' I shook my head. 'I can do this.' I took another deep breath, felt a little lightheaded. 'It's just, well, it is a bit intimidating meeting them all for the first time, y'know. All those new people you talked about, I mean not new to you but new to me—'

I stopped, realising I was starting to ramble. 'But Guy, darling, I think maybe I'm just a teensy bit overwhelmed by us, this whole thing that we have.' I waved my hand vaguely in the air. 'This marriage thing... I didn't know you'd already told everyone that we were getting married – I wasn't prepared for that. I'm still trying to get my head around it, and I tend to get a bit anxious if people make a fuss.' I stopped, blinked. It felt like quite a slow blink.

He smiled, touched my cheek. '*Bah*, Nicole, I did not tell everyone. I only tell Françoise, and I tell her not to tell anyone, not even my lovely nieces. And I will tell my children later, not now.'

He leaned over and kissed my forehead. 'I tell Françoise because I had to tell someone. I am so happy about it, even though I know you are scared and it is all quite fast. But I know it is right. I am right for you Nicole, and I know we will be very, very happy together. You must trust me. I know much more about these things than you know, *mon ange*. You need to trust me.'

He put a finger underneath my chin, turned my head gently so that we were gazing at each other. His eyes were big pools of liquid chocolate as he leaned in and kissed me very softly. I began to relax, and immediately started slipping backwards into the bath. He grabbed at me, pulled me back, laughed. 'How much Valium did you take, Nicole? How much are you supposed to take?'

I gazed into his lovely eyes. He was still smiling at me, didn't seem annoyed. 'Uhhhh, five milligrams on the train, and now, um, ten? Did you give me a whole tablet?'

'Yes. A whole one.'

'So, fifteen milligrams? One and a half tablets, anyway.'

'And how much normally must you take?'

'Mmmmm, depends. Normally, five milligrams. Ten, if it's very bad. I forgot that I took the one on the train, but this is why I took it, so that this didn't happen, but sometimes the bastard tablets take some time to kick in… Although I don't remember this happening before, where I've already, you know, er…'

My eyes wandered away from his, attracted by the Spanish dancer doll in a knitted red-and-black Flamenco dress on top of the toilet cistern. What the fuck was that doing there? Was it a normal thing to have in a French bathroom?

Eyebrows up. 'Three times the dose? And no food.' I had refused to eat the croissant he'd bought on the Eurostar on the grounds that it looked horrible and I was feeling nauseous, so he had eaten it.

I looked away, ashamed again. 'I'm sorry.'

'No, it's okay. It is me who is sorry. I should have been more careful. I did not think this would happen to you. I know you warn me about this, but I did not realise.'

I turned back to him, shrugged my shoulders and made big 'I told you so' eyes for a minute, before they started closing again. He laughed softly, kissed me again. 'Come, Nicole. We take you back to the hotel. You need to sleep. You will meet my brothers at the funeral, not now. We order some lunch and maybe we have a little dinner later, but just us two. I will cancel dinner with Manu and Charlotte, we will see them at the funeral also.'

'No! Please don't do that, don't cancel your children. I already feel bad, and that will just make me feel worse. You must have dinner with them. I'll stay at the hotel, you go to dinner. I'll be fine, I promise.'

He frowned, shook his head. 'No, Nicole. I don't want to leave you alone all evening in the hotel.'

I gazed into his eyes again. Everything was always so incredibly ... complicated with him. 'What's the time, darling man?'

He looked at his watch. 'Nearly one o'clock.'

'Well, I'll be fine by eight o'clock, promise. Well, mostly fine. I'll be really calm anyway. It will be fine, my darling, I promise. I have form, I know the drill, I know how this works.' I leaned in, kissed him, a big smoochy kiss. 'I love you so much, darling man. I'm sorry if I'm a bit fucked-up, but in my defence, I did warn you. We don't have to get married if you've changed your mind. It's okay. I'm okay with that.'

He stood up slowly, pulled me up carefully from the edge of the bath, and wrapped his arms around me, holding me tightly against his body. I positively purred with pleasure. He was soooooo lovely, his arms so strong, his body so warm, his gorgeous, familiar Dior scent so heavenly. My eyelids began to drift closed; I felt so safe, so happy, so relaxed.

'Nicole,' he said softly, 'open your eyes, look at me.'

I opened them again, dived back into the pools of liquid chocolate. 'I am never, ever, ever going to change my mind. I want you to be my wife, always, until I die. I cannot live without you. You are my angel, *mon ange*, Nicole. *Je t'aime infiniment, mon amour.*' And then the most wonderful, slow, sensuous kiss that went on forever; a kiss that I wanted never to end.

But eventually it did. Before we left the bathroom, my curiosity got the better of me. I pointed to the Spanish Flamenco dancer. 'Why is there a doll on top of the toilet? Is it a French thing. Does everyone have one in their bathroom? Is it normal?'

He laughed out loud, picked the doll up and turned her upside down; her legs were inserted into a toilet roll which the full-skirted Flamenco dress covered. 'It is to hide the *papier toilette* Nicole, and no, it is not at all normal!'

\-

So, stoned to the eyeballs, I spent the afternoon snoring my head off in a sumptuous room in a five-plus-star hotel off the Champs Elysées. Yeah, that one.

\-

And then we went to dinner. I woke in the early evening to find him stroking my cheek gently, whispering my name. I opened my eyes and smiled, and he gathered me up in his arms, held me tightly against him. '*Ça va, ma belle Nicole*? Are you feeling better?'

I nodded. 'Much better thank you, lovely man.'

I showered, dressed calmly in black, flared, Givenchy trousers, cream Gianfranco Ferro fluted blouse, the muted Louboutins I'd brought for the funeral, wore my hair up; he fastened the Cartier necklace around my neck, kissed my nape softly afterwards.

We descended serenely in the elevator to the restaurant. He introduced me to Emmanuel and Charlotte, who were both beautiful, charming, engaging young people with high cheekbones and almond-shaped eyes; they both had his mouth, though, the full lips, that slight pout. Emmanuel had dark, almost black hair, but the same olive complexion as Charlotte; her long, auburn hair fell in natural ringlets over her shoulders and down her back.

She had tears in her eyes as Guy enveloped her in a big hug. He spoke quietly to her for a moment after they'd embraced, rubbing her back comfortingly, and I heard the word '*mamie*', which is the familiar for grandmother in French. He hugged Emmanuel next; the hug went on longer than a normal greeting and there was quite a lot of back patting.

Although the mood was a little sombre at first, it lightened as the evening wore on. I was fascinated to watch him interact with his children; he clearly adored them and they, in particular Charlotte, adored him in return. I tried not to stare; so THAT was what a normal father/daughter relationship in adulthood looked like.

I think I last saw my father, Jeff, when I was twelve. It's difficult to remember when you were a kid, whether you were eleven or twelve when you last saw your dad but, having given it some thought over the years, I reckon I had just turned twelve.

He turned up in a red BMW at the apartment block where Tiffany and I lived just behind the Durban beachfront, all mirrored sunglasses, blond hair and flashy teeth. He took me to the ice rink nearby, probably because I begged him to as it was where I hung out when I wasn't on the beach.

I couldn't wait to show off to him, my cool, absent dad, lounging there in the plastic seats. I kept glancing toward him in delighted disbelief as I laced my ice-hockey boots with trembling fingers (they were a Tiffany guilt purchase after a particularly nasty slap across the face that had caused a black eye). I had an enormous grin on my face when he waved at me from the ringside as I skidded onto the rink, zooming off with the slick sound of metal grating on ice. I was a fearless skater (aren't all children?) and, as I crouched low and zoomed in and out of the other skaters, the music blaring tinnily, my heart was pounding with excitement that MY DAD was here, sitting just over there, watching me. All of the callously broken promises of visits, the forgotten birthdays, the promised-but-never-made phone calls – none of it mattered anymore because MY DAD was sitting just over there by the side of the rink watching me.

And then something happened. In my excitement, I either miscalculated and caught the tip of my skate in the ice or ran over a foreign object, but suddenly I was flying through the air and hitting the ice, sliding to a sprawling halt, unconscious, awakening groggily on the damp rubber matting off-rink, surrounded by concerned faces.

Jeff was still there when I came to (Yay! Go Jeff! Dad of the Year nomination!) and made sure to bring me back to the apartment where Tiffany was, by some small miracle, actually home. There was some discussion about concussion, there was some arguing about parenting (ha, ha), there was some yelling and swearing, a scuffle, another scream from Tiffany, and then the front door slammed shut. That was the last time I saw my father.

Emmanuel and Charlotte were warm and friendly to me from the moment we met, and it wasn't just because I was still stoned and everyone was warm and friendly. Even in my supremely serene state, I could tell that there wasn't a shred of animosity from either of them.

The whole evening was bathed in a slightly euphoric, occasionally sad, fuzzy-edged loveliness. I told Guy before we left the room that I would not be having any alcohol, and that he wasn't to offer me or pour me any, and he agreed without asking why. There are things I know too, and one of them is how dangerously exciting the black holes are that open up when I combine alcohol and diazepam.

Although I slept very deeply in his arms that night, his body spooned around mine, I was aware that he did not let go of me once.

Chapter Eight

Guy spent Friday with his siblings, dealing with the administration of his mother's estate, and the logistics of getting his mother's body to Bordeaux where the family burial plot was.

Over breakfast in the room, I offered to help in any way that I could bearing in mind my limited French, but he just smiled at me, reached over and tucked some loose strands of hair behind my ear. He was still more subdued than normal, and it was interesting to discover D'Artagnan Dialled Down. I was aware of a tenderness for him that I hadn't felt before.

'No, what you need to do today, *mon amour*, is to go and find a ring that you like. Go and look for an engagement ring. We will buy it in London, but you can look for what you want while you are here. Go to Place Vendôme, or if you want to stay inside and find lots of nice clothes too, go to Galeries Lafayette Haussmann, or Printemps next door. They have all the good French jewellers there, maybe not the full range but lots of choice. *La vie est courte, mon amour*: go and buy some clothes, spend some money. It will make me happy if it makes you happy, please, *ma chérie*.'

What wasn't to love about D'Artagnan Dialled Down?

Until he remembered, eyes narrowing, the pout becoming pronounced, a deep frown. 'But do not use the *connard*'s money. Please Nicole, not today, not in Paris! Here, you take one of my cards. I will get a card just for you when we are back in London in your name, but today you take my card.' He got out of bed, went to get his wallet. He had a very cute butt.

I leaned back against the pillows and watched him. Clearly there were still issues. I hadn't any intention of using the sociopath's card, had not in fact used it for the past six weeks. I felt that the arrangement with the sociopath had probably run its course. Our professional relationship had changed since I had accepted that things were getting serious with D'Artagnan; it was more tense, less symbiotic, and the clothing allowance no longer seemed appropriate. But Guy didn't need to know that; he might get ideas about his level of influence.

I decided to let it go, smiled sweetly at him instead. 'Thank you, that's very kind of you, sweetheart.'

A little smile as he handed the card to me, then he lifted the breakfast tray off the bed and put it on the table nearby. As he turned to get back into bed, it became clear that, despite the solemnity of our visit to Paris, he was no longer very Dialled Down.

I had to take a moment in Galeries Lafayette Haussmann, to lock myself in one of the loos, put my head between my knees and think calming, soothing thoughts – which just consisted of thinking I should be thinking calming, soothing thoughts, as I seem unable to access calming, soothing thoughts at will. They are not very biddable, I find.

It happened after I'd finished swooning over the beautiful jewellery on the ground floor. I'd taken the escalator to the first floor and turned to take it to the second floor. I was digging in my handbag for a tissue and looked up a nanosecond before the second and third-floor escalators ceased to intersect – and *he* had been there, there on the escalator on the way up to the third floor.

I was sure of it. I had seen him: the spiky sliver-blond hair, the angelic mouth, the dark sunglasses – he often wore sunglasses, even inside. He said his silver eyes were sensitive to light and I had no reason to doubt him: his eyes reflected light, it shimmered out through those incredible eyes, the gaze of a fallen angel. *He* hadn't seen *me* though: he was looking upward in that split second.

After I gave up trying to think calming, soothing thoughts, I focused instead on doubting myself. He was in the States, I *knew* he was in the States; there was no reason to think he was in Europe, in France. There were plenty of men in Paris with spiky blond hair wearing sunglasses inside. I had seen what I both wanted and didn't want to see.

And finally, when I felt calmer, when I had convinced myself that I had been mistaken, I took a deep breath and left the loo, put on my own sunglasses and kept my head down until I was out of the shop and on the street. Then I went back to the hotel, took five milligrams, lay down on the bed and deliberately and carefully replayed, with much rewinding, the sex Guy and I had had that morning. I was determined there was not going to be another Parisian meltdown, and it was impossible for Karl to intrude on my thoughts when my mind was so thoroughly immersed in D'Artagnan. By the time he got back to the room, I was serenely calm but also very wanton. This didn't pose a problem for him.

The next day he hired a car, which was delivered to the hotel, and we set off to drive to Bordeaux after an early breakfast.

'I thought we were going to take the TGV? Isn't there a really fast TGV now to Bordeaux? Like, two hours or something?'

'Yes, there is the LGV, the *Ligne de Grande Vitesse*. It's just over two hours, very fast.'

'So why are we driving? Surely it takes much longer to drive?'

'Yes, but I want to stop on the way. I want to show you something.'

The traffic on the autoroute south wasn't bad and the journey went quickly, especially since the speed limit did not, apparently, apply to D'Artagnan. The powerful Audi ate up the distance; after about three hours, he took the exit off the A10 for Cognac. Endless rows of bare, uniform vines flashed past the car window, and we passed through the occasional village, creamy limestone houses reflecting the bright winter sun.

Then he took a turn and the road became more potholed. We dived into a vine-filled valley, up the other side in a cloud of gravel and dust without a thought for the no-claims bonus, down into another valley of more uniform rows of vines, around a slight bend, and then, finally, there was more hard braking, more gravel.

Guy turned left off the road, manoeuvring the Audi between two biblical stone pillars off which hung enormous, white-painted wooden gates. We proceeded slightly more sedately up a chalk-gravelled driveway that wound its way through a small forest of bare trees, and then suddenly we were clear of them.

In front of us, a fairy-tale château, twin slate-roofed towers on each end of a classical, two-story façade, mansard windows jutting out on the third level between tall stone chimney breasts.

The car skidded to a halt on the gravel outside the château, and Guy turned off the engine. The silence was deafening.

He turned to me, smiled. There was a new look in his eye, a sly look. Or at least, in retrospect, I swear that there was. '*Voilà, mon ange!* This is my family's château. It belong to my grandparents. I wanted to see it again, I wanted to show it to you, Nicole.'

'It's very lovely,' I said, peering up at it. I was ignored; the perfectly symmetrical eyes of the château were disdainfully closed and shuttered.

'Yes, it is. When we were children, we spend most of our summer holidays here. It was the most wonderful place.' He smiled; it was a wistful, nostalgic little smile. 'We were completely wild when we were here – we build treehouses in the trees, we ride my *grandpère's* horses, we ride our bicycles into Cognac, swim in the river, sleep outside under the stars – it was a magic place for children.' His eyes sparkled wistfully. 'Come, get out of the car. I want to show it to you!'

He got out, slammed the door. I climbed out cautiously. I felt very small in front of the enormous house. He put his arm around my waist, pulled me close. 'What do you think? Do you like the château?'

'It's very, uh, imposing. Very big,' I said quietly.

'Nonsense! It is a *tout petit château*, only 600 metres square!' He kissed my cheek. 'Come, we go inside, I have the key.'

Brandishing an enormous iron key, he bounded up the stairs like a young suitor. After several failed attempts to find a keyhole to fit, he gave up and used the Yale key instead that happily fitted both the top and bottom Yale locks. The door swung open with a horror-film squeal.

The hallway was tiled with faded black-and-cream tiles, flooded now with morning sunlight through the open door; towards the back of the hall, a sweeping wooden staircase curved upwards. As I walked in, my nostrils were assailed with the smell of damp … fabric? Wood? Stone?

There were French doors off both sides of the hall. After a short negotiation involving wood and humidity, Guy opened the doors on the left and we entered the standard walk-in refrigerator that is, I have subsequently learned, common to many old French houses.

I pulled my coat closer around me, my scarf over my nose. 'Is double glazing a thing at all, here in rural France?' I tried for offhand neutrality.

'Not really!' he said cheerfully, coaxing open the first set of double windows, then pushing back the shutters, letting the sunlight flood in and illuminate the swirling storm of dust particles we had stirred up on entering. The humidity/wood negotiation went less well on the second set of shutters and he gave up for fear of breaking one of the fragile glass panes which rattled alarmingly at each tug.

We turned to look at the room. It was very large, longer than it was deep, populated with the ghostly shapes of sofas and sideboards under dust drapes, pale islands adrift on the dusty oak floorboards. An unpleasant, faded floral wallpaper covered the walls, darker in several patches where artwork had been removed. An enormous stone fireplace, straight out of Hogwarts, dominated the entire left corner of the room.

'This is the salon, of course.' He waved an arm vaguely. 'I don't really remember it; we never spend any time in here.'

We continued through the next set of French doors into a vast room that ran from the front to the back of the château, with large, shuttered windows at each end. He managed to open the one facing the front quite easily, and once again the light flooded in.

I turned toward the room and felt an unexpected surge of joy. It was simply beautiful, in the sense that it was both simple and beautiful. A long, monastically sturdy oak table occupied over half its length. On either side of it, intricately carved, solid wooden chairs. Enormous ivory-coloured stone flagstones, slightly shiny in places and smooth with age, ran the length of the room, merging into the creamy stone walls. An identical Hogwarts' fireplace about a third of the way along the wall backed on to, I guessed, the one in the salon.

More light flowed into the room from the left where the kitchen was. I wandered into it as he went to do battle with the windows at the other end of the room. Cream-painted cupboards and black-granite worktops followed the curve of the room, which I realised was in one of the towers. A large window, unshuttered, allowed the flagstones to reflect the sunlight that bathed the room in a warm glow. There was a heavy wooden door at the back, and a massive, smoke-blackened cooking range straddled a large part of the wall between the front-facing window and the back door. Copper pans of varying shapes and sizes hung on the walls either side of the window.

Guy came up quietly, put his arms around me from behind. 'I remember my grandmother cooking in this kitchen.' His voice was soft, wistful.

I nodded. 'It looks like a proper château kitchen.'

He nodded. 'It is sad that it has not been used for so long.'

'Why is that?'

I felt him shrug. 'My mother inherited it, but she didn't want to live in the country. She would stay sometimes in the summer, maybe, but she wanted to be near to her grandchildren. After my father died, she sold the house in Bordeaux and moved to Paris to be near to my brother and his horrible wife, who started to produce babies like contraception had never been invented. Six children! Like they are still living in the seventeenth century! And all horrible *pieux* – you know this word in English, what is this word, for Catholics that are like saints—'

'Pious.'

'Yes, that. So *maman* was very busy in Paris looking after Stephane's little tribe of *pieux* Catholics, she had no time to spend here in the Charente. So, the château has been empty and sad now for many years.'

'What's going to happen to it now that your mother has died?'

Another shrug, but he was still behind me so I couldn't see his face. 'I don't know. It will be part of *maman's patrimoine*, her estate. We will have to wait until the *notaire* reads the will to find out what will happen to it.'

'That's sad. I suppose it will have to be sold so that you all inherit equally.' Naïve little ex-colonial.

Another little shrug. 'We will see.'

He insisted on doing a thorough tour of the château, including the damp, spider-infested cellar. When we finally reached the upper floors, it became obvious that there was a problem with the roof as the ceilings were badly stained in places, and some of the floorboards on the top, mansard level felt spongy and a little scary underfoot. The walls were all papered with very, very vile floral wallpaper in varying degrees of decay, and the sole bathroom on the first floor was a swinging seventies' Peach Panoply. Guy laughed at my expression when he opened the door to show it to me. Some of the windows, those he managed to tug open, seemed fragile; their wooden frames creaked alarmingly, and it was clear that some of the shutters were about to fall apart.

On our way out as we descended the wide, oak staircase which was in surprisingly good condition, I felt a bit depressed for this big, old, dilapidated house that had been left to die on its own, no longer lived in, no longer loved. D'Artagnan clearly had spent some memorable parts of his childhood here, and I couldn't help but wonder if it had been a good idea to drive all this way just to witness another part of his life fading away, dying.

But he was strangely upbeat when we got back into the car. He took a final, long look at the façade and smiled. 'So, did you like your little tour, *mon amour*?'

'Yes, thank you, it was interesting. I've never been in a French château before.' I put my hand on his leg. 'I hope it hasn't depressed you too much seeing it in that state.'

'What state? It's fine. It just needs the roof fixing, a little bit of paint on the shutters and maybe a bit inside, and it will be just as lovely as it always was!' He started the engine, smiled at me again.

Wow, I thought. He clearly can't see it properly through the Champagne goggles he's wearing. Whoever bought it would need to gut it, or at least gut a large part of it. But I just smiled back at him and squeezed his leg.

If I had listened carefully as we careened over the gravel drive on our way out, I might have heard the Duchess sniggering. But I wasn't very perceptive in those early days.

We arrived in the early afternoon at his sister's home, an eighteenth-century *longère* just outside Bordeaux, set on a slight hill and surrounded by endless vineyards that swept away from the house in every direction under the cloudless turquoise sky.

On the way down, Guy had told me with tears in his voice about Françoise's husband – his best friend, Laurent – who had died of cancer when he was just forty: how much he missed him, how they had been very close, like brothers, how much Françoise and his daughters missed him. The pride in his voice evident, he explained how Françoise had fought with Laurent's family to keep the vineyards, how hard she had worked to improve the wine they produced, how she had raised her three young daughters on her own, inspiring them by her example to become passionate about wine, how their wine was now winning awards and being critically acclaimed in Paris and Lyon.

The family were just finishing lunch around a vast, circular table at one end of the terracotta-tiled kitchen when we arrived. Françoise introduced me to her three daughters: the eldest, Emma, was the spitting image of her mother, while the two younger sisters, Chloé and Amandine, were blonde and blue-eyed. All three were extraordinarily pretty, fresh and natural; all had their mother's warmth and charm.

Guy embraced them closely, asked them how they were, hugged them again after they'd answered. The word '*mamie*' was spoken several times. Emma introduced me to Conor, her Irish fiancé, and I immediately placed his accent: County Cork. He was fair-skinned, blue-eyed, and he gazed at Emma whenever she spoke as if he had only recently fallen in love with her.

We sat down and Guy proceeded to eat his way through most of what remained of lunch, putting things on my plate which I kept putting back on his plate when he wasn't looking. But I was actually hungry, so I had a bowl of leek-and-potato soup, which was lush, mopped up the rest of it with bits of crusty bread, tried all four of the wonderful cheeses on the cheese board, ate them with walnuts and almonds while sipping a glass of their excellent wine – *du* château, of course.

'Why did you drive down? Why didn't you take the train?' Françoise asked Guy in French.

He stopped chewing, fixed his eyes on her across the table. 'I wanted to see the château. I wanted to see what state it was in.'

'And? How was it?'

'It was good. It needs some work, but it is still in good condition.'

'Do you think you will—' she started.

He interrupted her abruptly. 'So, *maman*'s casket will be at the funeral parlour this evening, then? What time? I will need to go and pay my respects. I don't think that Nicole needs to come, I don't think it's necessary. Is our room ready, is it the same room? Will we go all together in the car to the funeral parlour later?'

Françoise held up her hands, laughing a little. 'Stop, little brother, stop! So many questions!'

He raised an eyebrow at her, took a sip of his wine. 'I just want to know. I wanted to take Nicole into Bordeaux, maybe this afternoon, but I don't know if we will have time.'

'Hmmm, the traffic on Saturdays... It might be difficult. The funeral parlour said we can come from 7pm, so you won't have much time this afternoon – look, it's already after 3pm.'

She turned to me, smiled and said in English, 'But Nicole can see Bordeaux another time. I'm sure she will be visiting us again very soon, and she is probably tired after a long journey from Paris – especially when you have probably been driving like a maniac as usual...'

I rolled my eyes. 'You're not kidding.'

There are digital noticeboards overhead on the autoroute that automatically detect excess speed, note the numberplate and flash it up, together with a warning. I had begun to suspect that Guy took it as a personal challenge to make sure his numberplate was flashed up on every one of them.

She groaned. 'Always. He doesn't care, he always drives too fast. One day he is going to have his licence cancelled, he will lose too many points.' In France the points system is inverse to the UK: you start with twelve points on your licence and lose them for traffic infractions.

'Not a problem for me,' he said smugly. 'I use my British driving licence when I hire the car. No points on my French licence.' A sly smile. '*Voilà, la mythique* Brexit benefit.' Which made the wine I'd just sipped come out of my nose, making Conor laugh even harder than he already was, while the others looked on bemused.

I met Guy's other two siblings the next day at the funeral.

'Nicole, this is my brother Stephane, his wife Catherine.'

'*Enchantée.*' I smiled the small, funeral-appropriate smile I had been practising in the mirror that morning. 'I am so very sorry for your loss.'

They both stared at me in silence as if I had crawled out from under something very unpleasant. Stephane was slightly taller than Guy and had the same eyes, but where Guy was solid and athletic, he was thin and gaunt. He drew the longest, loudest, most disdainful breath I think I've ever heard, at the end of which he gave an almost imperceptible nod, stirring his thin lips a fraction. Although there was no actual sound, I understood that I had been acknowledged.

Catherine made no such Herculean effort. Her eyes travelled from the top of my head all the way down to my demure black Louboutins (well, the demurest pair that I have) and then slowly all the way up again, her gaze coming to rest slightly below my left eye. 'You are very tall,' she said accusingly. Her small mouth puckered in disapproval, nostrils flaring as if she'd just smelled something really bad.

I wondered what the best way was to answer that: 'I'm not actually that tall, I just know how to rock a pair of heels'?

'Yes, she is tall, isn't she?' Dislike, perhaps even hatred, dripped from Guy's voice. His arm slid possessively, tightly around my waist. 'Nicole used to be a model before I met her.' He matched her hostile stare, which had become several degrees more hostile.

'A *WICKED* life!' She spat out the word.

It suddenly hit me exactly who she reminded me of: Blackadder's puritan aunt as played by the fabulous Miriam Margolyes! Not quite as robust a model, but every inch as repressed. My mouth began to twist in an effort to keep the edges down.

'Not as wicked as she is now,' said Guy childishly and, without waiting for her reaction, whisked me off smartly toward the church entrance, muttering about 'uptight *pieux connards, putain*' until I had to nudge him in the ribs to shut him up.

He introduced me to Antoine, the second-eldest brother, then spotted someone across the room and scooted off, leaving me with what was clearly the cuckoo-in-the-nest sibling. Wheatwhite blond hair, watery blue eyes, short, plump – and rabidly racist according to Guy.

'So, Nicole, tell me, when you were modelling, did you ever meet Karl Lagerfeld?'

I admitted that I had not.

'Ah, such a shame, I met him once. He was *fabuleux!*' Short pause. 'What about Jean-Paul Gaultier?'

'No, not him either, unfortunately.'

'Oh, what a shame. He is also *fabuleux!*' Short pause. 'Galliano? He was very unfairly treated, I thought. Did you ever meet him?'

I wondered whether I hadn't perhaps been a little harsh on Darth Vader and the Arch Bitch; I was starting to miss their witty repartee. 'No, not him either, I'm afraid. I did once meet Stella McCartney, and she was lovely.'

'Oh, I don't know anything about her.'

I finally saw a hint of family resemblance in the jowly pout Antoine affected. Somewhat relieved, I saw Guy heading back my way, followed by a very slim, extraordinarily elegant woman in charcoal-grey Chanel.

'Nicole,' he said, smiling broadly, taking my arm and turning his back rudely on Antoine. 'I want you to meet someone. This is Isabelle. Isabelle *je te présente*, Nicole.'

'*Enchantée*, Nicole.' She stretched out a small, slender, perfectly manicured hand. It was cool against mine, which suddenly felt hot. I immediately saw where his children got their almond-shaped eyes and cheekbones.

She wasn't very tall, although it was clear she could also rock a pair of heels – and then some. Her black hair was short, *très chic*; it suited her delicate, high cheek-boned face perfectly.

'Isabelle, hello. I'm so pleased to meet you.' I smiled nervously, resisted the urge to curtsey. Blimey, how the fuck had they ever agreed whose turn it was to be emperor on a daily basis?

Her long, black eyelashes swept slowly over her dark eyes. She smiled, a cool little smile, but not unkind. 'It is nice to meet you too, Nicole. I am sorry it is not under different circumstances.' Her voice was rich, low, her English only lightly accented.

'Isabelle! I didn't expect to see you here!' Antoine wriggled his padded little body between Guy and her. At that point I was reassured that she had not in any way been unfriendly to me. The eyelashes were lowered disdainfully, her upper lip contracted, nostrils dilated, and she tilted her elegant chin a little at him. 'Well, Antoine, here I am. Your mother was the grandmother to my children, and she was always very good to me. I have come to pay my respects.'

And then she turned, gave a positively Napoleonic sniff, nodded another little smile at me, and walked majestically across the room to embrace Charlotte and Emmanuel, who had just arrived.

'So, what did you think of Isabelle, *mon amour*?' Guy asked later that day on the way to the airport.

'Incredibly intimidating. Extraordinarily elegant, self-assured. Really scary. Like she was born in Chanel, the very quintessence of Paris, of France. '

He laughed delightedly. 'You must tell her that! Isabelle always calls herself a mongrel!'

'What?!'

'Yes, she describes herself as a Parisian mongrel. Her father was Algerian, and her mother is half-Russian, half-Hungarian. They met in Paris in the 1950s, so her French background is only from her father when Algeria was a French colony.' Then his eyes narrowed. 'This is why she hates Antoine so much. He is so stupid, always making stupid, racist comments about people who are not "pure" French, whatever that is!'

'Wow. He must be incredibly stupid to dare to piss her off. Does he live in Paris, too?'

'No, he lives in Nice. He is a big fan of that terrible blonde bitch Le Pen – or maybe it's her niece, I don't know – but *ultra-droite* in politics. He is always supporting the racists and the homophobes, which is even more stupid because he is gay! He goes to the *Rassemblement National* meetings with his boyfriend, even though they are full of *putain d'homophobes*!' He shook his head angrily. 'But he knows I will kill him if he talks about my children, about their mother, their heritage. I will snap his fat little neck in two pieces, *petit connard*!'

'Well, Isabelle seems a thousand percent Parisian to me, whatever her background.'
'Yes,' he nodded, calming slightly. 'She is. Like a lot of Parisians, it doesn't really matter what your family background is. If you are born there, you are always more Parisian than you are anything else.'
'Like Londoners.'
'No, Nicole, not like Londoners. It's not the same thing at all.'
Yadda, yadda, yadda: long lecture about France, the superiority of French culture, Paris the sparkling jewel amongst all the other negligible contenders, etcetera, etcetera. But at least he wasn't angry or sad anymore.

Chapter Nine

'This afternoon we go shopping!' Guy announced uncharacteristically cheerfully as we left the gym together the following Saturday.
I raised an eyebrow. 'You hate shopping.'
'Yes but today we go shopping for the engagement ring for my fiancée!' He pulled me close, kissed my cheek. 'This is good shopping. Not shopping for expensive clothes so that the *petit connard* can have another wank.' Eyes narrowed.
'Slippery ground there, Romeo.'

Chaumet was expensively quiet after busy Bond Street, crowded with tourists. I had spent a considerable amount of time in Paris perusing the *haute joallerie* in Galeries Lafayette, flirting gently with the immaculate, charming assistants, male and female, while trying on various rings. I was very clear in my mind about what I wanted, and gradually getting comfortable with the idea of being engaged. Engaged didn't mean married; it just meant engaged, a kind of flirtation with the idea of marriage. I was okay with that. And marriage, well, that could be a flirtation with the idea of divorce if things went wrong. Nothing was permanent, was it?

The salesman was the epitome of elegance: tall, olive skinned, exquisitely groomed. He greeted us in heavily accented English; Guy answered him in French. He showed me the rings from the collection I was interested in, which was called 'Bee My Love' and based on the honeycomb of a bee: a single honeycomb ring in yellow, pink or white gold, studded with small diamonds.

I picked up a pink gold one with diamonds to look at it more closely, glanced at Guy. He made a face. 'No, I don't like it. It looks cheap.'

The salesman smoothly intervened, showing us how the different coloured rings interlocked to create a wider ring. The three golds together, sparkling with diamonds, were beautiful – exactly what I wanted. The assistant helped me slip them onto my wedding ring finger; his hands were cool and smooth, perfectly manicured. I turned, fingers splayed, to show Guy.

Same pout, slightly more exaggerated. 'No, I don't like it. Not big enough. You need a big diamond, *mon amour*.' He focused on the collection. 'Here is one that I like.' He picked it up. The subtle honeycomb shape was disfigured by a solitaire diamond.

I stared at him. 'I don't like it. I like this combination, these three together.'

He stared back. 'So, take this combination instead. Three of these, with the solitaire in each, in the different gold colours you like.'

'It will look shit, Guy. It will look like a diamond-pooping bird has shat on my hand.'

The assistant looked slightly confused. He could sense that the sale might be imperilled. '*Monsieur* would like to see more *diamant solitaires*?'

'*Monsieur* can look at all the solitaire diamonds he wants,' I said crossly. 'I don't want one. I want this combination. I love this combination. It's discreet, playful, beautifully designed.'

More frowning. 'It's not expensive enough, Nicole.' Turning to the assistant, 'How much is this combination?' in French.

The assistant told him. He turned to me crossly. 'See? It is not nearly expensive enough for an engagement ring. And your finger will be full when the marriage ring also has to go on.'

I looked at him thoughtfully. 'Can we not just do away with all that bullshit? All that engagement-then-marriage crap, all the different rings? We're not twenty-two-year-olds getting married in a church after a long betrothal. We're adults, one of us has already been married, and we're getting married in a registry office.' I looked at the ring combination on my finger. It sparkled so prettily.

He sensed that I was not going to change my mind, but he wasn't happy. 'So, if that is the ring you want, I will buy you a wedding present as well.'

'Clothes?' I smiled sweetly at him.

'*QUOI*?!' A couple on the other counter turned to stare. 'Why do you say these things to me? Today, the important day when we are buying a wedding ring, and you are thinking about clothes

again so that *petit connard* will carry on masturbating and laugh when he sees the *tout petit* ring that you insist I buy—'
I kicked him on the shin. Hard. He yelped. 'Enough, or we are NEVER going to get married.' Hissed through gritted teeth.
He swallowed, glared at me. I glared back.
Big pout. 'Okay, I will say no more about it.'
'Anyway, I meant a special dress, not a dress for the office, Romeo.'
Which is how the dark-blue Balenciaga evening gown came to nestle silkily in my wardrobe. Guy also became enthusiastic about buying me more very expensive underwear, on condition that I never, ever, EVER wore it to the office.
I wore the Balenciaga gown over some of the very expensive underwear to dinner at Galvins. Guy theatrically presented the ring box after dessert and proposed to me in lavishly traditional fashion, excepting the kneeling stuff because I told him that I would kick him if he did that. The maître d' uncorked a bottle of Dom Perignon and poured us each a glass, and the tables close to us gave a little round of applause, which made me deeply embarrassed. But I said yes, even though there was still a part of me that was shocked, stunned, at what was happening.

At first, I took off the rings in the lift on the way up to the office. I wasn't exactly sure why; an aversion to the comments, the congratulations I knew a ring on that finger would trigger? I'd observed, even participated in the office rituals that my fellow personal assistants followed when one of their colleagues got engaged. The thought of being at the centre of one of those rituals horrified me.

Or perhaps it was a last bid to hold on to my independence for as long as possible.

I had dreamt of Karl again the night of the formal proposal, the traditional proposal. It was one of the worst dreams, one of the most painful.

I'd had it before, in Ireland after I'd been discharged, but this time it was more vivid. We stood, Karl and I, side-by-side gazing out over a perfect, light-filled, horizontally bisected ochre-and-blue world; it was hot, a hot wind was blowing on us. He turned his head to look at me and I turned my head to look at him; we gazed at each other in perfect symmetry, his silver eyes into mine, my green eyes into his. And then he smiled that beautiful smile, and his eyes travelled down to my perfectly formed belly, carrying the perfectly formed child we had created. And I smiled back at him. And then we both turned back to face the horizon. But the world wasn't bisected ochre and blue anymore: it was black and red now.

And then I woke, woke gasping, woke crying, my cheeks wet with tears.

D'Artagnan made a muffled noise in his sleep. His arms crossed over me, holding me tighter against him; a tear from my face fell onto his forearm. I kissed it off. My heart felt like lead.

Later that week, Guy was waiting outside our offices impatiently (so out of character!) in a taxi; we had tickets to *La Traviata* in Covent Garden and I was running late – the sociopath was being an arsehole. I had finally managed to get away, but it was pouring with rain as I climbed into the taxi feeling hassled, flustered, wet.

I leaned in and kissed him as the taxi drove off. He did not kiss me back. 'Why are you not wearing the ring I buy you, Nicole?'

Oh *GOD*. Flip through the list of possible excuses at lightning speed. Blank. Shrug. 'I dunno. Busy day, darling?'

'You don't want people to know we are engaged?'

'No Guy. It's not that.' I sighed. God, he was tiring. 'I don't know why, it's just that I don't want everyone to make a fuss. I hate all that cooing and giggling and girly shit that goes on, as if getting married is all that women dream about, that it's the fulfilment of all of their fantasies, all of their desires, ambitions. I hate all that shit.'

I dared to glance at him. 'It's not got anything to do with how I feel about you. I love you. I'm pretty fucking crazy about you, actually and I'm even beginning to be okay about the idea of getting married to you.' I looked him in the eyes, willing him to let it go.

He held my gaze, shaking his head slightly. '*Mon dieu* Nicole, you are very, very good at deflating the ego of a man.'

'For God's sake, Guy, did you not just hear what I said?! I said I love you, I'm crazy about you, it's just – I'm still getting used to the idea of getting married! It's not something I ever really thought about before you. It seemed something alien to me, weird, this idea of codified obligations, making vows and promises. Life isn't like that, it's messier than that, messier than neat little ceremonies that imply that love is something that can be governed by vows and rules and conventions.' I sat back, slightly surprised at what had just spewed forth from my mouth. It made quite a lot of sense, I thought.

He nodded slowly, thoughtfully. 'Okay, Nicole, I understand more now. You are frightened again.'

I stared at him. 'I'm struggling to hear the fear in what I just said.'

'Not real fear, not *aieee I am going to die* fear! When I say you are frightened, I mean you are worried, you are scared. You are scared that you are being asked to make a promise when you don't know how you will feel in the future about that promise you made in the past. And because you are a person that does not make a promise easily, this is what is worrying you.'

I continued to stare at him. That actually also kind of made sense. Was it possible we were going to see eye to eye on something for the first time?

'But this is normal, Nicole. We don't know what is in the future, we don't know that we can keep the promise we make in the past. But we try, we make the promise, we try to keep the promise. This is what being married is. Sometimes we don't succeed, for all different kind of reasons. We break the promise. It is hard to accept that we break a promise, that we fail. But it does not mean we cannot try to make a promise, that we cannot believe in this promise.' He reached over, picked up my hand, held it to his lips.

There was a scratchy noise on the cab intercom.

'He's right, swee'eart,' interjected the cabby. 'Your Frenchie, he's right. I know what 'e means. I been married four times, I believed every time in the promise, and now my lovely Cathy, my fourth wife – twen'y-five years we been married, still 'appy, never been 'appier!'

I started laughing at the absurdity of it and the cabby joined in, laughing uproariously over the scratchy intercom. Guy smiled at me, then leaned forward and flicked the intercom to 'Off'. He did not like being upstaged. 'So, Nicole, you will wear the ring? And you try to keep the promise, *mon amour*. That is all I ask you to do when I ask you to marry me.'

The sociopath clocked the offending finger first thing the following morning. He raised a fuzzy blonde eyebrow, his thin little lips twitched, his pink cheeks pinkened a little more. 'I see congratulations are in order, Nicole.'

I smiled at him, shrugged a little. 'Yeah. Who'd have guessed!'

That being the full extent of his congratulations, he moved swiftly on, smirking unpleasantly. 'I'm rather pleased actually, as I'm afraid I have some bad news for you. I've been offered a promotion to the New York Office,' the equivalent of the Nobel Prize, by the reverence in his voice, 'and the bank aren't going to be replacing my position here in London, so I'm afraid I have to give you notice of termination of your position. HR are just drafting the letter now.'

For once, I was taken by surprise. Either he really had only just been offered the posting or he had rather craftily managed to conceal it from me; there had been no meetings with HR in the preceding weeks that I'd been aware of.

'Oh well, congratulations Stephen.' I gave him a tight little smile. 'I'm sure you'll fit in just fine over there.'

'I imagine I shall do more than just "fit in", Nicole!' he guffawed, his pink, piggy little eyes scrunched up at his hilarious witticism as he swaggered back into his office.

I tried not to let the news of my impending unemployment bother me; after all, life was about to change in so many ways once I married D'Artagnan. But I hadn't been prepared for the idea of losing my job, and by extension my financial independence, quite so abruptly.

'It's almost as if he'd been waiting for that exact moment to tell me, as if he already knew we were engaged and was saving up that little nugget, a sort of revenge. I mean, he's normally not smart enough to be devious,' I complained to Guy, lying between his legs on the sofa. We were watching a French film on *Arte;* the plot was complicated, and my mind was wandering.

'Well Nicole, maybe he did know. I tell some of my colleagues, maybe he hear something about it from someone else.' A little shrug. 'Anyway, it's good news, *n'est-ce pas, ma chérie?* It means that we can take a long honeymoon after we are married. We can have three weeks in the sun. This will be very good for us.' He looked pleased. 'I extend the reservation tomorrow.'

When the honeymoon discussion had aired, I had explained that it wasn't going to be possible to take more than a week's holiday – my contractual year ran from May to May, and I only had five days holiday left until it renewed. The sociopath was not in a mood to be flexible about my going on honeymoon with the Frenchman who had, I assumed, physically threatened – or worse, actually assaulted him. D'Artagnan had never been forthcoming about exactly how the clothing allowance conversation had ended, other than to say darkly that the sociopath would not be mentioning it to anyone else in the future.

'Yes, I suppose it is convenient for that,' I mused, at the same time observing the tiniest little crack of dawn appearing in the darkness of my mind. Slowly, thoughtfully: 'It is all rather convenient isn't it, Guy? Us getting engaged, Stephen being sent to New York, me losing my job, us going on honeymoon. Almost, I dunno…'

I sat up, turned around to look at him, my elbow on his hip. 'Almost like it's been rather cleverly orchestrated by someone.' I stared at him. He carried on watching the TV, but I swear he was biting his lip on the inside. 'I don't suppose any of this has your fingerprints on it, has it?' I leaned heavily on my elbow, digging it into his side.

He squirmed and pushed it away, started laughing. 'No, Nicole, it's nothing to do with me. There are no fingerprints!'

'Is that because you were very careful to wipe them away? What else were you doing while you were in New York in January? I remember that you said you were having lunch with Francesca – did you do something, did you say something to her to orchestrate this?' Francesca was the MD of my bank's New York office.

'I was working!' He shot me a look, but there was a smirk hiding, not very well, behind it. 'But maybe. Yes, I had a lunch with Francesca. She is an old friend, I often have a lunch with her if I am in New York. I don't remember everything we talk about.' He shrugged, turned back to watch the TV, but I could see the small, upward curl at the edge of his mouth.

I carried on watching him watching the TV. 'Guy ... seriously. Did you do this?'

He turned back to me, earnest now. 'No, Nicole, I did not do this. You think I have this much power? I don't make decisions in your bank about who goes where, who has a job where, who loses their job.'

He seemed sincere, but his answer was clever, nuanced, wily, and he wasn't altogether answering the question. Of course he didn't have power to make decisions for my employer, but I knew that he knew Francesca well, and Francesca was powerful; even I, a lowly secretary in London, knew this. It was quite possible that my job had been collateral damage in his machinations to remove the sociopath from our lives, a topic that I knew was never far from his mind.

'Hmmm. Well, at least answer this honestly. When you had lunch with Francesca in New York, did Stephen's name come up at all?'

The tiniest pout, a twitched eyebrow, hint of shrug. 'I don't remember, Nicole. Maybe.' Turning back to the TV. But there was still that tiny, slightly self-satisfied curl at the edge of his mouth.

And that, as far as he was concerned, was the end of the conversation. My suspicions were not allayed.

Guy seemed to think that we had done all the discussing we needed to do about our future living arrangements: the Muffins and I would be moving into his apartment in South Ken immediately after we were married. There were times that his certainty made me stop and think: did we actually discuss this, and I didn't remember the conversation? Such is D'Artagnan's innate self-confidence that if he wants something to happen, to all intents and purposes it has already happened.

'So, when are you going to call the estate agents, Nicole, to sell your apartment? When are you going to move your furniture? You must rent some space, there is no room for it in my apartment. Maybe you should sell the furniture also.'

We were in my apartment after a not-very-good meal in the local 'gastro' pub, and were finishing a bottle of wine I'd opened the night before. 'When did we have that discussion?' I frowned at him.

He stared at me. 'What do you mean?'

'When did I agree to sell my apartment? I can't remember having that discussion?'

Pout. 'You are moving in to my apartment after we are married. Why do you still need your apartment?'

I shrugged. 'I don't "need" my apartment Guy, but maybe I should just rent it out? I'm not sure it's a good time to sell. I won't have a job anymore, so at least it will provide me with some income while I find another job.'

'It is a good time to sell, Nicole. You should sell it. You don't need to have income. I have a lot of money, enough for both of us. Sell your apartment. You can put the money in your own account, you can keep it, or spend it on anything you want, I don't care, because you will not need it when we are married.' He smiled smugly, as if it were all sorted.

'That's not very, er, responsible, though, is it?'

He shrugged. 'So put it in your savings account. What do you think the value of your apartment is? Five, six hundred thousand pounds? I think that is what it is worth. I can help you invest some of it if you want me to, but it will be your money, *mon amour*.'

'Less the mortgage. So, probably about £300,000 in equity, maybe £350K max.'

It was his turn to frown. 'What mortgage?'

'I have a mortgage on the flat. I don't know how much is outstanding on it, but I think it's about £350,000.'

'But Nicole, I don't understand. Why do you have a mortgage? Why do you need a mortgage? You must have made a lot of money in ten years doing the shows? For photo shoots, for *Vogue* and *Elle*? That is good money, surely enough to buy this apartment with no mortgage?'

After I'd finished rolling on the floor laughing (metaphorically speaking), I wiped away the (metaphorical) tears. 'Oh lovely naïve man, you really have no idea how corrupt the world of fashion is, do you? You have no concept of the level of exploitation that goes on! Let me enlighten you.' I took a sip of my wine.

'First off, no one ever tells you exactly how much you're being paid for shows or shoots because whatever figure you hear either is or isn't net of bookers fees, agency fees, sometimes hair and make-up fees. Sometimes the amount that you're actually paid is nothing like what you were told and, strangely, it's never revised upwards. But you don't care because your agent is taking care of it. That's what agents are for: they're looking out for you, you and all the other skinny little girls up there sashaying up and down under the bright lights. You don't care, you're twenty-two! Life is amazing, exciting. When you're not working, you're clubbing in London, in Paris, in New York, in Milan. You don't even remember where you are half the time. There's an endless supply of coke and Champagne, you get to wear lovely clothes, you never eat anything and everything you need is taken care of by your agent. Life is fast and groovy.'

I paused. He was listening quietly.

'But sometimes non-groovy things happen, and you get strung out and the coke isn't really cutting it anymore. Then someone suggests that perhaps a bit of smack might help to de-string you, so you do some smack, chase it with coke and you drink some more Champagne. Woo-hoo. The non-groovy stuff is muted again. Your agent tells you you're doing great. You're booked months ahead. You party some more. One day, you wake up and you think, fuck me, how did this happen – I'm twenty-eight years old! And you know that reaching twenty-nine is not a sure thing, let alone thirty. The thought that you will actually ever reach the age of thirty is so absurd that it makes you collapse in a fit of hysterics.'

I glanced at him. He looked sad.

'So you start to think about that a bit more, and you realise that maybe that isn't a good thing. And when you decide that you really need to get your shit together if you are ever going to celebrate your thirtieth birthday, you ask your agent how much money you have because you only have the cards for your bank account. He does all the rest – your accounts, your expenses, your rent, your taxes. And he tells you and you think okay, that's not a bad amount of money to have after nearly ten years of being completely out of control of your life. It's not as much as you thought it would be, but it's not bad. And it isn't until quite some time later, when you talk to your other, smarter, less messed-up ex-colleagues, the ones with useful skills like self-respect, and parents and agents who actually do look out for them, that you realise that you have been pretty royally screwed by the people you thought were looking out for you, and that in fact no one has been looking out for you.'

'I'm so sorry that no-one was caring for you, Nicole.' Guy touched my shoulder, smoothed the hair behind my ear, his voice gentle, sad.

I shrugged. 'I try not to hold on to all that anger about that part of my life or it will consume me. I left it back there; I focus on the now. And the now is good, my darling, because I have you in my life.' I leaned in, kissed him softly on the mouth.

Which ultimately, of course, led to the inevitable.

Chapter Ten

As soon as we'd returned from his mother's funeral, he had booked the registry office in Chelsea. There was a cancellation in mid-March, on day thirty after the obligatory twenty-nine-day pre-wedding registration period. He reserved it for us.

'But it's a Monday morning,' I said, frowning, when he told me the date.

Small Gallic shrug. 'It was available. The next one was not until two weeks later.'

'Was the next available date not slightly more ... I dunno, romantic?'

'I didn't ask. We need to get married, Nicole.'

'Yes, but why so quickly?'

'Because. Why not?'

I continued to frown at him. 'Because it will be difficult for Jules and Mark to come. Almost impossible for the kids, in fact. They'll be at school, and they'll be disappointed.'

We were at the opening night of a photographic exhibition that included several monumental, mesmerising Andreas Gursky prints. Guy slipped his arm around my waist. 'But this is just the formal marriage, *mon amour*, this is not for our friends. We have the proper marriage later, a big *fête* at the *ch— bah*, in France in summer. *That* is when we have all the family and the friends. *That* is when we have the proper marriage ceremony.'

I thought about that for a minute. 'I'm not doing that whole white dress, veil, flowers, aisle-bullshit thing, you know.'

He smirked, raised an eyebrow. 'I agree with you, Nicole, a white dress would not be very appropriate for you, for us. You can wear whatever you want, *mon amour*. You have time to think about it, to find a wedding dress in any colour you like.'

'Yeah, I suppose I do have time. Remind me again, why do we need to get married now when we could just get married in the summer?'

'Just because, Nicole! *Merde*, why are you arguing with me again about this?'

All those little clues. And I didn't pick up on a single one of them.

The marriage ceremony was short and shockingly, surprisingly, emotional. Jules had insisted that she and Mark were our witnesses. I was so grateful that they were there, as the temptation to bolt or faint or explode when the registrar said, 'These vows are a formal and public pledge of their love and a promise of a lifelong commitment to each other,' was off the scale. But Jules caught my panicked gaze just as I disengaged it from the fathomless depths of Guy's soft, soft eyes and she smiled the loveliest, happiest smile at me, tears in her own eyes.

That worked. I did not do any of the above. I repeated the words the registrar recited to me, Guy repeated the words he was required to say, and then it was done, and the registrar said, 'You may now kiss each other.'

Guy smiled delightedly at me, his eyes wet, and I found that I was smiling equally delightedly back at him, and that my eyes were wet too. I think the registrar was a bit embarrassed at the intensity of the kiss, though.

Jules eventually thumped Guy on the back, muttering, 'There are others present, people.'

The wedding day had not started well. I had been in Selfridges the Saturday before, trying on a banana-yellow Versace trouser suit that looked fabulous with an extravagantly funky guava-pink silk shirt. I wondered if it was appropriate for a wedding.

'Nicole?' I heard someone exclaim. I turned. My heart sank.

'Anthony! Hi! How are you?' I tried to sound pleased to see him, but I really, really wasn't. He had been one of Karl's fellow students at film school, had known us both quite well, had always been a nice, gentle guy. He'd been the one to drop the bombshell that fatal evening, only because he could no longer bear to ignore what was going on. Like I said, a nice guy.

'I'm fine, thanks. How're you, though? I thought you'd left London?' He still had those very sad, downturned eyes.

'Er, yes, I did.' I smiled brightly. 'Just visiting, actually.'

'Oh? Where are you living now?'

'Er...' The temptation to say 'Mars, actually' was strong. But instead, I said, 'France. Bordeaux.' It was the first thing that popped into my mind, but even saying that made me feel uncomfortable. We were bound to go to Bordeaux from time to time in the future: what if Anthony was still in touch with Karl. What if he told Karl?

'Oh, lovely. It's a great city, isn't it? I'm so pleased for you. You look so well, Nicole. Are you modelling again? That suit looks fabulous on you!'

I smiled at him. He really was a nice guy. 'Thanks, Anthony, that's kind of you to say. No, I'm not modelling any more. How's the film world?'

'It's good, thanks. I'm assistant director on a film for Netflix, we're shooting now, and I've got a short film showing at Sundance next year. Hey, did you hear about Karl? He won best new director last year at Sundance?' Then, as he clocked my frozen expression, 'Oh, I'm so sorry, Nicole. You probably don't want to hear about Karl...'

Nice guy, as I said, but a bit slow on the uptake.

Guy had insisted that we spent Sunday night at our separate apartments. 'It's traditional, Nicole. Then I take you home and ravish you after the wedding.' Wicked eyebrows.

I woke up at 3.30am on Monday morning, bathed in sweat, my heart hammering, the imprint of Karl's lips on mine, his intense, shimmering silver gaze so real, so tangible, the touch of his fingers on my face still fresh, and the usual enormous, unquantifiable loss filling the pit of my soul. It was very difficult not to think it was a bad omen for my marriage to D'Artagnan in seven hours' time.

I reached for Mr and Mrs Muffin, sleeping at the foot of the bed, stroked them quietly while I tried to forget the image of Karl's eyes, the feel of his lips, the acute sense of loss. I curled myself around them and finally fell asleep again.

In the end, I didn't buy the banana-yellow trouser suit; it seemed just a teeny bit too subversive for the Chelsea registry office on a cool, wet Monday morning in March. Instead, I bought a dusty-pink Valentino silk dress, backless apart from intricate criss-crossed satin ribbons laced tightly at the base of the spine, and a cream Erdem raw-silk fitted jacket. I wore them both with Roger Vivier cream satin heels with espadrille-ribbon satin ties. D'Artagnan was still going through a slightly obsessive ribbons, bracelets and other-things-that-knot phase, so I knew this would please him very much.

And it did. We were married, and afterwards I felt strangely happy, light, both in head and heart. Perhaps it was relief that it was done, but I also know that I felt different when I looked at him. He looked different, as if in some weird way I was seeing him properly for the first time. More ... strong, more solid, more just bloody gorgeous.

How the hell had this happened? How had I, little Miss Scared-of-Everything, married this tall, arrogant, gorgeous French man? It was extraordinary, now that I stopped and thought about it. I felt a bit shellshocked. This had never been part of the script.

We went to Galvin at Windows with Juliette and Mark for our wedding lunch. It was Guy's favourite French restaurant in London; it was where I'd worn the Balenciaga gown, where the formal proposal had taken place. We toasted with Champagne, ate a sumptuous meal, drank excellent wine, laughed a lot; the mood was elated, beatific. Jules took pictures of us against the London skyline, we smiled at each other, kissed each other with our eyes, our lips. Guy kissed my neck, my naked shoulder when I slipped off the silk jacket for some of the photos.

I heard him give a small groan when I turned slightly so that he saw the back of the dress and I felt his teeth graze the nape of my neck as he kissed it; it made me blink very, very slowly, tighten deliciously inside.

Our waiter took pictures of the four of us against the London skyline. We laughed; we were happy. I caught Guy looking at me too, as if *he* were surprised, as if I too were different, and he touched me constantly throughout the lunch, as if checking I was real. Covering my left hand with his, the thick gold wedding band on his finger metallic against the rings on my finger, he touched my hair and I touched his cheek with the back of my hand.

Later the sex, like a supernova fucking core-collapse. Look it up. Yeah, like that. It was our wedding night. It's private.

And then, on the Friday evening after I'd said my goodbyes to my colleagues and the sociopath (we were equally insincere), after I'd taken the lift to the ground floor of the bank for the last time, walked out of the building with my very few personal belongings (primarily pictures of Jules, Mark and the kids, the Muffins) in a bag and was standing there, hoping to spot an empty taxi, I thought, what now? What next? And I didn't feel nearly as much trepidation as I'd expected about the answer to that question.

We went to Mauritius on our honeymoon. *Quelle cliché.* It was fabulous. The hotel was five-star-plus; beautiful young people came around to our sun loungers from time to time and offered to bring us cold drinks, snacks, to polish our sunglasses in case one was feeling a little, I don't know, exhausted, overwhelmed perhaps, at the prospect of polishing one's own sunglasses.

On the eighth day, both darkly tanned by now, we were in the main resort pool. Leafy tropical plants grew abundantly in the central reservation. Guy was holding me around the waist in the water in one of the tiled seating recesses. We kissed.

'I like your hair like this, Nicole.' He did a slight upward movement of his chin, raised a lazy eye and an even lazier eyebrow at my hair, wild with the humidity, piled on top of my head and secured precariously with an elastic tie and a hair grip. I had given up trying to do much else with it.

'Yeah, it's a really easy style to master here. It's called "just been".' Indolent smile.

'Just been what?'

'Just been fucked.' I leaned in, kissed him. His mouth was cool, silky. I wasn't sure I was physically capable of having any more sex that day, but it didn't seem to stop me wanting more.

And yet he was physically very capable.

'Don't,' I murmured eventually, breaking off. 'Not here, not in the pool. There are people all around us, my darling.'

'So we go to the room, *mon amour.* Now, we go to the room.'

'Yes. Okay. No, we can't, not right now.' Another swooning kiss. 'Seriously, Guy, we're going to be in here the rest of the afternoon unless you stop doing that. You have to get out of the pool without looking like an ancient-Egyptian fertility god, so no, stop!'

I disentangled myself, moved away, stood in the water in front of him out of his reach. He gazed at me, the same lazy smile, sexy eyes at half-mast. 'So, you go first, *mon ange*, I come after.' An eyebrow raised itself. 'But you do the sexy model walk out of the pool, up the stairs. If you blow me a Marilyn kiss at the top of the stairs, I wait in the pool a bit.' Hard, lusty eyes. 'Otherwise,' he pronounced this '*ozzerwize*', 'I come after you immediately. Okay, Nicole? We are agreed?'

I gazed into his eyes. 'Remember, sweetheart, we talked quite a lot about manipulation and control? And here, all I'm hearing is manipulation and control.'

'*Pffft. Tant pis,* Nicole. This is the deal.' The eyes, even more sinful than usual.

'Or we can just stay in the pool, not doing anything about this.' I reached out, touched him gently, and he blinked slowly. 'And you can wait until the chlorine starts to destroy your swimming shorts, and makes you go all wrinkly.'

'It is a saltwater pool, Nicole.' Another slow blink.

I started laughing. 'Well, whatever kind of pool it is, we're at an impasse, my darling man. We can't have sex in the public pool, there are other people here. And you can't get out because you have a massive hard-on, so – I dunno, what do you want to do?'

'Like I say, Nicole, you do the model walk out of the pool, you stop at the top, give me a Marilyn kiss. I wait a bit so that it is not so obvious, then I get out of the pool. Then we go to the room and fuck.' He smiled. 'It's very simple.'

But as I walked out of the pool, doing a slightly reluctant (and at the same time not very reluctant because I kind of did want to keep him in that zone) catwalk swagger, a sudden gust of wind blew across the pool area. It snatched away the rather extravagantly brimmed sunhat of a woman on a nearby sun lounger; she gave a little 'oh!' of dismay as the hat took flight and bounced across the poolside paving slabs. I managed to grab it just before it landed in the water and brought it back to her.

'Oh, thank you so much, dear!' Her accent was pure Home Counties. I guessed she was in her sixties or thereabouts. The man I assumed was her husband, large bellied and vibrantly red with sunburn, was snoring on the sun lounger next to her.

'It's a pleasure,' I smiled. 'It got mine yesterday, and I had to fish it out of the pool. That wind, it comes up suddenly from nowhere!'

She smiled back warmly. 'Yes, it does, doesn't it?' Then, 'I hope you don't mind me saying, dear, but you're such a lovely couple. You seem so in love. It's really touching to see. Are you on your honeymoon?'

'Yes, we are, thank you. That's so kind of you to say!' I looked away, slightly embarrassed, hoping she hadn't been watching what had been going on in the pool too closely. 'It's a lovely resort, isn't it? Are you enjoying it?'

I glanced back at her, but her gaze had slid away from mine. Her face was transfixed as she watched something behind me; it was obviously fascinating because her mouth had dropped open a little.

I turned to see what it was.

D'Artagnan, with a very full, very obvious erection straining against his swimming shorts, casually emerged from the pool and walked – in fact, it was more of a leisurely amble – across the pool area towards where our sun loungers were as if nothing could be more natural.

'Oh God, I'm so sorry. Please ignore him, he's French. He's uncontrollable,' I gabbled, turning back to her, my face flushing hotly.

There was a pause. Then she said, 'I'm sure he is, dear.' Rather wistfully.

I went back to our sun loungers, head bowed, trying my hardest to attract as little attention as possible.

'Nicole,' Guy purred when I sat down next to him. He reached for my hand.

'Did you have to do that?' I murmured, *sotto voce*.

'What?'

'Walk out of the pool with an obvious hard-on? When we'd agreed you'd stay in until it wasn't quite that obvious?'

'*Pfffft.* You agreed, the model walk, the Marilyn kiss, but this didn't happen, Nicole, so I get bored. And this is an adult-only hotel. There are only adults here, no children. What is the problem?'

I rolled my eyes. 'Er ... not everyone is necessarily comfortable with outright displays of ... uh, virility!'

Full Gallic shrug. '*Pfffft.* The women here, they all have envy of you after they see me. The men here, they all have envy of me when they see you. We are all adults, we know about love, about sex. What isn't comfortable about this?'

I gazed at him. He really didn't give a rat's arse about what anyone else thought.

'So, Nicole, we go to the room now? We get rid of this?' He motioned towards his erection.

'No! Not now! It will be bloody obvious if we get up and leave! We're here for another two weeks and I don't want everyone here to be thinking about where we're going... Frankly, I just don't want them to be thinking!'

Exasperated exhalation and some muttering about '*putain* Anglo-Saxon *pieux* bullshit', then he folded his arms behind his head, closed his eyes and, after ten minutes while I read and re-read the same paragraph in my book several times, he started to snore gently. Gradually his swimming shorts became less – exuberantly occupied, I suppose one could say.

He never lets anything go, though; is always plotting his revenge. After a late dinner with an excellent bottle of Stellenbosch red (Me: 'easily as good as St Emilion'. Him: 'No, Nicole it is not at all the same', followed by a lecture about the superiority of French wine, etc, etc) we were back in the room. The Hermès accessories had, of course, come on honeymoon with us; in fact, I was wearing one of the bracelets that evening, which had not escaped his attention, I knew.

So when I was at that point, that breathless, pleading, poised on the edge of heavenly ecstasy point, he stopped. He stopped, sat back, and I knew he was smiling. I also knew that it was that self-satisfied, I-told-you-so smile when he said, 'So now, Nicole, you know how I feel today when you do not want to come back to the room.'

I heard him get off the bed, pad across the room in his bare feet, heard the rustle of clothes. 'Oh, you bastard,' I half-gasped, half-laughed. 'You can't leave me like this!'

'*Bah,* Nicole, but I can. I am going to have a cigarette outside on the terrace, I think, and then maybe I get dressed and go down to the bar. I quite like this idea. And then, when I am ready, I come back and maybe then, I make you come.' He sat down on the bed next to me. I felt his mouth on mine briefly, then on my nipple, his tongue, his teeth, first one and then the other, his beard slightly rough against my breast, his hand sliding briefly between my legs again. It was exquisite; my back arched against his mouth.

I heard him breathe in very deeply, the slightest groan, but then I felt the mattress shift as he stood up again. 'Not yet, Nicole, only when I am ready. You can spend some time thinking about it, hmmm?'

'I'm going to bloody kill you when this is over,' I whispered hoarsely.

'No, you won't. You will be too ... pleasured, when this is over.'

I heard him pad across the room, the glass door onto the terrace slide open. The warm, humid night air, thick with tropical scents wafted into the room. I heard the lighter flick on, off, smelt the faint smell of tobacco.

Everything was quiet, black behind the blindfold. My nose started to itch; I went to scratch it and was, of course, unable to. The bracelet felt very firm, almost tight, on my wrist.

My mind began to wander. I thought about going to the beach on the other side of the island the next day as we'd been discussing earlier, then I realised that I was actually quite tired. I yawned, went to cover my mouth, was prevented, felt slightly irritated, the muscles in my arms felt a bit taut, uncomfortable.

I wondered why he was so quiet. Was he still out there on the terrace? How long ago had he gone out there? Had he fallen asleep? Had something happened to him? Why was he so quiet? My heart gave a little skip, then started beating faster; I could hear it in my ears.

And then, faintly, I heard voices, a man's voice from a distance then another man's voice. They were coming down the corridor toward our room, they were getting closer, and now I could hear them clearly. They were talking loudly, laughing. They were right outside our room. And then I heard the sound of a key in the lock.

I froze. My whole body was instantly bathed in a cold sweat. I strained against the bracelets but there was no release. I realised I was utterly helpless, defenceless, and a wave of intense fear washed over me.

And then the panic slammed into me like a freight train. I strained with all my might against the bracelets, against the scarf, but could not free my wrists. My heart was beating so hard that it felt as if it were about to explode. I was gasping for breath, unable to get any air into my lungs, which were now starting to ache as my ribcage tightened and tightened around them.

And suddenly he was there, his voice near, then far away. 'Nicole? Are you alright?' Concerned.

I shook my head wildly, could not get any breath to answer.

His fingers on the bracelets, releasing one, then the other, lifting me up into his arms. 'It's okay, it's okay. I am here. I am here.'

I tore the scarf away from my eyes, flailed wildly against him, trying to get away, to get to safety, to hide. He continued to hold me against him. I started hitting him, pushing against him, but I felt increasingly weak. The black dots in front of my eyes were becoming bigger, were starting to join up with one another – and then suddenly everything went black.

'Nicole, Nicole, NICOLE!' When I regained consciousness, he was shaking me by the shoulders, his voice panicked. I took an enormous, wonderful, deep breath of air, but my heart was still hammering in my chest and my lungs still seemed to have forgotten how to function.

'Diazepam,' I gasped. 'Now, please, get diazepam!'

He got up immediately and went into the bathroom. I heard scrabbling and swearing and the sound of things falling on the floor, and then he was back, brandishing the life-saving foil wrapper and a glass of water. I was breathing in tiny little gasps, my upper lip tingling as if it were being electrocuted repeatedly.

I was soaked in sweat, trembling from head to toe, and the black dots were bouncing around the room again, in and out of my vision, taunting me.

'How many?' he asked.

I held up two fingers. He popped out two, put them in my shaking hand and held the glass for me like a child while I gulped the water and swallowed, swallowed the antidote. Then closed my eyes, focusing with all my might on the familiar mantra: The Drugs Will Start Working. The Drugs Will Start Working. The Drugs Will Start Working.

He held me closely against him, stroked my back, didn't say anything.

Chapter Eleven

I woke groggily after midday the next day. I battled to open my eyes; they felt swollen, glued together. I remembered I had been crying, and then I remembered all the other stuff too. I felt sick: sick at myself, my pathetic, stupid self, and ashamed. Yet another attack, just a few weeks after the last one. So pathetic. I closed my eyes again, started to pull the covers over my head, the familiar wave of self-loathing washing over me.

'Nicole? Are you awake?' Guy came in through the sliding door from the terrace and sat down on the bed next to me. He pulled the covers back and stroked my hair back off my face gently.

I couldn't bring myself to look at him. Poor man, I thought. He must be starting to realise he's made a terrible mistake; he's married a fucking basket-case. Oh well, I did try to warn him. Perhaps we could get a quick divorce. How difficult was it to get divorced, I wondered.

'How are you feeling, *mon ange*?' His voice was tender.

I sighed; I didn't want to have to speak. Shrugged. Tears pricked my eyes, and I mentally rolled my eyes at myself. Yay, more crying. What a fun honeymoon!

'What happened, Nicole? Why did you get so scared?'

I shrugged again. A tear insisted on rolling down my cheek. I wiped it away angrily.

He continued to stroke my cheek. 'I order you some tea, yes? Some chamomile tea, okay?'

I shrugged again. He got up and went to the hotel phone on the other side of the bed. I pulled the bedclothes over my head again, curled up in a foetal position and glumly let the tears flow freely from my eyes.

Some hours later, he insisted that I get up and take a shower. He stripped off his clothes and got in with me, held me against him while the hot water pelted down on us. It felt good, cleansing. He poured shampoo into his hands, washed my hair gently, thoroughly, carefully rinsed it all off, applied conditioner, but not enough so I reached for the bottle and made fleeting eye contact with him for the first time that day. Then I quickly looked away; his gaze was too intense. I combed a big gloopy blob of it through my hair with my fingers; he continued to hold me around the waist while I rinsed it out, eyes closed.

As I opened them again, we locked gazes and he gave a little smile. 'A bit better?'

I blinked, shrugged, nodded.

He reached for the shower gel. 'Would you like me to wash you all over, *mon ange*?'

I frowned, gave a little shake of my head. Although it was true that I felt better standing there in the cleansing water, the fog of uselessness, of disappointment in myself, was still thick in my mind.

'I just wash your ears, then.' He poured shower gel into his hands, rubbed them together until they foamed, reached for my ears with his fingertips.

My mouth inadvertently twitched into a twisted little smile; he knew that I was very squeamish about having my ears touched. I tried to push his hands away; he insisted, pushing mine away in turn, his elbows on my shoulders, rubbing the tops of my ears between his soapy fingers so that I tried to squirm away from him.

'They are very dirty, Nicole. I have never seen such dirty ears,' so that my smile turned into a snort and then into more squirming and eventually even some giggling as I tried to get away from his fingers in my ears. And then I was gazing into those deep brown eyes and his mouth was on mine, and we were kissing greedily, urgently, and the water was still pelting down, and then he was lifting me up, holding me against the smooth marble wall, and my legs were wrapped around his waist as I slid down onto him until he was deep inside me, and it felt utterly wonderful each time he lifted me up and slowly lowered me down onto him, so hard, so deep.

'Is that good my angel? How is that, how does that feel?' he murmured, his mouth on my ear, and I managed to gasp, 'It feels … exquisite,' just as my body closed hard on him so that I cried out, and he was saying, '*Oh, mon ange, je t'aime infiniment, je t'aime, je t'aime,*' and I felt him pulsing inside me, and all the stars in the universe exploded and I clung to him, my arms tight around his neck, my mouth pressed against his ear, whispering over and over again, 'Oh my angel, I love you so much, I love you so much, I love you so much,' because I was absolutely intoxicated, drunk with love for him in that moment.

Turns out, hot sex in the shower is the best kind of antidepressant.

Later, wrapped in our bathrobes, his arm around my neck, I lay against him on the terrace sofa as the sun was setting. He asked again what had happened.

I shrugged. 'I heard voices in the corridor and then I heard a key in the lock. I thought they were coming into our room, and I got frightened.'

He nodded slowly. 'So, it's not about the crazy bracelets, then? Because I am confused, Nicole – this is something I think you like before?'

'No, it's not about that. It's just because you weren't there and the voices seemed very close. I felt very ... vulnerable.'

'I understand. I am so sorry, *mon ange*, I should not have left you.' Then a pause. 'Something like that has happened to you in the past to make you this frightened?'

I sighed a deep sigh. 'Oh Guy, all sorts of shit has happened in the past. I really don't want to go into any of it again, if that's okay.'

More slow nodding, a deep breath. 'Okay, Nicole, we won't talk about it. But *mon amour*, I think maybe you must think about talking to a professional person about these things. I think maybe this might help you. This is not healthy, this fear that you have. It is not healthy to be so afraid, so frightened that you become unconscious.'

I swallowed, started to feel the sadness stirring again, made a determined effort to shut it down. 'Yep. Maybe, you're right. I'll think about it, okay?'

He hugged me. '*Merci, mon amour*. But you know, I am always going to be here if this happens, when this happens. You must not worry that it is a problem for me – it is *not* a problem for me. *Je t'aime, mon ange*. I will always be here if you are frightened, I will always protect you. And I will never leave you like that again, even though it was not very long, and I was there on the terrace. I was not far from you, *mon ange.*'

'Thank you, my darling.' I smiled up at him, lifted his hand, kissed the back of it.

The evening air was warm and soothing. I realised I was hungry. 'Anyway Guy, I'm bloody STARVING. Can we go eat something?'

He sat up abruptly, stared at me. '*Bah,* Nicole, you must be more sick than I think! You are NEVER hungry! There must be something wrong!'

I made a face. It's true, it's always him that's starving, him that demands that we go and eat, it's never normally me but I really was hungry. It felt like my stomach was trying to eat itself and that it might even be succeeding.

We arrived back in London on a cold, wet, rainy April day. In the cab on the way to his – our now, I suppose – apartment, he kissed the back of my hand. 'Should we go on holiday tomorrow, do you think, *mon amour*? Somewhere with the sun?'

I smiled at him. 'No. I miss my Muffins. I want to see my Muffins again.' The pet-sitting service had sent me photos of them every day, but they were timid cats and most of the photos were of them hiding under the bed or in some cupboard. Although the new apartment was bigger, about twice the size of mine (the second bedroom had been comprehensively filled with my clothing collection) the cats had only arrived a few days before we left on honeymoon. I felt bad that I hadn't been there to help them settle in to their new and unfamiliar home.

'Besides, doesn't at least one of us still have a job to go to?' I asked.

'*Pfffft.* My job....' He trailed off, looked out the window at the damp cityscape.

'Yes. Your job. You do have a job, remember?'

BIG Gallic shrug, a very languid shrug.

I watched him closely. 'What does that mean, Guy?'

'*Bah,* Nicole, I am thinking about my job quite a lot recently. I am bored of my job, a bit. I might change my job.'

I nodded slowly. 'Okay… What might you change it to?'

Another shrug. 'Something new. Something different. You remember, I talk to you about Bordeaux, about what I am thinking about doing with Guillaume in Bordeaux. And when I was in New York, I talk to Francesca, too. So we might do something together in Bordeaux, maybe also in Biarritz. This is where Francesca is from.'

'Will that be easy to manage from London?'

Shrug. 'Maybe.' Another smile, another kiss on my hand. End of conversation.

Oh, those heady last days, gambolling about in the meadows of blissful ignorance, the foothills of naivety…

A week passed, a week during which D'Artagnan seemed very chilled, only occasionally went into the office, seemed to have given up wearing suits. When I asked why, he said he was working from home on something.

On the Friday, he called me just after my yoga class had finished, said he'd meet me at a new Italian restaurant in Chelsea, WhatsApped me the address. I was starting to quite like living in South Ken, being a temporary lady of leisure; I had decided I would give myself the summer off and start looking for a new job in September. The flat was very handy for several underground stations. There were always taxis about, it was tantalisingly close to Harvey Nics, the V&A, great for walks in Hyde Park, and on a surprisingly quiet but elegant garden square with calm views over the pretty gardens in the centre.

I had found a great yoga class and was going every other day, Pilates on alternative days. I felt fit, supple, healthy and was eating well. I slept well in D'Artagnan's arms every night, and the Muffins had become quite excited about how shred-able the luxuriously upholstered sofa in the living room was proving to be. I bought throws to deflect any criticism about my cat-disciplining abilities.

'So *mon amour*, I have the date for the testimony of *maman* – it is next Wednesday, in Cognac. We will fly to Bordeaux early on Wednesday and hire a car to drive there, okay? We might stay some days extra.' He glanced up from his scrutiny of the menu.

I frowned. I had booked yoga and Pilates classes all the following week, and there was an exhibition at the Courtauld I wanted to see. 'Why do I have to come?'

Deep furrows on the brow, narrowed eyes, sharp intake of air. 'Because Nicole, you are my WIFE, *merde!*'

I weighed up saying, 'Yes, but I'm not your nanny. Can't you just do it on your own?' but thought better of it.

I shrugged. 'Whatever. I suppose Darth Vader and the Arch Bitch will be attending, too? Can I at least just wait in the car so I don't have to see them?'

'No Nicole, you have to be there. You will have to sign all the papers, too.'

I stared at him. 'Why? It's not like your mother left me anything in her will. That would be weird, given that I never met her.'

He sighed impatiently. 'You don't remember the contract that I explain to you we must sign before we are married? In France, this contract means that you inherit half of what I inherit so, because we are married, you must sign the documents to say that you also inherit. I tell you all of this before we are married, Nicole.'

'No, you didn't. You've never talked to me about inheriting anything in France. I would definitely have remembered that.' I was liking the idea of going to France for the will reading less and less. The idea of Darth Vader and the Arch Bitch's disdain on seeing the now-legally-married arm candy inheriting a part of their mother's estate did not make me feel warm inside. But then I thought, sod it. I hardly ever see them, I'll just ignore them. It's none of their business what Guy does with his share of the château.

Small shrug. '*Bah*, I thought I did. Well, it doesn't matter, this is what happens now. You have to sign all the papers. It is nothing to worry about, it is just a formality, it is just a bit boring. So, we go to Cognac next week *mon amour*, okay? And maybe we stay Wednesday night in Cognac, maybe Thursday night, too.'

I frowned. 'Why do we have to stay in Cognac? What's in Cognac that we need to see?'

He gazed at me steadily, as if he were thinking. Then he said, 'My cousin. My cousin Benoit is in Cognac. I need to see him about something. And there is a boutique hotel just outside the town. The owner is very friendly, she is a big supporter of young artists, so the bedrooms all have original art. It is very cool, very, *bah* – what is that word you like, Nicole, the word from the seventies?'

'Funky?'

'Yes, it is funky. And the food is excellent, very good vegetarian food. You will like it.'

The waiter appeared at our table at this point, and Guy insisted on quizzing him about the provenance of the parmesan cheese in the wild-mushroom risotto, almost to the point where he was demanding the name and immediate ancestry of the cow from which the milk had come to make the cheese. He knows I find his obsession with the provenance of his food wildly uninteresting and, sure enough, by the time the poor waiter finally crawled away, his spirit broken by the pedantic Gascon, I had forgotten all about why we had to spend two nights in Cognac in the funky boutique hotel after the will reading.

There was a biblical storm raging outside the notaire's office the following Wednesday. The bells were ringing ominously in the nearby church, and the opening bars of *The Addams Family* were looping endlessly in my head despite my best efforts to dispel them. Lightning flashed, the wind howled, and the rain clattered against the thin glass in the tall French doors. What light there was came from a chandelier with a total wattage of fifteen, and the sickly green desk lamp under which the notaire, a small creature with smudged round spectacles and a bun of escaping hair, crouched.

I sat at the far end of her vast desk as befitted my lowly status of second wife to the youngest child. Next to me sat D'Artagnan, and to the right of him Françoise, then Darth Vader, the Arch Bitch, and finally Antoine.

To add to the fun atmosphere, the notaire fancied herself as a bit of a comedian. She had been a close confidante of Guy's mum apparently, and as such, felt entitled to comment if she found something amusing in the text of the will. Comedic observations were accompanied by a combined snort and inhalation, which apparently indicated amusement, followed by a quick but sly scan of the audience to gauge how the gig was going. The last one (the snort/inhalation, not the joke which had gone way over my head and apparently everyone else's too) had made my eyes water with repressed hilarity, and I had been unable to stop a squeak escaping, which had caused much eyeball swivelling in the room. The will reading/stand-up routine was received with as frosty a reception as was possible in a room some degrees warmer than Pacha at 3am on a Saturday night in August.

Eventually, she got down to the nitty gritty. My French was still pretty rudimentary, but if I concentrated I could usually figure out what was going and, very occasionally, even contribute something to the conversation. I therefore gleaned:

- Each of the four of them, and the eleventy-seven grandchildren, inherited vast amounts of French francs, and all of the female grandchildren specific pieces of jewellery.
- DV and the AB inherited their mother's apartment in Paris and the family art collection.
- Antoine inherited an apartment in Nice.
- Francoise inherited a house in somewhere weird sounding, somewhere beginning with P in or near Arcachon, or something to do with Arcachon, anyway.

I realised I was frowning. Guy's mother seemed to have had quite a lot of property scattered around France, but there was still no mention of the château.

Et voilà, as they say.

Guy inherited the Chateau de Chantlette in the Cognac region.

I turned to stare at him. He did not look at me but looked straight ahead, the aquiline nose in perfect profile.

Slowly, slowly – way, way, way too slowly – the pieces of the jigsaw puzzle began to slide magically across the broad, flat, pristine surface of my naïve little mind, as if they had suddenly come alive and discovered their innate attraction for one another. When they were finally all reunited, there it was: he had known all along that he was going to inherit the château. The will had been made aeons ago when French francs were still common currency. It was no surprise whatsoever to him, or anyone else.

And there was more, there was oh-so-much more. Why we had to get married so quickly: so that I too would inherit the château. And why was that? Because he fully intended for us to come and live in the château, and he needed me to be invested in that particularly ... thorny little project. The way the pre-nuptial contract was structured, 50:50, for this very reason. His property venture in Bordeaux with his friend: he wouldn't be managing that from London, he would be managing it from France, from the château!

Oh, and more still. He wasn't going to 'change my job, I am a bit bored, Nicole', he was going to *leave* his job. Silly me! He had already given notice; at his level they were almost all on a minimum three months' notice, but as he wasn't going to a competitor bank, they would probably just let him go quietly. That was why he wasn't going to the office, why we had been able to take a long honeymoon, why he was so chilled.

All of that ranting on the phone from New York about how tired he was of his job, THAT was when he'd decided that he was going back to France, and I was coming with him. He'd had time to think about how to orchestrate it, to plan it, setting up the idea of marriage, the impossible-to-refuse proposal...

I continued staring at him while my brain finally finished the full system update and I was fully, comprehensively up to speed with how devious D'Artagnan was capable of being.

Oh no, wait ... BREAKING: he had DEFINITELY orchestrated the sociopath's move to New York knowing full well that it would almost invariably result in my becoming unemployed, which was exactly what he wanted. That made me cross.

The notaire was droning on and on. I think even she had got bored with the gig; she knew she'd lost the audience. But things were clearly moving towards some sort of conclusion. A pretty young assistant entered the room bearing what looked like the equivalent of *War and Peace* in octuplicate, which we were all required to initial and/or sign, starting at Antoine's end. Each piece of paper made its way gradually down the long desk before ending up in front of me.

I contemplated what would happen if I refused to sign, concluded it would probably be a bit nuclear. Guy still hadn't looked at me in all that time; to be fair, no-one was looking at anyone. Everyone seemed a bit tired, resigned.

I realised they'd all known exactly what they were getting. There was no animosity in the room, so clearly the fact that Guy had inherited the family château was entirely as predicted. I wondered if he would have preferred the apartment in Nice, then remembered our visit to the château; no, he'd wanted the château. It meant something to him; it was dear to him, where it wasn't dear to any of the others – I could see that now.

A fleeting mental image of him, the youngest child, running through that enormous, almost medieval, dining room popped into my head; he really had been happy there. And my angry, deceived little heart softened just a tiny bit as I realised that he loved the château and he wanted to live in it, but not on his own. No, he wanted to bring his naïve, young, newly captured wife whom he had lured into the trap so very, very cleverly, to live in it with him.

And in that moment, as if he'd been waiting for the complete download to finish, he turned to me and he smiled, and it was the wickedest smile that he'd ever given me in all the time we'd been together. It was a smile that said: 'You never knew I was THIS manipulative, THIS clever, did you?'

And I thought: 'Oh yes, you are clever. But you are mistaken if you think I am going to make this easy for you. I have the measure of you now, D'Artagnan.'

So, I just shook my head slowly at him, bit my lip, determined not to smile back. My mouth twisted with the effort of keeping it off my face.

He winked a big slow wink and turned back to signing the pages as they arrived in front of him, passing them on to me to do the same, which I did. What choice did I have?

Some hours later, we all filed out into the reception area gasping for fresh air. There was no display of emotion as we put on our coats, other than the usual icy disapproval from DV and the AB. Both Antoine and Françoise were already on their phones.

It was still pouring down outside as a small depression of *au revoir* air kisses perturbed the reception air, although Françoise gave me a lovely smile and squeezed my hand as she kissed us both warmly goodbye, still with her phone to her ear. Then everyone dashed out into the rain and disappeared in their respective cars.

That just left us.

'Clever.' I nodded slowly, gazing into the deceptive brown depths.

'*Bah*, Nicole, if I had told you, you would have been scared!' He laughed, reached an arm around my neck, pulled me close against him. He kissed my forehead, still laughing in a rather self-congratulatory manner, I thought.

I shook my head again, pursed my lips. 'But Guy, it worries me. You're so bloody devious, so manipulative! Why couldn't you just have told me everything from the beginning, instead of all the subterfuge, all the sleight of hand—?'

I suddenly remembered the little tricks he had performed that day for Josh and Katie that wonderful day in Marlow, the first day that I'd thought that perhaps I could love this man, this complicated, volatile, arrogant man. Perhaps I could trust him…

'Why couldn't you just be honest with me?'

Big Gallic shrug, jazz hands at half-mast. 'Nicole, I tell you why! You are scared of everything, you are like this little deer. I can't tell you, "Nicole, we are going to live in a château in France, you will be very happy there, we will be very happy there." This will make you run like a little deer into the forest!'

He slipped his arms around my waist. 'This way, you don't run. You already have a bit of the idea. You have seen the château, we are married, it is not so frightening now.' A soft kiss on the forehead, then finger underneath the chin, lifting my eyes to his 'Okay? You see this now?'

'Oh I see it, my darling. I just don't think you necessarily see it the way I see it. That château needs a FUCK of a lot of work before I am going to be happy living in it – much more work than you seemed to think was necessary when we saw it in March.'

Pout. 'I know, Nicole. It needs some work. I did not say that it does not need some work.'

'My darling, deceptive D'Artagnan, it needs A LOT of work.'

The slightest Gallic shrug. 'So, Nicole, you do the work you want to do to the château. There is money to do the work, you make it how you will like it. I want you to be happy, very happy *mon amour*.' His voice softened, a gentle kiss on the lips. 'I am *si, si heureux* that I have you in my life, that we are married, that we will live in my beautiful country, in our beautiful château together.'

I gazed into the soft, dreamy brown eyes and thought: Y'know, you go, girl. Ride this one out. It might not be so difficult.

Chapter Twelve

We left London early on the first Saturday in May, only slightly delayed by the Muffins' distinct lack of adventure when it came to getting in their cat baskets. They had not forgotten the trauma of their recent trip across London. For the first ten minutes, they conspired to deceive us into thinking that they were resigned to the journey; for the following eight hours and fifty-three minutes they let us know in no uncertain terms that this was not how they had planned to spend their Saturday.

It was utterly exhausting. At one point, Mr Muffin was suspended upside down in the cat carrier by his teeth, having taken a mouthful of the plastic cage front, all his claws deployed against the air vents and the roof of the carrier, howling his fury that, after forty-seven minutes, he was still imprisoned.

We stopped at the first service station after the Eurotunnel and I crawled into the back of the Audi to let them out to use the litter tray, or perhaps have something to eat, neither of which they had the remotest desire to do. Guy slammed the boot shut behind me, so I had to clamber with some difficulty back into the passenger seat because there was NO WAY ON THE FACE OF THE PLANET that the Muffins were going back into their cat carriers after I had let them out. EVER. Thereafter, it was my job to ensure that they didn't climb into the front seat and get in the way of his driving.

By the time we passed Amiens, I could feel the five milligrams of pharmaceutical calm begin to kick in. I was practically comatose on fifteen milligrams by the time we arrived in the Charente after a particularly challenging pee-stop just south of Poitiers. The pee-stop had involved an exciting cat hunt in the pouring rain, culminating in my trying to coax Mrs Muffin out from under the car of a family from Toulouse who were on their way home from visiting family in Paris.

Guy turned on maximum charm in order to distract them from his crazy-arsed wife lying flat out on the wet tarmac, wheedling 'Come on, Mrs Muffin, come to Mummy' over and over again to the underside of their car. We were all very relieved when I finally grabbed her by the scruff of her neck and hauled her out, the Toulouse family more than anyone. It was clear that they weren't a hundred percent certain there was a cat underneath their car and thought that we were a couple of psychopaths making up shit while secretly planning to murder them.

Apart from a brief but calm lecture about the importance of keeping the cats out of the front of the car, and in particular from under his feet and the foot pedals, Guy didn't once raise his voice or complain throughout the journey, even when a suspiciously unpleasant smell wafted around the car towards the end of the journey. Mr Muffin was sitting on top of his cat carrier making deliberate and angrily satisfied eye contact with both of us in turn in the rear-view mirror.

Occasionally he reached over and squeezed my knee sympathetically when a particularly furious stream of invective was hurled at me from somewhere in the rear of the car. For all his impetuosity, he has an intrinsic awareness of when I'm on the edge and it isn't appropriate to add to the drama.

Well, obviously, it isn't an infallible awareness.

When we finally arrived, we were too exhausted to make up the old four-poster bed in the bedroom, and just threw a clean sheet over it and climbed under the duvet we had brought with us. The mattress was a goose-feather quicksand; we sank deep into its centre and slept like the dead.

When I finally managed to claw myself out of yet another deeply realistic dream about chasing Mrs Muffin down endless corridors in the château, I realised I was desperate for a pee. I fought my way out of the mattress and ran, naked and shivering, down the cold, dark corridor to the only working bathroom – and more importantly, working toilet – on the first floor. I glanced at my watch lying on the ugly empire-style bedside table before diving back into the feathered pond: it was 10.45am.

We had brought only the essentials from London in the car. The apartment in South Ken was being let fully furnished, and the last boxes of our personal possessions had been collected by the removal firm the day before we left. They would be delivered towards the end of the following week.

I had finally agreed to sell my apartment. It had been interesting to discover that I was, in fact, quite fickle; I had expected to miss it when the cats and I moved to South Ken, but I had not given it a single thought since I'd closed the front door for the last time.

The idea of managing a rental from deepest rural France, even through an agent, did not appeal. I also felt that having a lump sum from the sale in my own account would be comforting. I had taken the time to actually read the pre-nuptial contract we had signed, and done some Googling to understand French matrimonial law, at least in outline. I now understood that everything we owned prior to our marriage remained separate, and everything we acquired after our marriage was shared.

I was still getting used to the idea of having joint finances. Guy had given me my own Amex card and was in the process of setting up a joint account for us in France, but it was still a little disconcerting. I had always worked, always had my own money, and I wasn't entirely comfortable with being a kept woman, even though by my calculation there was some personal financial retribution owing due to his deceitful machinations – not least ensuring that I became unemployed.

As far as the château was concerned, however, I had not a single qualm; money was going to be spent, that was for bloody sure.

The essentials that we brought in the car from London were: Guy's beloved coffee machine and several containers of his favourite coffee beans, in case he didn't like the French equivalent; the Muffins' beds and blankets, and several dozen tins of their favourite cat food in case they didn't like the French equivalent; and a suitcase containing practical but stylish clothing suitable for a long weekend in a country house because, while I knew there was no question that I wouldn't love the French equivalent, apparently we wouldn't be going shopping for clothes right away. I had even managed generously to cram a couple of D'Artagnan's cashmere sweaters in the suitcase on the grounds that I could always borrow them if I needed to.

Later that day we were watching the rain spatter against the windows while we sipped our coffee in the vast dining room. Guy had dashed out just before noon for bread and croissants from the nearest boulangerie and some other food essentials from the small supermarket nearby that was, by some miracle in stuck-in-the-1950s-shopping-France, actually open on a Sunday morning. I was wrapped tightly in my fluffy bathrobe over both of his cashmere sweaters, leggings, socks and furry slippers, but I was still shivering. I mentally ran through the capsule-clothing inventory. There was nothing in it; in fact, I was pretty sure there was nothing in my entire collection of clothing and shoes going back nearly eighteen years that was suitable for ankle-deep mud. I resolved to stay inside, unpack and start working on Project Bonjour 21C! until the weather became more clement and amenable to stylish cropped Prada trousers and my Vega trainers, which would be perfect for fresh countryside walks (on tarmac).

'Is the heating really on?' I asked Guy as my teeth chattered against the coffee mug.

'Yes Nicole, I tell you three times already. You need to eat more, this is why you are you always cold. Eat a croissant, I bought you one.' He pushed the brown-paper bag towards me and leaned back against the table. He was wearing a sweatshirt and jeans, his feet bare on the ivory flagstones and still suntanned from our honeymoon. He looked happy, healthy, robust. Very capable of being harassed about the need to make things happen, rather than 'ça ira, ça ira, mon ange' (the French equivalent of mañana, mañana) which seemed to be becoming his standard response to my questions about renovations.

I absently started eating the croissant. It was very good, flaky and buttery. 'It's nothing to do with how much I eat, Guy, the fact is, it's bloody freezing! It's because the windows haven't been done. You promised me that the windows would be done before we arrived. Why aren't they finished?'

After the revelatory will reading in early April, we had re-visited the Duchess. The damp, early-spring air made it feel as if I were literally walking into a freezer; however, I had once again felt that little surge of joy when I walked into the creamy, flagstone dining hall (it was more than a room) with the enormous stone fireplace and the high, beamed ceiling. Interestingly, there was already scaffolding up and roofing work going on; Guy had clearly been spending his time in London organising roofers as a matter of some urgency.

I spent a long while, wrapped in my coat, cashmere scarves (yes, two) and furry hat, exploring the Duchess's interior. I was pleasantly surprised to discover that she actually had quite a lot of charm. I investigated the first floor, deciding which bedroom was going to be ours, that it would have an ensuite bathroom and beyond that, a dressing room.

That, I think, was the tipping point for me. The idea that I could have my own bespoke dressing room for all my beautiful clothes, that they would be together in their own little heaven – that was the point at which I thought, maybe I can do this, maybe I can get used to the idea of living in a French château.

But I didn't let D'Artagnan know this. He was still in disgrace. Sort of. Apart from the rather fantastic sex in the funky boutique hotel after we'd left the notaire's office. He had slayed the dragon (the sociopath), overcome the enemy (quit his job), and was now riding triumphantly toward his castle, the captured princess between his arms as he spurred his horse onwards. D'Artagnan was *epic* that afternoon.

Nonetheless, I had made it an absolute requirement that the old, single-paned, almost-rotten windows were ripped out and replaced with new double-glazed ones. Guy had promised to get onto it straight away, find a company that would do the work, and complete it before we arrived in France to live in the château.

And yet… I hadn't noticed when we'd arrived late the night before, but it was very clear in the cold, clear (well, rainy) light of day that the windows were exactly the same as the last time we'd visited.

'*Bah, ma chérie*, these things, they take time. It is a big job. Do you know how many windows the château have?'

'Nope, and I don't care. When are they being done?'

Half-shrug. 'Soon, *mon amour*, very soon.'

'When is that?'

'*Bah,* Nicole, it will be done. You must be patient, sometimes these things, they take time!' He drained his coffee cup.

'We need to go and speak to the company that's doing it tomorrow and find out exactly when. Or you do. I can't go outside, it's too cold and wet. I thought France was supposed to be warmer than bloody England?'

'It is seventeen degrees outside. It is not cold, it is just raining. Put some jeans on, some boots.' A long, slow look. 'Or did you only bring the party dresses in the big suitcase?'

I ignored him. 'We need to make a list of all the urgent jobs, Guy. There is loads to do and we need to get things kicked off *tout de suite*. We need to find someone – a company or companies – to do all the renovation work. You said your cousin, the one who lives in Cognac, might know of someone. Can you talk to him please, get some recommendations?'

'Nicole, *arrête*! It is Sunday afternoon. We only arrive in France yesterday, and nothing is going to happen today. *Merde*!' He stood up, dusted his hands of croissant flakes, and bent over my chair, wrapping his arms around me from behind. His breath was warm on my ear. 'I think we should go back to bed now, so that I can take some time to welcome you properly to France and to the château, *mon amour*. Tomorrow we will think about windows and projects and renovations, *d'accord*?'

The next day I wore the only pair of jeans I had (Armani) tucked into a pair of slightly too large but surprisingly comfortable Wellington boots that I'd found amongst the vast collection in the back hall.

My jeans became mud-spattered instantly on the first of the two occasions I needed to go outside. The first was to catch Mr Muffin, who had escaped out of the back door and was wide-eyed and traumatised at the vastness of this new, big, cold space. The second was at Guy's insistence, because for some reason, he deemed it essential to show me that two of the tall horse-chestnut trees to the right of the château were both dead.

We stood underneath them in a light drizzle, while he snapped off a low hanging branch and held it out to show me. 'Do you see, Nicole? It is dead. And the one next to it. They are both dead. If there is a big storm, the wind will come from here,' he pointed south west, away from the château, 'and the tree will fall there.' He pointed at the château.

I gazed up into the tree. It was very tall. 'That will need to be added to the list of things to be done.'

'Yes. It is worrying me. I am going to see if the chainsaw in the *chais* work.'

'Chainsaw? What – are you going to cut them down yourself? I know you're very talented, light of my life, but I wasn't aware that you were also a qualified tree-surgeon?'

He ignored that and started walking around the tree. The trunk was close to a metre thick. 'Maybe I will need to buy a bigger chainsaw.'

'Fuck's sake, Guy! Have you ever even used a chainsaw?'

'Of course I have – during our vacations!'

'What – the freedom you had as children included playing with chainsaws? Wow, I hadn't realised raising a child in France was quite so ... hands off, in so many senses of the phrase.'

'When I was a teenager, my grandfather show me how to use one.' He waved his arm toward the small forest that separated the château from the road. 'The forest here needs to be managed. You have to cut out the trees that grow wild or that die so that the other trees can breathe and grow.'

I looked at him doubtfully. 'So, the last time you used a chainsaw was what – about thirty-five years ago? And now you're going to have a go at cutting down a tree that is—' I gazed up at the tree and a fat raindrop splattered my cheek '—about fifty metres tall, on your own, with a chainsaw that belonged to your grandfather?' I looked at him again, hard. 'What could possibly go wrong?'

'Nicole, you exaggerate, it is only about twenty-five metres tall.'

I shook my head in exasperation, turned to go back inside. 'I'm just going to re-read the will that I assume you've made, *mon amour*, and put the ambulance on speed-dial.'

I stopped, turned around again. He was gazing up into the tree again, calculating. 'Guy! I'm absolutely serious! You are absolutely NOT going to do anything to that tree! You are absolutely NOT capable of cutting it down, and I will NOT spend the rest of my life nursing you when you fall out of it and become a vegetable in a wheelchair!! We will find a qualified person to come and cut both trees down, someone who does it for a living.'

He looked at me crossly.

'If you so much as touch a chainsaw, I am getting in the car and the cats and I are leaving.'

The yeah-whatever mouth movement.

'I really fucking mean it!!'

'Okay! I will get someone to do it! But Nicole, you need to accept that we live in the country now. There is a lot of big work I need to do on the land, and I will sometimes need to use a chainsaw and other big, scary things that you think are going to kill me. You are just going to have to accept this!'

I really did need to find out how to call an ambulance, learn how to say 'My husband has cut off his leg with a chainsaw, please come quickly' in French.

'Fine, Hercules. Whatever. But not that. Not cutting down enormous bloody great trees on your own.'

I went back inside, left my muddy Wellingtons by the back door, and padded upstairs in my socks to find out whether Mr Muffin was still suffering from PTSD. He was not, apparently. The cats had both been on hunger strike in protest at their unfamiliar surroundings and had refused to eat anything since we'd arrived, but their curiosity and hunger were getting the better of them.

They followed me downstairs, Mr Muffin making a couple of half-hearted attempts to trip me up on the way. 'Food!' he shouted as he ran ahead of me. 'Food, bitch, I'm hungry! Hurry up!'

Mrs Muffin is much more polite than her illegitimate son. He is fluffy and black and white, of dubious and unknown paternal origin, while she is completely black, sleek and glossy. She was a skinny, stray single-mother when Mrs Robertson began feeding her six years ago. As has been noted, having been an only-kitten and therefore deprived of a normal kittenhood, Mr Muffin has issues around acceptable levels of play-biting and scratching. I often get the impression that Mrs Muffin wishes she'd had access to contraception.

I located one of the little tins of their preferred, expensive cat food in a kitchen cupboard and split it between their two bowls. They came over, sniffed the food, sat down and looked up at me. 'This isn't what we ordered,' they said. 'We hate this food. Why did you bring this food?'

'Oh, for fuck's sake,' I muttered, turning away to make myself a coffee. I sat down at the dining-room table, watching to see if they would change their minds.

They came over and sat in front of me accusingly. 'Dying of starvation here,' said Mr Muffin, making big green eyes at me.

'At least let me drink my coffee,' I snapped. 'And then, if you are both absolutely certain that you no longer wish to eat the very expensive food that I bought in vast quantities before we left, I might consider going to the supermarket to find you something that you might deign to eat.'

When Guy came back inside, I told him we needed to go shopping for cat food.

'Nicole, we need to go shopping for food for us, too! We will go to the *marché* in Cognac on Wednesday. It is a good *marché*.'

I frowned. 'Who's going to be doing the cooking, by the way? I don't see a whole lot of restaurants within walking distance. I hope your plan to imprison me in your château doesn't involve my having to learn to cook, dearest?'

He started laughing, like it was the funniest thing he'd heard in a long time. '*Mon dieu, mais NON*, Nicole! You are terrible in the kitchen!'

This is true. Tiffany taught me absolutely nothing about cooking; I lived on crisps and sweets when I wasn't eating with Juliette's family, until I got a bit older and developed traditional, tried-and-tested, food-based methods of controlling the chaos of my teenage (and later) years. My relationship with food is slightly complicated.

'The kitchen, *mon amour*, is MY *domaine!*' Guy said, wiping the tears from his eyes.

'What?' I stared at him 'You don't know anything about cooking!'

'Of course I do!' It was his turn to stare at me.

'Since when? You never cook! I've never seen you cook once!'

'Well Nicole, you remember I was working and I travel a lot, a lot of jetlag? I did not have time to cook when we live in London. But now, now I have time to cook.' He looked very pleased with himself.

'When did you learn to cook?'

He looked at me with an expression that implied I was slightly simple. 'I am French. *Merde*, Nicole!'

'What? All French children pop out of their mother's vagina with innate culinary knowledge?'

He laughed, grabbed me around the neck in mock-frustration, then kissed my forehead. '*Bah*, always the sarcasm *ma petite ange*! Of course not! We are taught all the time by our mothers while we are growing up, by our grandparents when we are on our vacations. We go to the *marchés* with *maman*, or *nounou* if *maman* is not able, or with *mamie*. From when we are very young, we are taught how to choose the *fruits de mer*, the fish, the meat, the vegetables, the fruit – it is just,' he shrugged, 'it is just what we do.'

'So, you go to the markets with your mum or nanny or your grandma when you're a kid. That doesn't necessarily mean you know how to cook!'

'*Bah, ouais*, but we are then taught how to cook what we have bought at the *marché!*'

I continued to stare at him. D'Artagnan on his own *territoire* was full of surprises. But I was actually very relieved that the kitchen was not going to be my *domaine*.

It gradually stopped raining that afternoon, and the following day the sun came out. I sat on the top step at the front of the château the next morning, sipping my coffee and supervising the Muffins' hesitant forays onto the weird, damp spiky stuff that was the lawn. The forest at the end of it was dressed in every possible shade of green, sparkling with residual raindrops from the day before. The stillness was full of the sound of birdsong and the bees in the flowering trees to the left of the château. The sun was warm on my skin and I closed my eyes, soaking it up.

Guy came and stood behind me; I leaned back against his legs, his bare feet. 'Happy, *mon amour?*' He smiled down at me.

I squinted up at him. 'Yes, I am. You?'

'I am very happy—' He broke off. I looked up at the sound of a truck coming down the drive, still partially hidden by the trees. 'And now I am very, very happy, because my fridge is arriving!' As the truck came to a halt on the gravel, he turned and went back inside to slip on his shoes.

An enormous, stainless-steel, double-door fridge was gradually coaxed into the kitchen by two large delivery men. Fridges it seems, can easily be ordered, delivered and installed in rural France. Windows, not so much.

After Guy had finished cooing over and smiling flirtatiously at, the shiny new addition to his kitchen, we went into Cognac to buy the Muffins French cat food (they approved, thank God).

'And I need some new clothes, Nicole. For being at the château, for doing outside things.' We went to a sports shop where he bought two pairs of jeans, some shorts, T-shirts and a couple of sweatshirts from Lacoste.

I bought two pairs of Levi jeans, a plain black T-shirt and a Coq Sportif hoodie. I was surprised at how inexpensive and comfortable they were, and resolved to rethink my countryside clothing choices. I was starting to wonder if perhaps I had mispacked after all; there didn't seem to be a whole lot of Dior, Dolce & Gabbana and Valentino in evidence on the streets of Cognac. Not a sniff of Louboutin, either.

Then it was lunchtime. We drove to a Michelin restaurant on the river Charente about twenty minutes from Cognac, were shown to a smart table under a cream sunshade with a view of the wide, sparkling river over which squadrons of swifts screeched, swooped and dived, the buzz of insects audible above the low murmur of the elegant *clientèle*. The white-linen tablecloths flapped lazily in the warm breeze as I sipped my glass of Champagne, sat back in my chair and thought; Well, this is very pleasant, I could get used to this.

I ordered from the entrée menu only: a sublimely good salad with walnuts and blue cheese and incredible-tasting tomatoes in several different colours, and as a main course, white-asparagus gazpacho with a green asparagus, hazelnut and parmesan-cheese topping.

D'Artagnan ordered half a cow. When the waiter asked how he would like it cooked, he said, '*Bleu.*'

'Did you really just ask for your steak to be blue?' I asked, puzzled, when the waiter had gone.

'*Ouais.*' He smiled at me, lit one of his rare cigarettes, inhaled, blew out a cloud of smoke.

I frowned. 'I don't understand. Is there some sort of weird colour-coding system in France? What does blue mean?'

'It means I don't want it cooked like they do in fucking England, Nicole.' 'Furking England' – I could not help smiling. 'In France, we know how to cook steak. There are three ways: *bleu*, which means twenty, maybe thirty seconds each side, nothing more; *saignant*, maybe forty seconds each side, or *à point*, maybe a minute each side for people who don't know how to eat meat.'

'What about if you want it well done?'

'Then you must order something else, maybe some vegetables, because this is sacrilege. It is only the English – oh, and always the Americans – who say they want *bien cuit*. It is a crime to do this to steak!'

My introduction to the intricate rules of D'Artagnan's bourgeois culinary world was just beginning.

Chapter Thirteen

Guy told me that we were going to visit his cousin Benoit, after lunch. 'He is my Aunt Sylvie's son. You remember, Aunt Sylvie? I introduce you to her at the funeral. And Benoit.'

'Yes, of course.' I nodded confidently. I had absolutely no idea who Aunt Sylvie was, absolutely no recollection of meeting her, or indeed her son Benoit. I had been overwhelmed by the number of people Guy had introduced me to, had smiled as charmingly as I could, shook hands and said *'Enchantée'* a lot. It had seemed to work.

'They have a Cognac house, an *entreprise* here. My Aunt Sylvie, when *mamie* Charente die, she inherit the Cognac vineyards that belong to the château before the estate was split, *maman* inherit the château, Sylvie the vineyards. She was always very interested in the making of Cognac. Now Benoit runs the distillery and he makes a very good Cognac, some of the best, I think. But not a lot, maybe only forty, fifty thousand bottles a year. It is very small. But they sell at a big price to the Cognac *connoisseurs*. We will taste some this afternoon.'

'Yay!' I said, raising my excellent glass of Margaux 2015 to him. I was starting to REALLY like living in France.

He grinned at me. 'Nicole, you need to eat some bread with the lunch. You cannot just eat salad and drink Champagne and wine, *ma chérie*.'

But the sun was warm on my skin, D'Artagnan in his sunglasses across the table from me was ravishing, the food and the wine were sublime. I wondered why I had ever resisted the idea of being imprisoned in *la France profonde*.

\---------------------

After lunch – including a detailed, passionate discussion with the chef of the restaurant (about the food, of course) – we were back in the car on the way to Benoit's distillery. 'One thing, Nicole' he turned to gaze at me as we entered and exited yet another roundabout at rally speed. I silently willed him to look at the road instead of at me, but he was not receptive. 'You will need to be careful of Uncle 'Arry.'

'Who is Uncle Harry?'

'Sylvie, when she was young, she goes all over the world to learn about Cognac, about whisky too, and she goes to Scotland. And she meet my Uncle 'Arry there.' He sounded glum.

'You had an Uncle Harry in Scotland? How did that happen?' I was confused. Perhaps it was the wine.

'No, no,' he said crossly. 'I didn't have an Uncle Harry in Scotland. She met a man called Harry and now he is my uncle. He is Benoit's father.' Big sniff. 'Unfortunately, he is a complete *connard*.'

'Ooh, family gossip. Tell me more.' I rubbed my hands gleefully.

'Well first, you need to know that he will be drunk, and next that he is going to try to grab your ass, that is almost for certain' – glancing at me sternly. 'It is best if you keep away from him at all times. Never let him get near to you, Nicole.'

'Wow. He sounds charming.'

'Yes. He is a disgusting old man, always thinking he is so charming to women. I don't know why Sylvie doesn't divorce him, but I think she is so used to him after all this time, she just ignores him. Also, of course, she is usually in the apartment in Bordeaux now because Benoit manage the *entreprise* with Harry, a bit.'

Another roundabout: on this one he took the third exit, cutting up the car on the inside quite hard. There was a blast of horn. I was reminded of that bumper sticker, the one that says 'Using your indicator isn't giving secret information to the enemy', while I observed the guy behind gesticulating and shouting in the wing mirror.

D'Artagnan ignored it completely, changed gear, accelerated hard.

I did remember Benoit. He had the same lovely brown eyes as Guy, curly dark hair; he smiled easily, laughed a lot. He was utterly charming and gave us a quick tour of the distillery, which was interesting and entertaining. It was obvious why their business was successful; Benoit was passionate about his craft, but he was also smart, and he knew how to sell his product. He spoke to us in French, but slowly so that I understood everything, and I was emboldened by the rather large and unfamiliar quantities of alcohol I'd had with lunch to answer him in French. It seemed to please D'Artagnan enormously: he smiled encouragingly at me and didn't correct me once.

After the informative tour, I was sitting on an old sofa at the far end of the kitchen savouring a glass of their cognac, happily squished between an ageing Labrador and heavily moulting cat, when the infamous Uncle 'Arry bowled in. He was a little overweight, short and stocky, with faded blue eyes and the classic alcoholic's bulbous red nose.

'Eeeeeh, well, helloo everybody. Well, well, well this is a pleasant surprrrrrrrise! If it isn't young Guy after all these yearrrrs. And, oh my, who is this lovely young hen on the sofa? Stand up, stand up, ya gorgeous gerrel, let's have a good look at you!' He was over in front of the sofa like a guided missile.

I had never in my life heard anyone speak directly from their nasal cavity, or with such a broad Glaswegian accent.

I am not a slow learner, even after a lunch with Champagne and wine and a sampling of some very good cognac. I remained seated on the sofa and extended my hand graciously toward him, channelling my best Maggie Smith. '*Enchantée*, Harry.'

'Budge up, budge up, ya filthy old fleabag.' Harry shoved the Labrador unceremoniously onto the floor and plonked himself down on the sofa practically on top of me. The fumes almost made my eyes water. 'So, what's a gorgeous gerrel like you doing out here in the middle of nowhere? Is it so that young Guy can keep you away from other men? He wasn't so good at that with the first one, were you, Guy?'

Raucous laughter, hand already squeezing my leg. I looked up at Guy in amazement. He made an 'I warned you' face as he marched over. '*Bonjour,* Harry. Please will you take your hand off my wife's leg, or I will have to do it for you.'

'Eeeeeeeehhh, Guy, it's good to see you again. Where did you get this gorgeous gerrel from?' More squeezing, some patting. Guy frowned angrily.

Benoit clocked what was happening, called across the room, 'Papa? Can you come over here, I need to show you something really important?' No response. Looking embarrassed, he came forward a bit further into the room. 'Papa? Now, please, it's important.'

'Eeehhhh, what is it, Benny? I'm just getting to know this lovely gerrel. What's so important?'

'NOW, Papa! *Putain*!'

At that, Harry grunted and climbed off the sofa effortfully, went over to where Benoit was standing at the kitchen counter with his back to us. There was a short, forceful conversation in hushed tones.

Guy grabbed my hand and pulled me off the sofa. 'Maybe also don't sit down anywhere near him, either.' He put his arms protectively around my waist. I took another sip of the cognac. It was very good, smooth and faintly woody, the forty percent alcohol content only a subtle hint in the aftertaste – unlike the walking distillery that was Uncle Harry.

After the hushed conversation, Harry turned back to us. 'Well, young people, Benny here tells me that I have urgent business in the distillery to see to, so I'll be running along there to take care of it.' He gave a sudden lurch sideways, righted himself and stepped forward. 'I'll be saying bye bye for now, lovely gerrel.'

As he leered and moved in for kisses, Guy stepped in front of me. 'Goodbye, Harry,' he said. Very firmly.

Harry peered around the edge of Guy and winked at me. 'I'll be looking out for you! I'll see you soon.'

Not if I see you first, I thought.

Just before we were about to leave, D'Artagnan finally got around to quizzing Benoit about recommended artisans for Project Bonjour 21C!

Benoit nodded, started scrolling through his phone and noted down the contact details of someone who had done some renovation work for him.

'He's quite good,' he said. 'But you must be very careful not to pay him more than thirty percent when you sign the *devis*, because he will disappear for a long time, and you will have to chase him to finish. He made a new bathroom for me at the back of the distillery, and he renovated a kitchen for a friend of mine.' He paused. 'The work is okay, no problems. No big problems, anyway.'

Even with my limited French, that was hardly a glowing recommendation. 'Don't you have anyone else you can recommend in case he's busy?' I asked.

He thought for a moment. 'No, I'm sorry. The other guy who did some work for me was really good, but he moved to the Basque country. But you will find, Nicole, that it is very difficult to get good French artisans who are not booked many, many months in advance. And Guy said you want the project done urgently?'

I nodded. D'Artagnan muttered something. I frowned at him. 'What did you say, darling?'

A sniff. 'It's not urgent, Nicole. There is already a bathroom in the château.'

I stared at him. 'Sweetheart, remember, renovations to the château, MY project, okay?'

Benoit looked from one of us to the other, eyebrows raised.

D'Artagnan sniffed, pouted a little, did not say anything. I smiled. 'Thanks so much for this Benoit.' I put the note in my pocket. 'And we also need a—' I turned to Guy. 'I don't know what a tree surgeon is in French.' He told me. 'We need a tree surgeon, someone to cut down some dead trees, and that's very urgent. They could fall on the château, apparently.'

'Ah. Yes, I know exactly who you need.' Benoit pulled out his phone again and scrolled until he found a number, wrote it down on another bit of paper, and a name below it.

Guy picked up the piece of paper. 'Gabriela? This is a girl's name, Benoit.'

'Yes, it is a woman. She is very good. She works with her partner who is also a woman. They are both very good.'

I looked slyly at Guy, waiting for it... Not disappointed!

'This is not a job for women! These are not small trees, Benoit, these are very big trees. They will need to have ropes and big ladders, BIG chainsaws!'

Benoit looked a bit nonplussed. 'Yes, but they are qualified to do this work.'

'What Guy means, Benoit,' I interrupted, 'is that an essential necessity for tree surgery is a penis.'

Benoit burst out laughing. 'Very funny, Nicole! Yes, many men in France still think that women can't do certain jobs if they don't have a penis, but we are learning that that is not true. Look at Françoise, my cousins, they are doing fantastic things in Bordeaux! Previously, there were hardly any women vignerons and now there are many, and many really good ones. I tell my daughters all the time that they can do anything they want to do, anything at all!'

'Yes, I tell Charlotte that too. I do believe it,' said D'Artagnan, a bit sheepish now. 'And I am so proud of what Françoise has achieved. But—' he looked at the piece of paper in his hand again '—chainsaws...' He caught my eye. 'Well, I suppose if you say she is good and professional, I will call her.'

'She's not French,' said Benoit. 'She's Portuguese, but she speaks good French, and some English, too. She lived in England for a while.' He smiled at me. 'I think you will like her, Nicole. She has a big character.'

A big-charactered, chainsaw-wielding, female Portuguese tree-surgeon, and a slightly sexist, arrogant, French micro-manager. Must remember to buy popcorn, I thought.

I stood at the dining room window watching D'Artagnan as he stood underneath the tree, coffee cup in hand, staring up at Camille suspended from her harness twelve metres up, the chainsaw snarling in the morning calm. Gabriela reappeared from behind the trunk and went over to say something to him, and he took a step back. She made a shooing motion with her hand and he took another step back, then she grabbed him by the shoulders and forced him to step back several metres until he was standing on the driveway.

There were words; there was gesticulating. I turned away. I really hoped he didn't piss them off too much; yesterday, when he hadn't been around, they had done a fantastic job. One of the dead trees had already disappeared, magically transformed into a neat stack of wood at the side of the château.

A short while later the front door slammed and Guy marched through the dining room into the kitchen. 'She is very bossy, that woman,' he said peevishly.

I decided that soothing the French cockerel's plumage was probably the best approach if there was to be any chance of peace.

'She's just concerned for your safety, my darling. You're not wearing a hard hat, and a branch could fall on your head.'

A grunt. He stood at the kitchen window watching them again.

'They did a great job yesterday, Guy. I really don't think you need to supervise them.'

'I am not supervising them, Nicole. I am just keeping an eye on them to make sure they don't do something stupid – fall out of the tree, for example.'

I shook my head slowly, doing the full eye roll behind his back.

'I can see you doing that Nicole, in the glass of the window.' Warningly.

Fortunately, another exciting morning of bickering was headed off by the appearance through the trees of a truck, bouncing and shuddering its way along the drive at some speed. I heard Gabriela turn and shout '*Putain!*' and fling an appropriate hand gesture after it as it passed closely by her in a cloud of chalk dust and skidded to a halt on the forecourt.

'Ah *bon*! The plumber is here!' After I had nagged him quite a lot, D'Artagnan had made a rendezvous with the artisan Benoit had recommended. I think he was pleased that he was no longer surrounded by women. 'Do you need to come and meet him, Nicole?'

I stared at him. 'Of course I do Guy. It's my idea, it's my project!' He ignored that and bustled me out of the kitchen ahead of him.

Monsieur Duprés was still climbing laboriously down from his mud-spattered flatbed truck that had once, possibly, been white or something close to white. He was overweight, bordering on obese, and his black hair gleamed greasily as he smoothed his hand across it. He landed on the ground heavily, made a stomach-churning nasal sound in his throat, and spat a fat yellow globule onto the drive, at the same time hoiking his trousers up from behind with both hands in his pants, taking the opportunity to rearrange his balls a bit at the same time. He hadn't yet seen us standing there.

'Oh I LOVE him. Isn't he a charmer?' I murmured into Guy's ear.

When he finally did notice us, a toothy, insincere smile began to spread across Duprés' jowled face. He barrelled across the drive towards us, hand outstretched.

'This one's all yours, *mon amour.*' I shrank back behind Guy. D'Artagnan's body was rigid with distaste, but he shook the proffered hand.

'Enchanted to meet you, sir, madame. It is my grovelling honour to make your acquaintance. My name is Ludovic Duprés. A pleasure to meet you both.' Or the equivalent in French, slathered in obsequiousness.

'*Enchanté.*' D'Artagnan's voice was strained. 'Guy du Beauchamp. My wife Nicole,' trying to pull me out from behind him.

I smiled brightly over his shoulder, tinkled my fingers in a little wave. '*Enchantée*, Monsieur Duprés.' There was no way on the planet I was going to touch that septic appendage.

By the time Monsieur Duprés had reached the first-floor landing (panting), the mood had changed to one of gloomy scepticism. As we walked ahead of him up the stairs (upwind, obvs), I explained that we needed an entire new bathroom created at the front of the house where there hadn't been one before. He started sucking his teeth even before we had entered the smaller room off the main bedroom that was to become the new ensuite. The gloom became almost terminal as Guy tugged at the windows to allow fresh, cool air to dilute the new and unusual fragrance in the room.

'It will be very, very complicated to do this.' Monsieur Duprés put both hands in the vicinity of his body where his hips might once have been.

Guy shot me an 'I told you so' look. I had already had the first of many, many long explanations about why putting a new bathroom in at the front of the château was ludicrous, positively insane. He could not understand why the existing bathroom could not be renovated.

'One bathroom, my darling, for the WHOLE château? Really? What about when we have people to stay?' I shook my head crossly. 'Anyway, fuck's sake, Guy, are you going senile?

Have you forgotten that you said that I could do ANY renovations I wanted? That was the deal, remember?'
Very big pout.
So I ignored him as we stood in what would become our new ensuite bathroom.
'Where is the water supply?' Duprés asked.
We traipsed out of the room and down the corridor, where he inspected the Peach Panoply that was the existing bathroom. More grunting, some peering behind the toilet, a laborious stretch to inspect the pipework behind the bath, which very nearly toppled him into it. Some slightly scary bouncing on the floorboards outside the bathroom, then back into the small room for a fiesta of teeth-sucking, head-shaking and general Gallic misery.
Finally, Duprés drew a deep breath and looked at us both sorrowfully. 'It is possible to do, but it is going to be very, VERY expensive. I will need to rip up some of the floor in the corridor outside and the floor in the other bathroom to bring the water supply in here, and to take the waste back out to join up with the other bathroom.'
Guy turned to me triumphantly. 'I told you, Nicole.'
I ignored him again. 'Well, Mr Duprés, please would you make an estimate of how much the work would cost? And give us an idea of how soon it could be done?'
He nodded, slowly, joylessly. 'Yes, I can do that.'

After the plumber had hauled himself away, arse hanging halfway out of his sagging trousers in an unforgettable parting image of horror, Guy scrubbed his hands pink under the kitchen tap. I made us both an espresso.

'I can't say I have a whole lot of confidence in him,' I mused as we stood at the kitchen window, watching Gabriela effortlessly toss two enormous pieces of wood to one side. 'But he does seem to know what he's talking about, and he has done some work for Benoit, so he can't be THAT bad.'

'*Bah.*' The gloomy Gallic mood had infected him, too. 'He said it was going to be very difficult, Nicole. I told you it would be.'

'Oh for God's sake, Guy. If the human race was capable of building a rocket fifty years ago to go to the moon, surely it isn't asking too much to install a new bathroom on the first floor of an old building? I'm sure I've heard somewhere that it's been done before.'

'*Bah,* Nicole, you don't know about these old buildings. They don't like to be touched too much. You should instead put a new bathroom close to the other bathroom at the back of the château, maybe next door. Like that, it is easy to have the water and the waste supply.'

I took a deep breath. 'No, my darling, I want my dressing room to be next to the new ensuite bathroom. There will be an entrance to it directly from the ensuite.'

He frowned. 'What dressing room?'

I felt a tiny bit of the will to live leave my soul, perhaps forever. 'My dressing room. It's going next door to the new ensuite, which will be off the main bedroom, our bedroom. I'm sure I've mentioned it.'

'Why do you need a dressing room, Nicole? The bedroom is a very big room. You can easily put all your clothes in there.' He sniffed.

I ran through a range of possible responses in quick succession:
- Pickaxe through his forehead (the favourite).
- Make a big sign that said 'FUCK OFF, MY PROJECT', underline and embolden the MY, and carry it around with me for the foreseeable future.
- Use my feminine wiles.

The latter was the least messy, the most immediately accessible.

I slipped my arms around his waist, stroked his back, gazed into his dark eyes. 'Because, my darling, I can finally create something I've always wanted, I've always dreamed about. My very own, perfect little piece of heaven, my sanctuary, where all my beautiful clothes can live together in perfect harmony. It will make me so very, very happy. I will be the happiest princess in the loveliest dressing room in our gorgeous château, and—' I kissed him very softly on the mouth, which was starting to curve into the sexy smile '—if you are very good, I will occasionally let you come and visit me on the cream velvet chaise longue that will be in it.'

The dark-chocolate eyes melted. His hands slid down over my bum, pulling me against him. 'Okay, Nicole, I like this idea more now. A dressing room is a good idea.' Another soft kiss. 'But tell me more about this chaise longue, *mon amour*. Do you think it will have some special silk ribbons for the princess's *exquisite petite* wrists?'

So no, that obsession hadn't ended, despite the honeymoon meltdown.

Chapter Fourteen

I insisted Gabriela and Camille come inside to eat their lunch with us as it had started to rain, a light but soaking drizzle. Benoit had been right: I liked Gabriela straight away. She was a tall, sinuous woman, dark skinned and black haired, with deep brown eyes set in deep purple eye-sockets. She had a leisurely but serious manner, and a strong don't-mess-with-me undertone.

D'Artagnan had been less enthusiastic when we'd first met them a few days earlier to show them the trees that needed taking down. 'She is very butch, I think.'

'I don't think so at all!'

'Well, she is clearly the man in the relationship, Nicole.'

I sighed. Sometimes it was really tiring having to explain modern sexual politics to him. 'That isn't something you can say, or that you should think, anymore.' I did not add 'Grandad', even though it was on the tip of my tongue.

'Why? They are two lesbians, one plays the male part, one plays the female part. I have gay friends Nicole, a lot of my work colleagues were gay. My brother is gay. I know these things.'

Count to three. 'No, my angel, that's a very outdated way of thinking. They are two homosexual women who are, we assume, in a sexual and emotional relationship. That's the beginning and end of it. It isn't relevant to define that relationship by reference to a heterosexual one.'

A little pause. 'It seems you know a lot about lesbians, Nicole.' There was definitely a question in there, but he wasn't entirely sure how to phrase it.

'Yes. I spent a lot of time working with women, as you know. Quite a few of them were lesbians. Some of them were bisexual. Some of them were heterosexual. By the time they stopped modelling, some of them were asexual too.' And with good reason.

'And you?'

'Oh, I'm absolutely a lesbian, my darling. Can't you tell?'

Big, sexy smile.

Gabriela and Camille sat side by side opposite us at the big dining table. I couldn't stop surreptitiously staring at Camille when she wasn't looking. She had a fascinating, changeling quality about her. One instant she would seem the epitome of French *'petite'* – demure and pretty; an imperceptible moment later, she seemed defiant and almost feral. Her eyes were inky black, her skin olive, but when she took off the safety-helmet she'd been wearing, a cascade of wheaten-gold curls fell about her shoulders and down her back. The eye/hair colour contrast was so absurd that it had to be fake, but a nanosecond later it was patently obvious that it was as natural as the day she was born. This changeling aura was enhanced by the fact that she hardly ever spoke.

'Where are you from, Camille?' I asked, unable to keep the curiosity from my voice.

'She is from the Camargue,' said Gabriela. She opened a variety of Tupperware containers that she had taken from a big cooler bag, spreading them out on the table in front of them. Then she started filling their plates with a selection of the Tupperware contents: small bright red peppers; enormous green capers and olives; potatoes covered in some sort of dressing with flecks of orange; a salad with fat, prune-skinned, black olives and cubes of white cheese (feta, I assumed); sliced tomatoes in three different colours – red, yellow, green with black edges, bathed in olive oil; sliced salami; oily anchovies. The ubiquitous baguette. It was an amazing spread, straight out of a food magazine. I could see Guy studying it all with interest as we ate the mushroom-and-cheese omelette he had made for our lunch.

'The Camargue,' said Guy thoughtfully, breaking off a piece of his baguette and popping it in his mouth. 'St Maries des Mers? Arles? Aigues Mortes?'

'Yes,' said Gabriela. 'There.' A tiny smile flitted across Camille's mouth.

That topic of conversation clearly exhausted, Gabriela now fixed Guy with a hard, direct look. 'What was that *connard* Duprés doing here this morning? You are going to let him do work in your house? That would be a very, very, stupid thing to do.' She said it slowly, as if he was a very, very stupid man indeed.

Sproing! went the French cockerel's feathers. 'Why do you say that?' Chin up, nostrils flared.

'Because he is very, very bad. He is a terrible plumber. He is a liar, and he will charge you a big amount of money, and the work he does will be terrible. Terrible!!'

'How do you know this?'

'Because I have seen what he does! I have fixed the messes he has made! And it is always foreigners that are taken in by him. Everyone local knows he is shit!' Eyes flashing.

'I am not a foreigner.' Icy imperialism.

'Did you ever live here before?'

'This château has been in my family for over five hundred years.'

'But did you ever live here?'

'No, but my grandparents lived here, and we spent all of our childhoods here.'

'Did you have a chequebook when you were here?'

'Don't be stupid, I was a child!'

'Did you ever live here when you had a chequebook?' Deadpan.

'No.'

'*Voilà*, you are a foreigner!' Her tone softened, almost imperceptibly. 'To that *connard,* anyway, you are a foreigner. He will take your money and he will do a shit job.' She spooned a big mouthful of a bit of everything into her mouth, chewing meaningfully without taking her eyes off him.

Camille nodded sagely in agreement, raising an eyebrow for extra emphasis, her black eyes momentarily anchored on Guy's face.

Guy took another mouthful of his omelette. 'He did work for my cousin, Benoit. He had no problem,' he said sullenly.

Gabriela gave a small shrug. 'I know Benoit. I know the work Ludo did for him.' She sat back in her chair 'It's shit! The tiles are badly done, the grout is falling out and the washbasin leaks all the time! Benoit is too kind and too busy, and the bathroom is in the distillery, not in his house, so he doesn't care!'

'So, Gabriela, is there someone you would recommend instead of him?' I interrupted, trying to head off the impasse.

She turned a slightly softened gaze on me, gave a little shrug. 'Maybe. What is the job?'

I explained my plans for the ensuite bathroom and also the dressing room leading on from it. 'I can show you, if you like?'

'Okay. Show me after lunch.' She turned to Guy again. 'I am sorry if I have offended you, Guy, but it makes me so angry when I see *connards* like Ludo allowed to do such terrible work and to steal money from people for it.'

The plumage started to subside. 'Yes. I see. But I would probably not have agreed the *devis* anyway.' Airily, just to underline that he wasn't a stupid foreigner.

That's not what you said an hour ago, I thought. I also thought, she's really good, she even knows how to handle The Ego. Smart woman.

After lunch, I showed both women around the rooms upstairs and explained what I wanted done in detail. D'Artagnan stayed downstairs and washed up. Gabriela looked at everything closely, asked lots of questions, opened windows and stuck her head out, unscrewed panels in the bathroom wall with the screwdriver she had in her pocket, looked at the water connections, and even found a loose floorboard in the corridor, which she lifted carefully to see what was going on underneath.

At the end, when we were standing in the hall downstairs, I asked again, 'So, do you know someone who can do this job?'

'Yes,' she said simply. 'We can do this job. Camille and I can do this job. We have done this before.'

Guy was standing in the salon by the window, slightly off stage, supposedly removing something from the architrave. There was the tiniest sound of air being expelled through pursed lips.

Gabriela's eyes swung around to fix on him. 'I have references. I will give you the name of some of my clients, all here in the Charente and in the Charente Maritime. You can talk to all of them. If you are happy, I will prepare a *devis* for you, and you can decide if you want to accept it.' She turned back to me with a little smile, the first I had seen her give. 'And now, we must go outside and finish the tree.'

Guy and I had gradually, tenuously, started to develop a routine – well, a morning routine anyway. He would get out of bed first, go downstairs to make coffee, feed the cats and let them out, and bring the coffee back up to bed. I would roll out my mat and spend half an hour doing yoga, while he showered and dressed. I liked to shower before bed. Then I would dress and go downstairs, channelling calm and positive thoughts for the day ahead, confident that I could deal with whichever version of D'Artagnan I was living with today.

The most irritating one was the Supervisor. 'What are you going to do today, Nicole? I have some ideas for you.'

Flip the bird, sip coffee, carry on scrolling.

The next most irritating one was the imperious Employer. 'Nicole, I need you to go to Paris on Friday.'

'I'm not double-O-fucking-seven, Guy. You can't just order me to go places.'

After that, the Hobbyist. 'Nicole! Today we must go to the DIY store. I need to buy a new chainsaw, the other one is not big enough. And I think I need to buy a machine to split the wood as well. Here, look, there is one for sale here. And maybe we need to buy a quad bike. I must do some research. Finish your coffee, hurry up. Come on we need to go, the shop will be shut soon.'

This really does still happen in rural France: shops shut for lunch at noon *precisely*. That Renault Clio overtaking you on the blind bend at 110km an hour at 12.10pm? Do not get in the way of it; that is a Frenchman on his way home to lunch, and he has dangerously low blood sugar. Breakfast was an espresso and a fag at 7.30a.m. Out of the way, *putain de merde*!

D'Artagnan went to Bordeaux about once a week where he had lunch with his friend, Guillaume. He was excited about their property venture, frustrated that the lawyers drawing up the joint-venture documentation were not working harder, faster. He constantly nagged me to come to Bordeaux with him.

'I will come, I promise, but not right now! There's loads of stuff I have to plan and organise. If I don't do it, it won't happen and that will drive me nuts!'

We finally had a date in early June for the windows to be replaced, which was a relief, but I was beginning to realise how much work it was planning, designing and sourcing materials for a completely refurbished bedroom, entire new bathroom and the creation of Heaven. I spent hours in the library, a cosy room in the matching tower at the other end of the château from the kitchen. I installed myself in the shiny-with-wear, red-leather captain's chair behind the enormous green-leather topped desk, and gradually honed Project Bonjour 21C! (Phase One).

But the Duchess had begun to flex her old, surprisingly sprightly muscles. She had been throwing sporadic tantrums about electricity usage, tripping part of the château on occasion, sometimes the whole château. She enjoyed making us scurry about trying to guess where the fuse box she had tripped might be. It was possible that there were more than six.

'It's your fridge,' I told him. 'Nothing else has changed since we got here. The electricity worked fine until the fridge arrived, and now it doesn't.'

'*Pfffft*, Nicole, it is not the fridge. The fridge does not use a lot of electricity – and we need the fridge.'

'Well, the château is unhappy about something. This morning the electricity went off while I was blow-drying my hair!'

'*Mais voilà*, Nicole, that is the problem! The hairdryer uses a lot of electricity!'

We were eating lunch in the dining room; I was starting to realise that he was actually pretty good in the kitchen. Apart from the feathery omelettes and crunchy grilled vegetables he made for us, he had quickly identified which salads were my favourites and had made one that day: raw spinach, blue cheese, walnuts, sun-dried tomatoes, capers and olives; a seared duck-breast and new potatoes for him in addition to the salad. He had put a couple of new potatoes on my plate; normally I don't eat potatoes (why would I? Tasteless carbs!) but these were spectacularly good; they were small and firm, they tasted of salty earth. I told him so.

'*Bah ouais*, Nicole,' he smiled. 'They are from the Ile de Ré. They have the sea in them, they are the best potatoes in the world. I will take you there; the Ile de Ré is really special, and it is only an hour away.'

'Guy, I am not going to stop drying my hair just because it upsets the château. Fuck's sake.'

'But, Nicole, why don't you just wear your hair like on our honeymoon? I like it like that.' He waved his fork at me, gave me the lazy smile.

I smiled, remembering. 'Yes, I know that, my darling, but sometimes I like to look like I haven't just been clubbed over the head and dragged down a mountain. It's not a very chic look. And the electricity problem really does need sorting out. It's starting to become really annoying, and I don't know how to do it. Please, can you do something? Pretty please?'

Small Gallic shrug. 'Because you ask so nicely, I find an electrician. I promise. But tomorrow, I have another meeting with Guillaume in Bordeaux. Why don't you come with me, *mon amour*? You have still not been in Bordeaux. I want to show you my city, and maybe afterwards we go to Pyla, we take some days in the sun, we swim in the sea, we have a lot of sex…' The smile became even lazier.

Françoise had inherited the family holiday home in Pyla-sur-Mer in the achingly cool Arcachon basin, summer playground of the wealthy Bordelais. It did sound tempting. 'How about a compromise? Once the windows are installed, and I've had the devis from Gabriela for the work on our new bedroom suite and I've ordered all of the bathroom stuff, and the units for the dressing room, and the furniture for the new bedroom…'

'You are trying to find an excuse, Nicole?' His voice was sharp.

'No! It's just you don't seem to understand. If I don't organise all of this, nothing bloody well happens, Guy! We can go away on holiday, we can go away loads, apart from that I don't think it's very fair on the cats to be away' – to be honest, the cats were becoming increasingly, happily feral – 'but apart from the cats, then what? We come back home again, and the château is exactly the same as when we left it. Nothing has been organised or done, and it still doesn't feel like a proper home!'

Sulkily: 'It feels like a home to me.'

I successfully managed to suppress yet another scream of exasperation at the eternally circuitous discussion we seemed to be having.

Then, new hobby! Guy joined Benoit's cycling club and spent hours and hours, days, researching which bicycle to buy, where to order it from, how light it was, how fast it was going to be. 'Look, look at this one Nicole, do you see? It is made of carbon fibre. I think this is the one I need, don't you think so?'

Shortly after it arrived, he went out for his inaugural Sunday morning 50km ride in a fairly undulating part of the Cognac region. He came back grey-faced and trembling, collapsed onto the bed and lay there groaning and whimpering for hours about his age and lack of fitness.

I tried to be sympathetic. 'My darling man, Benoit is at least ten years younger than you, and has been cycling probably twice a week for most of his adult life, whereas you have been working in the city, stuck in an office or on a plane, and you maybe get to go to the gym once a week if you're lucky. How about starting a bit more realistically? Maybe join a different club, with people that are a bit older, slightly less athletic?'

Another muffled groan. 'Benoit is one of the young ones in the club, most of the others are my age or older! I cannot believe how unfit I am!'

'Well then, if they can do it so can you. Here's an idea: perhaps don't try to climb Everest on your first day out hiking, idiot! My darling idiot.' In case I sounded a bit harsh.

Fortunately, his innate antagonism meant that it was inconceivable that he wouldn't be entering – and quite possibly winning – the Tour de France the following year. He started going out on the bike on his own, which allowed me a couple of hours of peaceful tranquillity. On his return, triumphant and sweaty in his Day-Glo, logo-ed Lycra, he would give me a detailed account of the route, the distance, the elevation, the descent, the speed, the traffic that had passed him, his mental state of mind and, of course, his physical state at every stage of the entire bike ride.

I usually contrasted wallpaper samples with upholstery fabrics and paint colours, and sometimes even mentally redecorated a whole room in the château while this went on, all the while nodding occasionally and making appropriate noises of interest at appropriate times.

The other hobby was cooking. This was a whole-day hobby, starting with the morning visit to the market in Cognac. The market took place most days of the week in a beautiful late-nineteenth-century wood and metal building, flooded with light from the enormous arched windows that lined the upper part of the structure. The array of fresh fruits, vegetables, meat, fish, seafood, cheese, olives, breads, honey and tinned, potted, preserved and bottled local delicacies was breath-taking. It was noisy as we wandered around: occasional shouts of the bargain of the day, detailed discussions between stall owner and customer which were sometimes serious, sometimes flirtatious, always good-natured.

There are cultural clichés about all nations. The French love of food is not one of them. It is a hardwired FACT.

D'Artagnan would put his arm through mine, hold my hand with our fingers intertwined against his chest as we wandered slowly past the stalls. A full inspection circuit was necessary before there was any hint of an actual purchase.

Then he would make a decision, and we would spend the next couple of hours standing in different queues waiting patiently to be served (yes, I too was surprised that D'Artagnan was capable of patience), pointing to various fruits and vegetables while the stallholder filled and weighed each brown paper bag. A casual exchange of words while the transaction was completed, and the sexy smile if the stallholder was female, then on to the next anointed stall, where the same procedure was followed but with fish, seafood or cheese or (more rarely, given my vegetarian "affliction") meat as the neatly wrapped bounty. I found it fascinating to note that the fishmongers were the most raucous and bawdy, while the cheesemongers were by far the most serious.

Afterwards, we would have a coffee outside the *boulangerie*/coffee shop opposite the market. Guy would smoke one of his rare cigarettes, and I would pretend that I was actually French too. I loved these mornings, even if they were long and it could be tedious queueing up for each different stall. I loved to stand quietly beside him, his body under his shirt warm against the back of my hand, and observe everything that was going on around me without having to engage with anyone. I loved us sitting together with our coffee afterwards, watching the market gradually wind down at the end of the morning, the shouts between the stallholders, the stalls starting to be packed away, the vans reversing up to be filled with unsold produce. And I loved the thought that this was happening almost every single day throughout every year, in this and hundreds of other small towns and big cities all over this vast, beautiful country.

I tried to articulate this to Guy, but just ended up saying, 'I love – all this,' and waved my hand about vaguely in the direction of the market.

He nodded. 'Yes, I love it too. It is why it is so important, Nicole, not to do shopping at the big supermarkets. It is very important that we support the small business people, the *marchés*, our local producers. This is an essential part of French life.'

'Spoken like a true non-capitalist ex-investment banker, my darling.'

He ignored that. 'But it is changing in France. French people don't go to the *marché* anymore, they are now too lazy to buy fresh food and cook it properly. They are happy to buy processed food, food full of sugar and industrial grain. They feed their children on American breakfast cereal, pizza and hamburgers from McDonalds – Happy Meals, *putain!* There is nothing happy about them, it is a death sentence for the children!'

'Well,' I said carefully, 'maybe they don't all live in châteaux and have a whole day free to prepare a proper meal. Maybe they have to work all day and they are exhausted when they come home, and they don't have the energy to prepare a nutritious meal for their children.'

'Yes. That is probably true.' More gloom. 'La France is going to be like Britain and America in a few years' time, you will see. People sat on the sofa wearing sweatpants, drinking bubbly sugar, eating pizza with cheese in the crust – cheese in the crust! What is this disgusting thing that has been invented? Why would you think to create, and then to eat, this abhorrent food, *putain de merde...?*'

And on and on, until I could think of something to distract him and change the subject.

Food. The British talk about weather when they are making small talk, but if you are struggling to make small talk with a French person, mention food. The conversational universe yawns before you.

Chapter Fifteen

There had been a very short discussion about celebrating our wedding later that summer in proper French style, *au château*.
'No.' I said. 'Just no, Guy. There is WAY too much renovation work to do, to organise, and my head will literally fucking explode if I have to organise a bloody wedding celebration as well. We'll do it next summer when everything is a whole lot less chaotic, okay?'
He gazed at me. 'You are not a very romantic woman, Nicole.'
'No, I'm not. Not when I'm stressed out, anyway.'
'This is why you need to take a break, *mon amour*. Come, we go to Bordeaux, to Pyla, next week. I don't want any more argument about it, Nicole. We need to take a break.'

His last sentence was almost lost in the sound of drilling as the second new window in the salon was fitted. It was the third week in June and the work had only started the day before. I was starting to understand that project start dates were anything but; they were simply an indication of a best-case scenario, kind of like doing a renovation lottery. You might be lucky and win, but the chances were slim.

I opened my mouth to respond just as the drilling began again. It was ear-shattering. When it stopped, I said, 'Okay.'

We asked Anna, Benoit's sixteen-year-old daughter, to feed the cats and lock up after the artisans had finished for the day. I asked Gabriela if she and/or Camille wouldn't mind popping back from time to time to check that they weren't doing anything outrageously stupid while we were gone, and insisted that I would pay her for her time and petrol to do so. She gave me one of her rare smiles and said it wouldn't be a problem; she often oversaw projects for her clients' holiday homes. I felt very relieved. I liked her more and more; she felt like an ally in my quest to negotiate this new, multi-dimensional maze that renovating a château in rural France was becoming.

We went to Bordeaux. D'Artagnan had booked a suite in the hotel overlooking the Grand Theatre, and I stood at the open French windows, the gauze curtains gently wafting into the room, gazing at its perfectly symmetrical Grecian beauty. He came up behind me, put his arms around my waist, kissed the side of my neck. 'It is a beautiful building, *non*? We will go to the opera one night, not this time, another time. You will be impressed, it is very *merveilleux* inside.'

'That would be nice. I'd like that.' I smiled at him, he smiled back, more kisses gradually progressing toward the nape of my neck. 'Darling man, stop that, not now.' I wriggled away from him. 'Come on, we need to go explore the city. I need to walk, Guy. My back is killing me after sitting in the car all that time.'

Bordeaux is a fabulous city but the traffic getting to it can be absolutely dire.

So, we went walking; we walked for miles that warm June day. We walked around the posh part (Hermès, Vuitton, Cartier, etc), down wide avenues lined with classical, butter-coloured buildings, across the vast twelve-hectare square that is Quinconces; admired the voluptuous Monument des Girondins, its frothing marble fountains full of galloping wild stallions, pert-buttocked men and bare-breasted women watched over by Liberty poised elegantly at the top of a marble column. Then a slower amble, hand in hand, along the banks of the Gironde, busy with walkers, joggers, bladers, cyclists, all the way up to the spectacularly engineered Pont Chaban-Dalmas. As we were walking towards it, it was gradually opening, the central eight-laned part of the bridge rising seeming effortlessly between four pillars, in order to let one of the enormous ocean-liners cluttering up the quay back out of the port.

'Wow.' I was impressed. D'Artagnan took this as an indication that I wished to hear a long lecture about the brilliance of French engineering. I smiled vaguely at him, enjoying the feel of the sun against my back and the warm gentle breeze, put him on mute while he droned on.

Then we took one of the zippy electric trams that make a lovely, soft 'ting-ting' sound at seemingly unscheduled moments all the way back into the centre and wandered around the cool, student *quartier*; bars, restaurants, narrow cluttered streets that opened unexpectedly into small squares lined with honey-coloured neoclassical buildings adorned with intricate wrought-iron balcony grills, filled with more bars and restaurants and laughter and chatter. We found a table, sat down, and ordered Lillet spritzes (Lillet is the locally made aperitif) which are like Aperol spritzes but less … sugary.

'So, *mon amour*, what do you think of my beautiful city?' Guy smiled at me from behind his sunglasses.

'I love it! Why don't we come and live here?'

Frown. 'You don't like the château?'

I thought about the château for a moment. 'I do like the château,' I admitted. 'But it's a little bit exhausting, all the stuff that needs to be done. Whereas this—' I waved an arm at the pretty, busy square we were sitting in, 'this just seems lovely, easy, really relaxed. It's a really cool city.'

He paused while the waiter set our drinks down, then touched his glass to mine, smiled at me again. 'I am happy that you love it, *mon amour*. You will love Pyla too, the *bassin d'Arcachon*.'

I smiled back at him, took a sip of my spritz, gazed around the square. 'Which part is your renovation project in?'

'We didn't go there today. We go there tomorrow. It is a great *quartier*, you will like it, it is *très chic*, *très bio*, and lots of vegetarian restaurants.' He grinned at me.

'I like it already,' I said enthusiastically.

'I suppose I will tell you a little secret too, *ma chérie*. I am thinking that we will keep one of the apartments that will be renovated, I don't know which one yet, but we will keep one for us. We need to have an apartment in Bordeaux, I think.'

My smile got a lot bigger. 'That would be wonderful! When can we go and see it? Or at least where it is – the organic, vegetarian *quartier*?'

He looked at his watch. 'Not now, Nicole. We go back to the hotel now. We are meeting Guillaume and his new girlfriend for a cocktail a bit later, so I think…' He dropped his chin, looked at me over his sunglasses, brown eyes warm, half lowered. 'So I think we go back to the hotel, take a shower, and I take some time to make this first visit to Bordeaux special, *mon amour*. What do you think?'

Later, lying nose to nose on the pillows, the gauze curtains billowing into the room, my legs still wrapped around him, I decided that Bordeaux was my new favourite city in the world.

We met Guillaume and Léa in a rooftop cocktail bar. They were already there when we arrived and stood up to greet us as we walked toward them. Guy murmured, '*Salut, les amis,*' and kissed them both in greeting, then turned to me. 'Nicole, *je te présente*, Guillaume, Léa.'

I smiled, segued effortlessly into '*enchantée*', which I had now thoroughly mastered, exchanged kisses with Léa, a very pretty, very skinny girl with long, straight dark hair and enormous brown eyes, long, long eyelashes, while thinking 'surely a bit young!' before turning to Guillaume.

He smiled lazily at me, the same sort of lazy, sexy smile that Guy was so very good at, only his smile stopped dead at his eyes; they were hard eyes, dark, almost black, and they weren't smiling.

'Nicole, *enchanté*. I have heard so much about you from Guy.' His English was lightly accented, his voice smooth, low. As we exchanged kisses, I distinctly heard him breathe in, as if he were ... sniffing me, which was disconcerting.

'Oh, thank you. I hope it was all good,' I felt slightly flustered. He was very good looking: tall, dark-haired, lightly bearded and suntanned. His face was narrow, perfectly chiselled.

White teeth flashed briefly as he smiled again. 'Oh, all very good, very interesting. I have been looking forward to meeting you.' A direct look from the unsmiling black eyes.

I didn't like him.

I didn't tell Guy. 'Oh, he seems nice,' I said the next day when he asked me what I'd thought. 'Although isn't his girlfriend a little, I dunno, young for him? I thought you said you were at school with him?' I was aware of the irony given our own age difference, but Léa couldn't have been more than twenty-two or thereabouts.

Guy gave a little shrug. 'Maybe. Sometimes his girlfriends can be a bit young.'

'He has lots of girlfriends?'

He shot me a look. 'Yes. Are you interested in Guillaume, *mon amour*?'

'Quite the opposite, Guy. I'm merely observing that if he's the same age as you perhaps he is going through the traditional male-menopause phase, the one where older men shag impressionable young girls. Remember, I did see quite a lot of this when I was modelling. It's very familiar to me.'

He turned his gaze fully on me; we were walking through the pretty park toward the part of Bordeaux that their development project was in. 'Yes Nicole, I remember. Is this what happen to you? Was this man you were in love with older than you? Were you very young too?'

'No, I'm not a silly fucking bimbo. I never fell for that bullshit!' I said crossly. I had not slept well; Karl had kept me awake. I could not stop thinking about *that* poster. That title. Remembering. I had taken five milligrams at 4am, and another five milligrams at 9.30am just before we'd left the hotel because the first five milligrams didn't seem to have had any effect. My heart still felt as if it were being alternately squeezed, wrung out and then massively inflated. I was not calm.

On the way back to the hotel after dinner the previous night, we had passed a cinema. It was an independent cinema and there were posters of forthcoming films. One of the posters immediately caught my eye: it was split perfectly in two, vibrantly brick-red on the lower half, deep blue on the upper half. It showed a jagged, monumental red land mass and a sapphire-blue sky, swirls of bright, ephemeral white cloud scribbled across that wide, endless blue sky. Beneath it were the actors' names – and the director's name.

Karl's name. The name of the film was *Chaque Fois: 5m30s*. *Everytime: 5m30s* in English.

There is a LOT of shit 'trance' music out there, and some truly excellent stuff; 'Everytime' on *Gatecrasher Wet* falls in the latter category. Five minutes thirty seconds into 'Everytime' was our code. We waited, we abstained, eyes locked together in the silver-and-green gaze, his full lips slightly open, always just a breath away from mine. But we always waited. We whispered to each other 'five minutes thirty seconds', his mouth just touching mine, his silver eyes heavy: we never fucked until five minutes thirty seconds into 'Everytime'. When the full, glorious refrain really kicked in ... then we did. It was insanely good, that rush. It was orgasmic. Literally. Five minutes thirty seconds was code between us.

There was a very direct message from him to me in that poster.

It made me ache, made my heart ache, every time it trespassed into my mind. And it made me very anxious. Because I knew I wasn't over Karl – and having seen that poster, I knew that he had not forgotten about me.

I had absorbed the poster as we walked, Guy's arm around my shoulders, his fingers brushing gently against my breast. I had already clocked the blue-and-red horizontal split, before I'd even focused on the text below, and I knew exactly where it was from. Karl and I had gone to that place; we had been there in Arizona. We had stood on the terrace in that hotel, that super-chic boutique hotel where the world was split into two colours, where the cloud formations flirted with leisurely atmospheric updrafts.

We had walked out onto the terrace into the bright sunshine, and Karl had sneezed. I was reminded of the note he'd left in my apartment one day, early on at the start of our relationship when we were still fascinated by each other. In the beginning, he always left me notes if I left the apartment before him. Sometimes he drew me a picture. This note said simply: 'Today, I sneezed to greet the sun. I miss you. I love you.' A stick figure, with a disproportionately large hand over its heart; the sun behind.

We had still been in love at that time, standing there on that terrace in Arizona gazing out at the red-and-blue landscape. It was after the first IVF procedure, and it had been more than six weeks. I had not miscarried. Yet. We still believed in the future.

Guy made a face. We carried on walking, the gravel crunching under our feet. 'But you know, Nicole, you never tell me about this man who break your heart. Who was he? This Anglo-Saxon? I think he was Anglo-Saxon.' He nodded sagely, in full agreement with himself.

Karl's mother is English, his father is German. You pretty much can't get any more Anglo-Saxon than that. I wondered, not for the first time, whether D'Artagnan was telepathic. The thought made me go cold inside.

'Why is it relevant, Guy?' The anxiety that he had picked up on something manifested itself as annoyance in my tone.

He shrugged again, squeezed my hand. 'I am curious, that is all. You have met my ex-wife, my children, my family, and I have met Juliette and Mark. You don't have any other friends. You never talk about your life before, about your family, about this man that you were in love with, that you wanted to have a family with.'

It was my turn to shrug. I looked away from him, across the lawns towards a pretty curved footbridge in the distance. I took a deep breath. 'I didn't stay friends with anyone from that period. They were mostly his friends, and you know how things are when couples split up. Often the friends will be loyal to only one of the couple.'

He let go of my hand, slipped his arm around my shoulders instead. I was wearing a loosely knitted linen sweater, a long cream linen scarf knotted at the back; the morning was fresh but sunny.

'And my parents – well, I told you about my parents. They were pretty shit. They were crap parents, accidental parents. I'm not in touch with them anymore.' I threw a glance at him. 'Is that a problem for you? If so, it might be a little late to flag it up.'

He raised one eyebrow a little, looked at me sideways 'You are very defensive, Nicole. I am not your enemy, *mon amour*. I just maybe want to know more about the woman I love, about my wife.' He reached for the scarf, hanging down my back, wrapped it around my neck then pulled me in against him, stopped in the middle of the pathway so that a cyclist had to swerve around us. He held the two ends of the scarf while he kissed me, softly.

'But it's okay, we don't have to talk about this. I only want that you are happy, *mon ange*. Okay?' He gazed into my eyes, waiting for me to respond.

'Okay.' I made an effort to smile at him but the anxiety remained. I loved D'Artagnan, I really did. I drew a deep breath, kissed him back, smiled properly at him, and mentally polished the only solution to the problem that had worked so far: avoid Karl and anything connected to him. At. All. Costs.

Guy and Guillaume's development project was in the part of Bordeaux known as Chartrons, the old part where the Bordeaux *negociants*, the wine-traders, had historically located their warehouses near to the quays and the ships that transported the Bordeaux wines all over the world. The main, largely pedestrianised street running through the quartier was lined with organic bakeries, art galleries, vegetarian and other restaurants, small boutiques, a fabulous vintage clothing shop specialising only in designer labels (I fell in love with a dark blue, beautifully cut Yves Saint Laurent cape/jacket from the 1960s; Guy indulged me). We passed several signs for yoga studios. I felt immediately at home; I hadn't known it was possible to love Bordeaux more than I already did.

'It's very boho. I love it,' The second five milligrams had kicked in and I was feeling peaceful, happy again. I slipped my arm around D'Artagnan's waist; his body felt firm under my fingers, warm and strong under his soft T-shirt.

'In France we don't say boho, Nicole, we say bobo – *bourgeois-bohémien*. We say Chartrons is very *bobo*. Also, that it is the 21st *arrondissement* of Paris. Since the fast train, all the Parisians are coming to live or to buy a *pied-a-terre* in Bordeaux for the weekends. This is why our development is going to be very successful.'

Their development was on one of the side streets off this main street; a series of unrenovated *negociant* warehouses.

'When can we move in?' I asked, as we stood outside looking at the enormous, industrial windows. Most of the windowpanes had been smashed, but it had loads of potential, even I could see that.

He frowned slightly. 'It will be an apartment that we come to sometimes, Nicole. We are not going to live here all the time. We live in the château, remember?'

'Mmmmm.' The château seemed very far from my mind. Like I said, fickle. 'Can I have a say in decorating our apartment?'

A hard stare. He was weighing up how to answer that. 'Will it need to have a dressing room?'

'Not necessarily,' I said airily. 'But it might need a little space for my visiting wardrobe.' Then I gave him a naughty smile 'And of course, it will have to have a chaise longue, don't you think?' He laughed, slipped his hand around my waist. *'Bah, bien sur, mon amour...* I will have a special one made for you.' Suggestive eyebrows.

The next day we drove to Pyla-sur-Mer. France has coastline on three oceans, the Med, the Atlantic and the North Sea. I have spent time on the Mediterranean part, the Côte d'Azur, at various times in my life. As is well documented, the coast is jaw-droppingly beautiful, picture-postcard stunning, all pinks and blues and greens and white sand – it oozes five-star beauty. It is, however, massively overcrowded and it feels supercharged, loud; there's always an undercurrent of menace accompanying the ubiquitous bling, four-wheeled, hairy-chested or otherwise. I'm aware that's a massive generalisation, that it isn't all like that, but the parts I've spent time in are.

The Atlantic coast is different. Its colours are more subtle than the Mediterranean: pastel blue, oatmeal sand, frothy cream surf, dusty, faded pink. The coast around which the lagoon, the *bassin d'Arcachon*, curves is the distilled essence of the Atlantic *esprit*. The holiday towns dotting the 70km curve around the shallow, sea-water lagoon are a bit shabby chic, a bit sand-blown, sun-bleached cool, a bit bare, sandy feet under the lunch table. The curve culminates in Cap Ferret, which is so sun-bleached cool and laid back, it's positively comatose.

Pyla, directly across the oyster beds on the other side of the lagoon, is not quite as supine as Cap Ferret; the wide, pine-tree-lined avenues are occasionally disturbed by the throaty backfire of a Ferrari or an Aston Martin.

In July and August it is HEAVING. Bordeaux and a lot of the interior of France, of Europe, has drained like an empty bathtub and all of it is now stuck to the Arcachon basin. Fortunately, it was late June when we were there; the weather was perfect, the restaurants were not all booked solid and the atmosphere was still relatively chilled.

Françoise had promised to come down at the weekend with Amandine and Chloé. We spent three slow, lazy days before she arrived, getting up late after leisurely morning sex, wandering to the boulangerie for croissants and bread, back for coffee on the terrace overlooking the garden, a swim in the bay around midday, drying off flat-out like starfish on the hot sand, walking back barefoot to the house, a cool shower, some lunch mid-afternoon, more sun, occasional cooling off in the pool, another cool shower, maybe more sex, a bottle of rosé or Champagne and then a wander down to a restaurant for a late dinner on the main drag, then blissful, luxurious, sun-kissed sleep. The next day rinse and repeat, more or less.

By the time the others joined us on Friday evening, we were about as animated as sloths, drugged up to the eyeballs on sunshine, sea and sex.

On the Saturday afternoon, Emma and Conor arrived; including Chloe's boyfriend, Thomas, we were eight in total for dinner. Guy and Françoise had been to the market in Arcachon that morning and were preparing the evening meal together in the kitchen with a lot of bickering about how things should be done, and occasional giggling scuffles. The rest of us were sitting around the table on the terrace next to the pool, which was now shaded from the evening sun, sipping Champagne. I was basking in Conor's soft Irish accent (the Irish accent always makes me feel slightly weak-kneed) by asking him lots of questions about how he'd come to meet Emma.

'It was me dad, really,' he said, pronouncing it 'da'. 'He's always been crazy about wine, always really interested in it, particularly in Bordeaux wines. He loved France and he spent a lot of time in Bordeaux when he was younger, before he went back to Ireland and met me ma. He educated us, my brother and me, about wine so I was interested in it too. After I finished school and while I was at uni in Dublin, I always came for the grape harvest in Bordeaux – you know, working in the vines and meeting other people. It's always such a great atmosphere at the end of summer, even if it's hard work. The evenings are always fantastic, like everyone's on a high.'

He paused, turned to gaze at Emma next to him. 'And then one year, I met Emma, and there was no question that I could ever go back to live in Ireland.' He smiled at her and she smiled back. My heart gave a little pulse. They were SO in love.

I tried to modify the stupid, goofy grin on my face. 'Do you miss it at all? You're from Cork, aren't you? County Cork?'

'Yeah,' he nodded. 'From Cork city.'

'It's a great city. I loved it,' I said.

'Oh, you've been there?'

I nodded. 'Yes, I stayed in Cobh for a while. For quite a long while, actually, about six months.'

'Cobh is great, isn't it?! Such a fantastic atmosphere, and being right there on the harbour, it's really special. When was that then? When were you there?'

'Uh ... about, maybe four years ago?'

'You never told me you live in Ireland, Nicole.' I hadn't heard Guy come up behind me. He brushed my hair away from the back of my neck gently with his fingers. 'Where were you living? Where is this place, Cobh?' I tried not to tense up. I had forgotten about Inspector Clouseau for a moment.

'It's a small town on the southern Irish coast, just below Cork where Conor comes from,' I said, smiling up at him brightly. 'He was just telling me how he came to meet Emma. I didn't know they met while he was working over here in the vineyards!' Change the subject. I smiled at Emma again. 'It must have been so romantic to meet like that. Was it love at first sight?' I realised I was starting to witter.

She laughed. 'Not really! Well, maybe a little bit. I noticed his blue eyes. But I also thought, oh my God, he shouldn't be out here in the sunshine with no hat on, not with that Irish skin! So, I thought he was a bit of an idiot, too!'

He turned to her, laughed, squeezed her leg. 'Yeah, I reckon I did have a bit of sunstroke that first time we met.' They gazed at each other, eyes dancing.

'Why were you living in Ireland, Nicole? You never told me this.' Softly, mildly. Guy reached for the bottle of Champagne in the ice bucket in front of me, took my glass and filled it, waited until I looked up at him before handing to me.

'Thank you, sweetheart.' I took it from him. 'I was just – I don't know, taking a break? I took a break from London for a while, and I'd always wanted to go to Cork, so I took some time out and stayed in Cobh. On my own,' I added, a bit defiantly.

Which wasn't really true. I'd got as far west from London as I could in my car, then got the first ferry from Holyhead to Dublin and continued to drive west until I'd panicked and thought – Ireland is too close, I need to go further. So I'd driven to Cork to get a ferry to Roscoff in France, but I'd got lost trying to get to the ferry port outside Cork and ended up in Cobh, on the other side of the harbour. I'd found a hotel and passed out in a deep, exhausted sleep, woken up the next day and had a wander around and thought, actually, this feels safe. This feels far enough away. I can stay here for a bit. He won't look for me here; he won't find me here.

So I found an estate agent and rented one of the colourful terraced houses overlooking the harbour for a month, spending hours standing at the window watching the ships and ferries slowly navigate their way into port, numb with pain and grief. That was cathartic, in a way, and the month became two months, and I started to think that perhaps I might heal after all.

I went for walks; sometimes I walked for hours. It was very beautiful, the countryside: green, so many different greens, and blue, so many different blues in the ever-changing seascape. Even after I fell on one of those walks, even after the night in hospital where—

But no. I was NOT going to allow my mind to wander into that dangerous, sulphurous swamp.

Four months passed, Jules visited, hugged me close while I sobbed, and then after six months she swore to me that he was gone, that he'd gone to the States and it was safe for me to come back to London.

'Oh. I see.' Guy's eyes held mine for a moment until he turned away and went to refill the others' glasses.

Despite this slightly weird interlude, we had a lovely evening, definitely drank too much Champagne and ended up doubled over, weak with laughter when Conor pushed Guy in the pool fully clothed after he'd thrown Françoise in. Guy tried desperately to keep his Champagne glass out of the water while alternately ducking Françoise and swearing and splashing water at Conor.

It was a wonderful evening; my stomach ached by the end, and just as I was falling asleep in Guy's arms I realised that these wonderful, warm, funny people were now my family too, in a way. And that was a curious but very pleasant feeling.

We arrived back at the château. The Duchess was very miffed indeed about her new windows, and was determined to make me pay. The electricity went off when I was in the shower, combing conditioner through my hair with my fingers. Three days of 'just been' hair needed quite a lot of conditioner, and I had turned off the water while I did it (I am eco-conscious; D'Artagnan, not so much).

I reached blindly for the extremely unreliable shower control in the pitch dark, succeeded in activating the overhead shower instead and was doused in freezing cold water. I screamed, cursed the bitch Duchess. The water gradually got warmer. I washed out the conditioner, carefully turned off the water, stood there dripping in the pitch dark, wondering how getting out of the bathtub (we were still using the Peach Panoply bathroom at this point) and finding my towel, etc. was going to go.

I called for Guy. No answer. I yelled again, heard him coming up the stairs. He appeared at the bathroom door holding a candle.

'Ah *mon amour*, you look beautiful in the candlelight,' he purred.

'Fuck off! I thought you were going to get the fucking electricity sorted?'

'Nicole.' Patient voice. 'We just get back tonight. It is going to be difficult to get someone to do it tonight. I am still trying to find the fuse box where the electricity has gone off.'

We had gradually discovered, in a kind of intensely frustrating electricity-supply treasure hunt, that the Duchess actually had seven fuse boxes. Well, to date she had seven fuse boxes. It was possible that she had more and we hadn't found them yet.

Guy came into the bathroom, stood by the bathtub to stabilise me while I climbed out, handed me my towel. 'Sometimes, I fucking HATE this house,' I muttered.

'Forty thousand euros?!' his eyes widened in … surprise? Perhaps a little stronger than that. Big surprise?

'Yes.' I smiled brightly at him.

'But it is a bathroom, *mon amour*, just one. Why does it cost so much?'

'Because it's from Bisazza, darling man. It's by this wonderful Belgian designer, Jaime Hayon. The double sink unit, the bath, the bathroom cabinet – and the gorgeous mosaic mural on the back wall is a mural of the Emperor Napoleon's face. It's very classical – I chose it because I knew you'd appreciate it.' Given your Napoleonic personality traits, I added silently.

'But not the shower unit. I economised on that. Sort of. And the macerator toilet. That's not Bisazza either.' I continued to smile brightly, encouragingly, at him as if to say: You can do this, just run with it! I had signed Gabriela's devis; it had seemed very reasonable. Now I just needed the materials to make my beautiful bathroom happen.

We were in the dining hall. It is a dining *hall* I have decided; I feel the ghosts of the Musketeers are only a slight shift away in the time/space continuum, that one day I'll walk through the doorway and catch them all mid-banquet at the table, gnawing on the flesh of some animal, flinging the bones over their shoulders for the waiting peasants to pick up.

D'Artagnan had prepared dinner and was carrying through the salad bowl and the bread basket. I was leaning against the table, sipping the glass of wine he'd poured me. I had decided that this was the evening to lay it all out in black and white. I needed him to transfer the money directly to Bisazza's UK account so that Bisazza Italy would send the beautiful goodies I so desired directly to the Duchess. I had decided it wasn't going to be possible to surreptitiously Amex it: the Amex would be Amaxed out pretty damn quickly.

'Forty thousand euros, just to Bisazza? Nicole, this is a lot of money! This is not even all the costs, or including the cost to pay for the installation of the bathroom! Bathrooms do not normally cost this much, Nicole. I know this. I am doing the cost for all of the bathrooms in the apartments we are developing in Bordeaux; none of them are costing more than ten thousand euros in total!

How are you spending more than forty thousand euros on one bathroom?'

I stopped smiling. 'You said – do you remember, Guy? – you said: "You make it how you will like it, Nicole. There is money to do what you want to do. I just want you to be happy."' It irritates him enormously when I parrot his French-accented English.

He put the salad bowl down hard on the table, turned to me angrily. 'But be reasonable, Nicole. I don't expect you not to be reasonable! Forty thousand euros for a bathroom – this is crazy!' said the man who had chartered a private jet to Rhodes TO GO ON HOLIDAY at a cost of fifteen thousand euros just because we absolutely NEEDED to be there, because he wanted it, he couldn't wait and there were no commercial flights that suited his timetable. His selective memory about acceptable expenditure, particularly ephemeral expenditure, was one of the things that drove me nuts the most. But then D'Artagnan is soaked in French philosophy, as are all French people; it's a compulsory part of the educational syllabus. And French philosophy in a nutshell is: life is short, soon you will die, probably miserably. *Carpe diem*, people!

That was the extent of the explanation I'd got from him when I had last mentioned the transient/tangible expenditure dichotomy in one of our many disputes about renovations.

'You said,' I glared at him, 'you PROMISED – in fact, no, before that, you LIED to me, you LIED, Guy. You made sure I lost my job, and you deceived me about moving to France. You kept it a secret that you were going to marry me and drag me over here to your château!! You knew this all along, you DECEIVED me!'

'And? Are you so unhappily DECEIVED, Nicole? Are you so unhappy here, with me, you would instead be in London, working in an office for that *petit connard*, living alone with your cats, scared, so scared to have a real life, to fall in love—'

He broke off. We were staring at each other, both equally angry. Mazzy Star was streaming on the music system – there'd been quite a lot of epic, achingly sensuous sex while listening to Hope Sandoval's dreamy, luxurious voice non-stop in Pyla.

His voice softened a little. 'You were happy then, Nicole? Before I was in your life?'

I stared at him. His eyes were slightly narrowed, watchful but softer now, not so angry. But the pout was still there, the imperial pout.

I looked down and affected my own pout, though I knew it was less impressive. 'No.' I shrugged slightly. 'No, I wasn't happy,' I admitted. 'But you said, Guy, you said I could do whatever renovations I wanted in the château, and I want this. I WANT this bathroom, and I want my dressing room, and it's not as if we don't have the floor space. Yes, it's going to cost a bit, but I have thought about it a lot, I have dreamed about it, and it is finally possible, I think, for my dreams to come true, to create the most beautiful suite of rooms. I want it to be perfect, a place of beauty, touched by God – a tranquil place for us to be in love in, away from all the crap in the world, all of the shitty, shitty stuff that happens, that has happened, that I don't want to think about any more—'

And then he stepped forward, took my head in his hands, his body warm against mine, his mouth on mine, a deep, hot, lustful kiss. When he stopped, I was already melded against him; he radiated heat under his shirt. He traced the outline of my lips with his thumb, gazed into my soul and saw in that moment, after that kiss, that I was consumed with desire. He gave the slowest, most sensual blink of his eyelashes and lifted my T-shirt over my head in one easy motion, pushed me back onto the table, strong hands framing my ribcage, thumbs brushing my nipples. My back arched involuntarily, voluntarily, under him; he unbuttoned my shorts, pulled them and my knickers down roughly, his fingers sliding into me, all the time watching me.

'*Mon dieu,* Nicole, *je t'aime...*'

A deep groan as my body bucked against his hand, then, 'Nicole, you need to turn over, my angel,' his voice, hoarse. 'I need to fuck you very, very deeply.' Which led to an orgasm that I swear began with the sound of him unbuckling his belt, his hands lifting my hips slightly so that each penetration was slow, leisurely and deeply profound, every cell in my body pulsating with rapture at the feel of him inside me, his voice low, thick, murmuring, '*Mon dieu, mon ange, t'es serré, douce comme du velours* ... so fucking beautiful, my velvet angel, *je t'aime je t'aime je t'aime,'* until my very core closed tightly, convulsed around him as he came, my nails digging into the table so hard that I later had to remove a splinter that was deeply embedded under one of them.

I love my Bisazza bathroom very much for all sorts of reasons.

Chapter Sixteen

In August, Jules, Mark and the kids came to visit. I was so excited at the thought of showing them the château, showing them around this beautiful part of France that I somehow, almost magically, found myself living in: the neat, leafy green vineyards, the bucolic countryside, the pretty chalkstone, ochre-roofed villages, the picturesque stone towns dotted with ancient Roman monuments and the fantastic coastline. I was looking forward to showing them our region.

I stopped for a moment when that thought crossed my mind; how had that happened so quickly? How was it that I already referred to it as *our*, and by implication, *my* region? I had a brief, fleeting awareness of the reason why D'Artagnan was so attached to his *territoire*.

I really wished I had taken a picture of Josh and Katie's faces when their car stopped on the gravelled forecourt in front of the château. Both of their mouths were a perfect 'O'. I gave them huge hugs, lifted them off the ground, twirled Katie around and kissed her face all over. Josh squirmed and wriggled when I tried to do the same to him. Jules enveloped me in a wonderful tight embrace, and Mark patted my back awkwardly as he always did. Guy went to kiss him and he recoiled in horror, quickly stuck out his hand. We laughed at him.

'*Bah, les Anglo-Saxons*, always afraid to touch.' D'Artagnan ruffled his hair, which was also too much physical contact for Mark, so he made a fuss of giving Juliette and the kids kisses instead. It was clear he was pleased to see them again, too.

We helped them bring their luggage inside; they were only staying for three days before continuing down to the Basque region, where most of the rest of Jules' family were scattered.

The kids raced around, wide-eyed; they loved the Hogwarts' fireplaces, were fascinated by the damp, stone steps leading into the cellar. Guy gave them a small, ornate metal key and told them it opened a secret door that was hidden somewhere in the château. In the ensuing peace after they had disappeared in search of it, we opened a bottle of Champagne to toast their arrival. Guy filled an ice-bucket, put in the Champagne, and we went outside again to sit at the big wooden table under the horse-chestnut trees.

D'Artagnan had been in the kitchen most of the afternoon and had baked an entire salmon in the oven, stuffed it with herbs and lemons, and roasted an enormous tray of fresh vegetables: tomatoes, beans, potatoes, broccoli, artichokes, asparagus, all drenched in olive oil and sea-salt so that they were still a bit crunchy. I'd been to the boulangerie as instructed for bread and the *pièce de résistance* of the meal, a three-tiered white, milk and dark chocolate mousse dessert which, when I brought it outside, made Josh and Katie's drooping eyes very wide again.

It was a wonderful evening and we drank, laughed, and ate copiously as the sky gradually bruised from the east. The warmth from the sun was still radiating from the château façade after sunset as the bats swooped and dived silently in front of it, feeding on the insects at dusk.

It was close to one o'clock when I glanced at my watch as I got into bed after my shower, yawning enormously. D'Artagnan, seemingly without waking up, pulled me against the curve of his body, wrapped his arms around me and carried on snoring gently. I fell asleep immediately.

The next day we went to the Atlantic coast; I had reserved a table at Chez Bob, a popular bistro situated directly on the promenade overlooking the delightful beach of St Palais-sur-Mer, an idyllic little town with a gorgeous bay. There was a lovely, cool ocean breeze; we sat under the sunshades on the promenade, drank rosé wine, ate oysters (the kids and I did not, we made noises of disgust instead) and this time, I was allowed to order *moules marinières* as 'it is okay now to eat *moules,* Nicole, it is the season'.

Even though the last time we had come to Chez Bob everyone around us had been eating *moules marinières,* apparently it wasn't acceptable to eat them then because, 'They don't come from our region, these are *moules* from somewhere else, no, maybe not France, maybe Holland, and that is not acceptable. *Non,* Nicole, have the *burrata salade,* or the *octopus salade.* Well, just don't eat the *poulpe* if you don't want it. *Non,* I don't know where all the ingredients for the *salade* come from, but I am sure they come from France. *Non*, Nicole, I don't know which department they are from. *Merde*, can you just order something?'

Food, it seems, is very complicated for French people too. In D'Artagnan's bourgeois little culinary world, I have learned that it is unacceptable to do the following:

1. Eat mussels before 1st June on the Atlantic coast, on the grounds that the mussels for which the Atlantic coast is famous are not harvested until after Mother's Day, which is at the end of May.

2. Eat crunchy, delicious, green asparagus when the thick, slightly bitter, slightly buttery, local white asparagus is in season (April to June).

3. Eat fresh tomatoes outside of the summer months of June to September because they have not been ripened by the sun and might, horror of horrors, come from Spain.

4. Eat potatoes from anywhere other than the Ile de Ré or the Ile de Noirmoutier.

5. Ditto sea salt.

6. Eat fresh mushrooms outside the months of September to mid-December; or May and June for the first cèpes of summer.

7. Not eat foie-gras at Christmas and New Year (never gonna happen...).

8. Not eat three dozen oysters at Christmas and again at New Year (ditto).

9. McDonalds. Frothing fit.

10. Snack. At any time, ever.

The last one really is true. In my opinion, the French traffic death rate would be reduced if everyone just had a chocolate fucking biscuit at 11am, but it is unthinkable. French people do not snack between meals. Meals are serious, important business, and should be approached with the lowest possible blood sugar bordering on hypoglycaemia. Perhaps this goes to explain those often-heated dinner-table exchanges for which French people are famous and, come to think of it, Italian and Spanish people, too. I reckon there is a strong probability that snacking in all Mediterranean countries is *interdit*.

After lunch, we sat on the beach while Guy and the kids swam in the sea. He loves the ocean and he always swims when we come to the coast (my sub-tropical blood requires an outside temperature of at least thirty degrees Celsius) even when it's a cool day and the water is arctic. Occasionally, he brings his surfboard if the surfing forecast is good, although he always complains that the waves are not as good as they are at Biarritz or San Sebastien, where it seems he spent a lot of his youth surfing. Afterwards, he comes and shakes himself and his hair all over me like a big wet hairy dog.

Jules and I sat watching them. Mark lay down on a towel, put a hat over his face and was snoring almost immediately, but only after Jules had insisted on rubbing suntan lotion into his pale, exposed arms.

'Thank God you insisted,' I said quietly. 'I've seen some English people here who are so shockingly sunburned it's painful even to look at. I don't understand why they don't understand how strong the sun can be. Although having said that,' I admitted, 'I don't wear any. The sun here seems just right for my skin.'

'Yes, but you have olive skin, and you have a really deep base tan. That's the best protection from the sun.' She turned and grinned at me. 'You're a proper west-coast Frenchie now, Nicky, all brown and sun-bleached around the edges. How did that happen so quickly? One minute, you're this slightly uptight, perfectly dressed, super-efficient secretary in the City – literally, Nicky, it feels like one minute ago – and now you're this suntanned French babe, all long sun-kissed hair and pretty summer dresses – and slides! My God, Nicky, I never thought I'd see you in a pair of slides! No heels! It's hilarious!'

I laughed, slightly embarrassed, pushed her gently on the shoulder. Her eyes were so blue, even behind her sunglasses. 'They are Givenchy slides, Jules.'

'Of course they are, sweetie darling.' She laughed back at me.

I slipped an arm around her, hugged her against me. 'Oh Jules, I miss you so much! Please, please come and live in France. Come and live near us – come on, the kids will love it. Mark will love it. I *need* you here. D'Artagnan is a bloody handful on my own – I need back-up!'

She laid her head on my shoulder momentarily, her long ringlets soft against my arm. I caught her familiar Chanel No.5 scent and breathed it in deeply; it was always so comforting.

'I would love to Nicky, more than anything, but it's complicated – you know it's complicated. And besides, I think you're doing fine with D'Artagnan. You seem really happy, really well, healthy. More healthy and happy than I've ever seen you. He's good for you.'

I took a deep breath, exhaled. 'Yeah. He is good for me. He can be sodding annoying though, Jules. Sometimes I think he genuinely thinks that I work for him, that I'm one of his minions. And as for the renovations… Oh my God, every single bloody thing I want to do requires negotiation – so much for "you can do whatever you want, Nicole".' I rolled my eyes. 'I swear he's even more arrogant and interfering on his home soil than he was in London, which I didn't expect!'

She snaughed – somewhere between a snort and a laugh. 'Foolish woman, of course he is! He's lord of the manor now! Did you think he was going to settle down quietly in his château and take up gardening?'

I giggled at the idea of him actually planting anything. 'Oh, you'd be surprised, Jules. D'Artagnan does do gardening, it's just rather niche-gardening. If it doesn't involve petrol, diesel, chains or blades, he's not interested.' I paused. 'But yeah, you're right. I didn't really think about what he'd be like in his own country, on his own soil. But then it all happened so quickly. I only met him at the end of last year, it's not even been a year since he swaggered into my life. Don't you think it's a bit insane that we're already bloody married? I know I do. Sometimes I get vertigo just thinking about it!'

Clearly the Gallic shrug is hereditary, as Jules did a pretty spectacular one. 'On the one hand … yeah, I kind of agree. On the other, when I see how crazy he is about you, no, it's fine. He's just someone who knows what he wants and goes and gets it, makes it happen.'

'Yes,' I mused. 'Those exact words have crossed my mind. In fact, I think I've even spoken them aloud.' I sighed, hesitated, then said, 'But you know, Jules, that worries me a bit. He might know what he wanted, but he might not have got what he wanted.'

She frowned. 'What do you mean, Nicky?'

I thought for a minute. 'Without meaning to sound melodramatic, I worry that he thinks he's got someone who is whole. Not perfect but complete, with a bit of wear and tear of course, but basically whole. And I worry that he doesn't know that I'm a bit broken. I had a MAJOR panic attack on our honeymoon, actually fainted – it was pathetic. And also, Jules,' I bit my lip, 'I still dream about Karl. And it's stupid. I love Guy. We're married. Fuck's sake, it's ridiculous to still be thinking about Karl!'

She didn't say anything for a while. We sat watching the sea; I could see D'Artagnan and the kids quite far out in the surf. Guy had Katie on his shoulders, her feet just touching the water, and he was holding Josh's hand, lifting him slightly as he tried to jump every wave that came in.

Jules took a deep breath. 'Well, Nicky, there's two things there. Regarding the first, I don't want to say it again because I feel like a stuck bloody record, but I'm going to anyway. You need to speak to a therapist. You have all this shit locked down inside you – that bitch of a mother you had, the shitty childhood, all that pain when you were trying to get pregnant, not to mention the non-groovy stuff you obliquely refer to when you were modelling. You don't talk to anyone about any of that stuff. It stands to reason that it all gets too much from time to time, and your brain expresses that in the form of panic attacks.'

She paused, put her hand on my shoulder, squeezed it. 'I don't mean to sound harsh, but you have to turn and face it because it's not going away. And that brings me to the second thing. The reason you're still dreaming about Karl is because you haven't dealt with that, either. One day you walked out on five, nearly six years of an intense relationship, on someone who was everything to you, someone you'd planned a whole future with. No, sorry, you RAN out, you ran as fast and as far as you could, and ever since then you've done a spectacular job of not dealing with the end of it. That saga is hanging out there, pages fluttering in the wind, completely unresolved. It's no wonder you still dream about him! You need closure, Nicky. You need to see Karl, discuss what happened, forgive him. Or not, if you don't want to, but either way you need CLOSURE.'

She took a deep breath, exhaled, and her voice softened. 'And he needs closure too, Nick. I didn't tell you this because it was just before your wedding and I knew you'd totally flip out if I did, but he called me earlier this year. He's back in Europe this summer, shooting a film, I think he said. He wanted to get in touch with you. He really wants to speak to you, to explain himself, to apologise.'

My heart shrivelled like a fresh plum dropped into a vat of vinegar but with the process sped up: like Peter Greenaway's dead-swan decay sequence in *A Zed and Two Noughts*. 'What did you tell him?' So, it probably *had* been him I'd seen in Paris. My mind had not played a trick on me.

'I told him you were about to get married, and if he dared to interfere in that I would personally hunt him down and castrate him in the most painful way I could imagine. Then I'd kill him.'

I could not help a little laugh at that.

'And then I told him that I would tell you when I felt the time was right. So I'm telling you now. I have his number. I think you should speak to him. I think you owe it to him, despite everything, and I think you definitely owe it to yourself.'

She paused. 'And actually, Nicky, you owe it to Guy, too. It bothers him that you won't talk about it. He's quite anxious that the reason you won't talk about Karl – obviously he doesn't know who he is, but he calls him "*ze Anglo-Saxon*", which I thought was quite perceptive – is because you're not over him.'

'When did he say that?'

'Last night, when you were in the kitchen getting more wine and Mark was putting the kids to bed. He asked me about it, and I told him it wasn't up to me to tell him. Nicky, I know you're anxious about how quickly things have happened with Guy, but I genuinely think he loves you. He adores you, and having that Karl thing out there ... unresolved, it's like a poisonous little satellite in orbit around the both of you.'

I felt the sadness start to seep into what had been a sunny day, literally and metaphorically. I shrugged. 'Well, maybe that is the problem, Jules. Maybe I'm not over him. Despite everything, despite what he did.'

And just saying that out loud made my stomach knot instantly; I felt slightly nauseous. And, I wanted to say, it seems perhaps he's not over me, because he's made a film that clearly features our relationship in some way. But I didn't say anything; I didn't want to contemplate that, to dissect what that might mean.

She shook her head. 'No, I don't think that's true. I think you *are* over him, but because you haven't seen him in four years, because you never had any closure, never allowed any closure, you have doubts. I don't think you're still in love with him, I think you're pretty bloody madly in love with the gorgeous D'Artagnan. But because he's so –bombastic, demonstrative, intense, you're kind of a bit dazzled, overwhelmed, maybe even a bit scared. Not by him, but by the idea of him. But you are in love with him,' she said confidently.

My stomach unclenched and the nausea abated a little. Was it possible that she was right? I loved the idea that she might be.

I turned and smiled at her. 'Thank you for saying that, Jules darling. And thank you, as ever, for the free therapy sesh. I'm so sorry you have to listen to your basket-case best friend rabbiting on yet again about her messy life and all her insecurities. One day, I promise, I'll grow up and become an adult and not need constant free therapy.'

'Ah, Nicky, I love our therapy sessions! Sometimes I think I might change careers one day, retrain…' She looked thoughtful for a moment. 'Anyway, have a think about what I said. Please, Nicky. There is stuff you need to start dealing with, but Guy is there for you. He loves you very much, and he only wants to help you. I'm sure he finds it distressing to see you having those horrible attacks. I know I did.'

D'Artagnan was coming out of the sea. Katie was still on his shoulders, her feet bouncing against his tanned biceps. Water droplets glistened on his chest, on his legs. He was talking to Josh, still jumping waves beside him, as they chatted animatedly. My heart suddenly felt like it was going to explode; he was, as Jules said, so gorgeous, so solid, so real. I loved him so much.

I slipped my arm around her again, hugged her against me. 'Thanks, Jules. I really will, I promise.'

'And tell me if – when – you want Karl's number. You need to deal with that, sweetheart.'

I nodded, took a deep breath, watched Guy walk up the beach towards us.

'Okay,' I said. 'I'll let you know.' And then I smiled a big, wide smile at my gorgeous, bronzed musketeer as he bent down, deposited Katie in her mother's arms, leaned forward and gave me a big, sloppy, salty kiss on the mouth. Then he shook himself all over us like a big, wet, hairy dog.

The one thing I have never stopped doing throughout my life is reading. All through the screwed-up childhood and teenage years, and the even more fucked-up modelling years, I continued to read. I remember some of the books: I remember their names, I remember who wrote them, I remember their plots. They stayed with me, and I have read some of them again with enormous pleasure in my sober, older years. Some of them I don't remember at all, not the slightest bit – name, author, plot, nothing. And some I just remember a bit about.

I read one of the latter, but don't remember at what age, perhaps in my late teens, perhaps in my early twenties. I don't remember where I was when I was reading it, or how I came to have it, or what it was called, or who wrote it, or even whether it was fiction or non-fiction. But I clearly remember one thing about it: it was set in the Pacific Ocean and concerned a tribe of island dwellers sometime in the eighteenth or nineteenth century, before there was any sort of electronic communication. The author hypothesised, in some detail, about this tribe. They had a gift for seeing into the future; they knew days in advance when a ship or a boat was going to sail over the horizon destined for their island, even though there was absolutely no means of communication, no ordinary way of knowing this. They could predict the return of their fellow tribespeople because there was some sort of ripple in the ocean, or in the air, or in the sky that they could see. Like a stone thrown into a pond, they saw the outer ripples arriving some days in advance before the boat itself appeared on the horizon.

I have never forgotten this idea. Although I don't understand it, can't explain it and haven't done any real research into it (aside from fruitless Google searches for the book itself), I believe it is possible for such a phenomenon to exist, especially when there are repeated ripples, little ripples like static electric shocks, that keep happening.

I knew, even though I didn't want to know, that Karl was just beyond the horizon. He'd plopped into the pond, and I'd seen the ripples in Paris, in the poster in Bordeaux, in what Juliette told me that day. And Europe isn't a very big pond. The question was, did I call in the boat, was I ever going to be brave enough to call it in myself, or was it going to find its own way to the island?

Being me, I decided to park that particular conundrum for a while, let it ripen a bit while I mulled it over. If there was an Olympic event in procrastination, I would be a strong contender for gold.

The summer holidays were over, everyone went back to school, or college, or the office. It was the *rentrée*! I was fascinated; it literally means 'to re-enter' but in France it seems it's a mini-festival of some strange variety, to be celebrated like Easter or Christmas. The supermarkets all have signs up heralding the onset of the *rentrée;* the newsreader on the television wishes everyone '*Bonne rentrée!*' and everyone seemed quite buzzed by it. It's really weird, considering how much French people love summer, love the beach, love to be on holiday.

We were having our own *rentrée* in the château. In mid-August, Gabriela and Camille had started working on what was to become our bedroom. Our suite of three rooms would take up the front half of the first floor of the château – the east wing, I suppose, in *Downton Abbey*-esque posh-speak. The enormous new bed would be in the curved tower; a small, but reassuringly expensive, bedroom sofa, my dressing table and a large armoire would be the only other furniture in the very large room that extended from the tower to include one of the tall newly double-glazed windows. All the understated, classical-modern furniture had been ordered from Roche Bobois.

The ensuite bathroom was a slightly smaller room off the main one, and beyond that, through a newly created doorway, Heaven. One entire wall of floor-to-ceiling mirrored, fitted wardrobes, drawers in pale beech underneath a long sweep of frosted glass on the other three walls and, slightly off centre, a purpose-built shoe island, also topped with frosted glass. The room would be carpeted in thick, cream wool, the two tall windows swathed in gauze, and finally, there would be the enchanting, cream-velvet chaise longue, from Poltrona Frau.

D'Artagnan had been astonished to discover that Heaven really was going to be exclusively mine, purpose-built for my clothes and shoes; it had kicked off a fairly animated episode of eye rolling, head shaking and muttering, which I just ignored. The new armoire in our bedroom was easily large enough for his clothes and shoes and, as a concession, I graciously allowed his cashmere sweaters a couple of drawers in Heaven (mostly because I considered them to be shared clothing).

Gabriella and Camille stripped the vile wallpaper in the bedroom and replaced it with a very pale marbled-gold paper, created cornicing around the perfectly finished ceiling, replaced all the skirting boards and polished the oak floorboards so that they glowed with love and attention.

I waited breathlessly to see if we were in with a chance for the Bisazza Delivery Lottery – and we were! Everything was delivered exactly as scheduled at the beginning of September, and the bathroom began to take shape. All the dressing-room units had, by some small miracle, been delivered in late August, so our *rentrée* was proving to be quite noisy.

The Duchess was furious about the noise, the disruption, the messing about with her innards. She regularly disconnected the electricity until finally, FINALLY, D'Artagnan got onto EDF and had the electricity supply to the château increased to a wattage more appropriate for the twenty-first century, where things like coffee machines and kettles and fridges and hairdryers weren't just a figment of some wild-haired crazy scientist's imagination.

Nevertheless, the Duchess was still unhappy; the electricity supply was definitely more reliable after the EDF upgrade, but she remained capricious about electricity generally. Where previously she had an electrical wattage supply that allowed a light to be turned on upstairs, on condition that one hadn't been turned on downstairs at the same time, she now allowed both. But not ... other stuff, not always. And NEVER when there was a big storm. Storms were her big, theatrical moment. She made the most of them.

In summer, when it was hot and humid, when the clouds on the horizon gradually built themselves up in threatening shades of ever-darkening grey, and the local vignerons hunkered down and prayed for small hailstones, not the golf-ball sized ones that destroyed the grapes (a phenomenon they were becoming resigned to) – she loved that. The Duchess loved that. A bit of drama. She no longer had vineyards; she didn't care about hail!

During the big storms, she shut down ALL of the fuse boxes. When we knew there was a big storm coming, we closed all the shutters except one in the salon, sat there on one of the painstakingly re-upholstered nineteenth-century sofas (I was pleased with the result and pleased that I had successfully preserved some of the original furniture), the room lit only by scented jasmine candles, the rain hammering against the window. I leaned against D'Artagnan's warm chest, his arm around my neck, his bare brown feet caressing mine while we watched the lightning flash above the trees.

The Muffins were less comfortable with these phenomenal weather events; they hid upstairs under our bed. They were not used to the power, the passion of the Atlantic storms.

The Duchess pondered how else she might demonstrate her displeasure at the *arriviste*'s audacity.

Guy pulled the tray of tiny, tiny, blackened bits of coal out from the bottom of the range cooker. 'What is this shit, Nicole?'

I stared at it glumly. 'Well, before your bastard cooker decided to carbonise it, it was my muesli, actually.'

'Ah, the cocaine for the rodents!' He was very pleased with his nickname for my muesli mix.

I gave him a withering look. 'It isn't supposed to look like that.'

He raised an eyebrow. 'Really, Nicole? I would never have thought… But maybe it is because you try to play with my *piano* when I am not here, *ma chérie*? You need to ask me to do it, Nicole. You don't understand the *piano*, how it works.'

Really. It's true. A range cooker in French is a *'piano de cuisson'*: literally, a piano on which to cook; an instrument on which one makes music – food music, apparently.

Did I mention the obsession with food?

'It worked just fine the last time,' I said sulkily. And it had. I had bought organic walnuts, hazel nuts, almonds, pumpkin seeds, sunflower seeds, chia seeds, oats, all locally sourced, from the excellent organic food shop in Cognac, lightly blitzed them together with a bit of olive oil, and roasted them for fifteen minutes on a low heat. The result: divine. I ate it with yoghurt, in the wonderful salads Guy created, on its own with a slice of my favourite Ossau Iraty cheese if I needed a snack (bad, bad, non-French snacking person). Rodent cocaine was a fundamental, essential part of my diet.

He shrugged. 'Maybe you were lucky the last time. But you need to ask me, *mon amour*. The kitchen is my *domaine*.'

'Well, the bedroom suite is *my domaine*, and that doesn't stop you interfering in that, does it?' I said crossly.

Pout. 'I am not interfering Nicole. I just go to see what the girls are doing up there.' He pronounced this *'ze gerls'*.

'Well, darling man, *"ze gerls"* don't need supervision. They kind of find supervision by an ex – although sometimes I do wonder how "ex" the "ex" actually is – investment banker, who knows precisely fuck-all about plumbing or anything to do with renovations, really bloody annoying.' I stared into the imperial brown gaze.

'Pffffft. I know some things, Nicole. I am doing the development in Bordeaux. I am learning a lot. I know about renovation.'

I tried really, really hard not to roll my eyes. 'You're kind of a bit removed from the actual, hard-core, silicone-sniffing reality of it though, aren't you? You're kind of on the spreadsheet end, aren't you?'

Gallic sniff. He turned away, tipped the tray of carbonised muesli into the bin.

'So, Nicole, do you want to make some more rodent cocaine, and I show you how the *piano* work, *chérie*?'

Chapter Seventeen

The hypothesis wasn't wrong; the ripples had been real. It just took until late October for the boat to come unbidden over the horizon.

It was a cool, damp morning. D'Artagnan was out the back somewhere, cutting up a tree that had fallen the previous winter. I could hear the chainsaw in the distance from the library where I was poring over yet another bathroom catalogue, this time to replace the Peach Panoply. Negotiations were in the very early stages and had not yet required active coercion, sexual or otherwise, although I had fallen in love with some rather expensive wall tiles and intended to tile most of the bathroom with them.

Our bedroom suite had been a phenomenal success (excepting the Duchess's massive hissy-fit in the bathroom) and Gabriela and Camille had done an outstanding job; Heaven was exactly as I had imagined it and gave me an enormous sense of peace and well-being every time I set foot in it.

I vaguely heard a car pull up on the gravel outside, then the knocker tapped loudly on the front door. I looked at my watch; it was late for the postie to deliver something, but Guy was constantly ordering crap that he didn't really need (IMO) off the internet, so things were being delivered at all times of the day now. I went through to the hallway and opened the front door. And froze.

So. Karl. Sometimes I wonder how many people have had someone like Karl in their lives. I don't actually mean like Karl himself; I mean someone like Karl was to me. Someone that, the very first time you set eyes on them, you are instantly smitten. Floored. Helplessly, hopelessly in love, almost unable to breathe, transfixed by their beauty, their physical presence, irresistibly drawn into their orbit. Is that a thing that happens to most people? Is that what happens in normal relationships, ones that continue, lead to marriage, children, a happy ever after? Or is it a rare thing, too intense to last, are they the ones that burn up on re-entry into ordinary life?

I was twenty-six when I first set eyes on Karl. I was booked for an *Elle* shoot with a photographer I had worked with a few times previously. It was late March and I had arrived back in London two days earlier from Paris fashion week, which had not gone well. I was still struggling with the non-groovy thing that had happened in Milan the month before.

As I walked up the stairs and into the studio, Karl was the first person I saw. He was standing next to the light projector, talking to the photographer across the room. As I entered, he turned and looked straight at me. I swear there was something extraordinary that passed between us in that instant, an arc of electrical intensity, an instant connection, a certainty that we were made, only and exclusively, for each other.

If I had to describe Karl in one word, it would be silver. He projected, reflected, *glowed* silver in an odd, all-encompassing way. He had messy, spiky, silver-blond hair, the palest silver-grey eyes, and his skin tone was weirdly silver, almost shimmering. He never took any colour from the sun, wasn't interested in the sun and the sun was never interested in him; in all the time I knew him, they ignored each other.

He was tall, slender, had a cat-like elegance, the face of an angel and the aura of a fallen one. Dark eyebrows and long black eyelashes, chiselled cheekbones, a full, cherub mouth. His natural resting expression was a slight pout.

Karl is a year older than I am, almost to the day. We are both Leos. We are both single children. We both had chaotic childhoods, but there the similarities end. Karl's mother was a model and he is her only child; she had remarried and lived in New York. They were close and he visited her often. She hated me, so I only ever went once. His father was German, lived in Zurich and was spectacularly wealthy – he ran a hedge fund or something.

Karl was spoilt. He was indulged, doted on by his parents, but he was also talented and artistic. He drew a lot, doodled in ink and pencil, and his drawings were edgy, clever. He had a sharp sense of humour and a way of expressing himself that drew people to him, a kind of charismatic slyness. When I met him, he had grown bored with pencil and ink and become obsessed with photography, so Mummy had pulled some strings and got him a rare internship with the photographer.

Karl also had an extremely addictive personality. He was well-travelled on the rehab circuit, having spent time in luxurious 'health' resorts in Switzerland, California and upstate New York. The week before we met, he had just finished three months at one in Surrey. He was already using again. It was Karl who introduced me to his siren, his mistress: heroin.

Our relationship was utterly manic, soaked in drugs, completely uncontrolled right from the outset. We couldn't get enough of one another. There weren't enough drugs, there wasn't enough intensity, there just wasn't *enough* of anything in the world to satisfy us.

We spent weeks in Ibiza at his father's villa, the hours from midnight to dawn clubbing, soaked to the skin, welded together, lost in worship at the Church of Trance, and every other waking hour fucking, taut with anticipation for the 5m30s rush, trance constantly pulsing through the whole-villa audio system, totally blown on E, coke, smack, unable to be apart for even ten minutes. It was insane. It was totally unsustainable.

About two years into the relationship, when my modelling career was starting to wobble pretty badly because I'd become so unreliable, Karl didn't come home one night to the flat we shared. Neither did he come back the next night.

I was beside myself, calling all of our friends, my agent, the photographer, anyone that I could think of including the hospitals, trying to find out what had happened to him. The next day he was back, and I knew he'd been with someone else. In fact, he admitted it when I screamed the question at him. He shrugged, said it wasn't important, it was just a thing he'd done and he was sorry. I crashed really hard, and it was messy. I don't like to remember what I was like then because it wasn't pretty. The agency took pity on me, booked me in for three months rehab in Surrey.

When I came out, he was waiting. I tried to push him away, but he insisted he had changed, insisted that it had been a one-off, insisted that he was also clean, that he was still completely in love with me, that he couldn't possibly live without me.

The second time in rehab, just over a year later, I was determined that I wasn't going to relapse. Sure enough, Karl was there when I came out. This time he had also been in rehab. I would be thirty in a few months' time; he would be thirty-one. He was studying film production in West London and was very serious about it, focused in a way he hadn't been since I'd known him.

We were both clean, sober. We had been talking throughout the manic years about the silver-haired, green-eyed children we would have; now we were going to make those beautiful silver-haired, green-eyed children become real. It was the time.

We spent a year trying. I ate healthily; I even experimented with gaining weight. I started to have periods, but they arrived irregularly and their arrival became increasingly devastating. It was obvious that I might have some gynaecological problems, so we went to Harley Street.

We saw specialists; I saw gynaecologists. There was much prodding and poking, and they all suggested IVF. I started the course of hormones, held on tightly while that intense emotional rollercoaster unspooled... I held my breath until the first bleed, a little at first, then a bloody, bloody torrent. Then I cried. We both cried.

Three cycles of failed IVF later, emotionally and physically drained, utterly exhausted, we decided to stop trying. Two weeks later, Karl didn't come home one night, then a second night. I started ringing around our friends but more resignedly now, less hysterically. I was tired of the drama, just wanted to shut myself away and weep in a warm, dark place for a long time.

Finally, Anthony took pity on me. He came over to the apartment, sat me down with a glass of wine and explained that Karl was about to become a father of twins with an American girl he was at film school with, and that he was on a massive full-on bender because he couldn't bring himself to tell me about it.

So. Karl. Just a whole bundle of silver pain and agony, really.

And here he was, standing on the doorstep of the château. I clung to the door, felt as if I were trembling inside from head to foot, my heart and stomach taking turns to somersault over one another.

'Nicky,' he said.
'Please go away,' I managed to say, as I started to shut the door. My face felt frozen, my ears were ringing.
'No, don't do that. Please don't do that. I need to talk to you. Please. Please Nicky.' He stepped forward, put his hand on the door then his foot in the gap, pushed it back open.
I pushed back. 'Just fuck off, Karl. Really, sod off. I have nothing at all to say to you. I don't know why you're here and I don't want to know. Seriously, fuck off.'
He still had silver eyes, silver hair; he was still beautiful. Heart-breakingly beautiful; for a split-second my heart felt like it might break all over again.
'I can't, Nicky. It's taken me so long to find you. I have to talk to you, I have to apologise. I have to explain—'
I could feel the anger starting to rise inside me, my lungs filling, my eyes widening.
'Explain? For fuck's sake, Karl, what do you think I am, a complete imbecile? What the hell is there to explain?! It really, REALLY wasn't very difficult to understand what happened, what you did. Don't fucking INSULT me!!'
I was starting to shake uncontrollably and my heart was pounding in my chest. My cheeks were flaming. It felt like my eyeballs were jumping in their sockets, and everything around Karl was blurry except for him – he was crystal clear. Everything about him, it was all exactly as I remembered.
He flinched a little, then said, 'I'm so sorry, Nicky. I'm so, so sorry. I was such an absolute fucking bastard – but you didn't know I was using again at the time. I'd started using again and I couldn't tell you, and I couldn't stand what was going on. I was so upset at what you were going through it was—'
'YOU were upset? My GOD, poor little you!' I was enraged. 'Just FUCK OFF, Karl!!' I shoved a hand at his chest, pushed him. He was unbalanced, took a step or two backwards off the threshold, but managed to put his foot back in the door again before I could close it.
'How dare you come here?' I shouted. 'How dare you come to my house, to try and fuck up my life again? How very DARE YOU? Get your foot out of the door! Get out, Karl. There is nothing you can say that will change ANYTHING!!'

He didn't take his foot away. Instead he grabbed my wrist, held it tightly, stared into my eyes. His silver gaze was dazzling, exactly as I remembered it, exactly as it always was in my dreams.

'Nicky, Nicky, listen, LISTEN, please. I need you to try to forgive me. I can't carry on like this. I loved you so much – I still love you, Nicky. I know that you've moved on and you're married and that's okay, I can deal with that. I realise that I've lost you. But I need to move on too, and I can't do that unless I've told you honestly, sincerely, how utterly, utterly grovelingly sorry I am about what I did.'

We were less than a metre apart, staring at each other. 'Please let go of my wrist,' I said in a tight voice.

He did, but he held my stare, silver beams unwavering. 'I've never stopped thinking about you. I tried to find you, but you just – you just disappeared, I didn't know where you'd gone. I looked everywhere in Europe, then I thought maybe you'd gone back to South Africa, so I looked there too. Then someone told me you were in Australia, in Singapore, I looked there, but I never found you. I wanted to explain, I wanted to apologise. I felt so fucking awful.'

One of the things I had done in that pink house on the Cobh harbour front was to change my surname by deed poll. It had been surprisingly easy, and it worked. I wasn't, after all, very attached to Tiffany's surname (or maybe it was Jeff's, I was never sure). But I was determined Karl would not find me again because I knew, I knew how weak I was when I gazed into those silver eyes.

'Aw, diddums. Poor you.' But the anger had dissipated as quickly as it had arrived. I had none left; I just felt desperately sad, a sadness tied tightly to a heavy rock, a sadness falling softly, slowly, to the bottom of a deep, deep ocean. The rock made a slight 'puff' in the sand it dislodged as it came to rest.

All of those dreams, those plans we made, our future together, our green-and-silver future together, all gradually dissolved, there at the bottom of the ocean. And in that moment, I actually contemplated telling him. I finally allowed it to play across the full screen of my mind, I gazed upon it, the full agony, the full, ironic agony of it.

And I thought, 'Should I tell him? After what we went through, and after what he did, does he have a right to know? Or do I just want to twist the knife?'

Because I'd never told anyone. I hadn't even told Juliette. I had absorbed it, packed it away neatly in the box of sadness with all the other pain.

I'd slipped on one of those long coastal walks on the Irish Atlantic coat; I'd slipped on a muddy path, and I'd bounced and tumbled down that slippery, rock-strewn hill, hit my head and come to rest, unconscious, at the bottom of the path. Other hikers had found me and I'd woken up in hospital the next morning. I was still groggy, disorientated, and the bandage was quite tight on my head, but I was not too groggy to see that the nurse had tears in her eyes when she told me how sorry she was. I frowned at her, was confused by her sorrow, and she said, 'You lost it, my love. I'm so sorry to have to tell you this, but when you fell you lost the baby.'

I stared at her, confused. She saw my confusion, frowned. 'You didn't know you were pregnant?'

I shook my head, ever so slightly. She patted my hand, stroked it, smiled a glum smile.

And finally, I asked, 'How old... How long... How many months?'

And she said, tears glistening in her eyes, 'We can't be sure, but more than sixteen weeks – at least three months.'

I wanted to howl out loud then, but I didn't; I howled inside instead. I had never managed to stay pregnant for more than two months any of the times. We had stopped the IVF five months earlier.

My mind spooled backwards, forwards, furiously calculating what might have happened, how it might have happened. And then I remembered the last time we had made love, just before he'd left, before he'd done his usual disappearing act. We'd had sad, slow sex; he had seemed removed, I was not really present. But something else had been present, had started to be present, and I hadn't known. I hadn't been aware of another presence.

I stared into those silver eyes and I decided not to tell him. I decided not to tell him that actually, if things hadn't been so fucked up, if he hadn't messed up so monumentally, and if I hadn't slipped and tumbled down that slippery, rocky Atlantic coast path, there was a possibility that we could have had one of our green-eyed, silver-haired children.

What would be the point in telling him that? Sharing the pain would not lessen it, and it would wound him terribly. Even he didn't deserve that. But I couldn't resist saying, 'So, how are the twins? Or do you have other children too now?'

He had the grace to look away, and when he looked back his silver eyes were bright with tears. 'They're fine,' he said. 'They're four now. I don't have any other children. I didn't stay with their mother. Since you left, I haven't been in a relationship, Nicky.' He wiped his eyes, gazed at me, a glittering gaze. 'I don't think I realised how much I loved you until you left. I'm so sorry.'

'Well Karl, it never seemed to stop you shagging other women, did it?' I stared at him, shook my head slowly, but I was conscious that I still found him beautiful. For a second my heart felt like it was physically aching when I remembered how we had been together, how right it had felt, how much I had loved him.

He lowered his head, closed his eyes and pinched the bridge of his nose with his thumb and forefinger; it was a gesture he always made when he was sad, or ashamed, and it was so familiar to me. He opened his eyes again. 'I can only say again that I am so, so sorry I was such an arsehole. You can't believe how much I hate myself. I didn't realise how important you were to me. I never thought I would lose you, that I would be without you.'

'Well Karl, you are without me,' I said quietly. 'I'm married now. To someone else.'

He looked away from me again. Finally, he shrugged. 'Okay.' He said it very softly. Then he lifted his eyes. 'But Nicky, please. It would mean so much to me if you could try to forgive me. If you might be able to forgive me. That's all that I'm asking. Please.' A tear ran down his cheek. He wiped it away.

I carried on staring at him. Finally, I said 'I don't know, Karl. I don't know what to think. I don't know how I feel. I didn't expect to have to see you again, to have to think about all that shit again. And I can't just say "oh, it's fine, of course I forgive you". I don't think I have the capacity to do that now, today, in this moment, even if I could ever forgive you. I have so much anger, so much pain buried so deep – I just don't know.'

'I can understand that,' he said quietly. 'But can you think about it? Please think about what I've said, I would do anything to have that time again and to behave differently, not like the selfish cunt I was. What I did was so wrong, so awful, and I have never forgiven myself for how much I hurt you. That's why it's so important to me that *you* forgive me. I can't continue—' His voice choked. 'Nicky, I don't want to go on with my life and know that I haven't told you how much you meant to me, how much you still mean to me, and how sorry I am about what I did.'

Then I started crying, and he was crying, and we just stood there locked in a green-and-silver gaze, both crying. It was horrible. He pulled out his wallet, removed a business card, handed it to me. My hand was shaking as I took it.

'Please call me, Nicky. Even if you can't forgive me, even if you just want to shout at me some more, or if you want me to explain what a stupid, stupid cunt I was, then please call me. I'm in Paris for another week, then I'm going back to the States but I'll come back if you ask me to. You only have to ask.' And then very softly, 'I'm still in love with you, Nicky.'

A great, heavy vice tightened around my heart, and I thought instinctively, *oh my God, it's true, it's everything I feared. I'm still in love with him, too, even after what he did. We could still, it is possible...*

He touched my arm, the lightest touch, a touch infused with silver, then he turned and walked back to his car. He got in, started the engine, gave me the saddest smile and slowly drove off.

I stood in the doorway, still holding onto the door. The tears carried on rolling over my cheeks as if they would never stop and I thought, *if Guy comes around the corner now and sees me like this, he'll go into meltdown, I have to stop crying, I have to get a grip.*

And then I thought, *I can't hear the chainsaw, I haven't heard the chainsaw for a while now.* A cold, cold hand wrapped itself around my heart.

I stepped back inside the hallway and looked into the salon through the open French doors. He was sitting there on the edge of the sofa, watching me, his eyes glassy with tears too, and so, so white. His face was the colour of parchment.

'So, Nicole, your Anglo-Saxon found you,' he said, very quietly and then his eyes rolled back into his head and he crumpled sideways off the edge of the sofa and collapsed on the floor.

It was only then that I saw all the blood, saw his torn, dark-blue jeans stained black with blood, saw the pool of blood on the wooden floor around his feet, the deep-crimson stain spreading onto the corner of the rug.

I still don't know how the ambulance people understood anything, because I must have sounded absolutely hysterical when I called them. But they did, because the ambulance came screeching down the drive, full sirens and lights blaring, about fifteen minutes later.

I had spent the first ten minutes tying tea towels as tightly as I could above the massive, jagged slash above his knee on his left thigh. Fresh blood was still oozing out between the caked black blood in the wound. The last five minutes before the ambulance arrived were the longest and most terrifying of my life. I sat there on the floor, covered in my D'Artagnan's blood, cradling his head on my lap, watching his lips gradually turn blue, willing him with all my might to keep doing that faint, shallow breathing, bargaining with every god, demon, deity, being, to let him live because I couldn't contemplate the awful, yawning chasm of grief I would feel if he didn't.

Gazing through my tears at his long, dark eyelashes against his white, too white, skin, closed over those beautiful, expressive brown eyes that might never open again, I knew.

I stroked his beard, stroked it with my trembling fingers sticky with his blood, so that the hairs lay uniformly straight against his face, and I knew. It was knowledge that was blindingly, astonishingly clear: I wasn't in love with Karl. Karl was inconsequential. Maybe I hadn't yet accepted that the dream of our future was dead, but Karl was collateral damage from that dream. I could live without Karl – four years had proved I could. But I couldn't live without D'Artagnan.

They lifted his prone body and strapped him onto the stretcher quickly and efficiently, put an oxygen mask over his face, and wheeled him out to the ambulance. By then, a second medical car had arrived and one of its crew had set up the drip and was busy inserting it into Guy's arm as another of the medics started pulling the doors closed.

I made as if to get in to the ambulance too, but he put a hand out, stopped me. 'No.' He shook his head firmly. 'You must follow us. You can't come in the ambulance.' Then the doors slammed shut and the sirens started again, and it skidded off in a hail of stones and blue-and-red flashing lights, back out through the trees toward the road.

I stood in the drive watching it go, shaking from head to foot like the last leaf on the last tree post-nuclear apocalypse. The remaining medic took pity on me, put his arm around me, led me back inside and sat me down on the staircase. He asked very gently where my phone was and brought it to me. 'You need to call someone,' he said. 'You must not drive like this, you will have an accident.' He told me that Guy was being taken to the A&E in Cognac.

'Is he going to be alright?' was all I could manage in the tiniest whisper.

He tried to smile reassuringly, but it wasn't convincing. 'We hope so,' he said. And then he left too, in a cloud of dust and flashing lights.

Chapter Eighteen

I called Benoit. He answered immediately, and thankfully he was in Cognac. He came straight over. As soon as I heard his car, I ran outside, waiting for him to pull up so that I could get in the passenger side.

He got out as I reached for the door handle. 'Nicole! Stop, STOP!' He ran around the front of the car, grabbed my arm.

I tried to pull away and stared at him. 'Benoit, we need to go straight there. They've taken him to Cognac A&E. Please, quickly! We need to go there! NOW!'

'Nicole, try to calm down. They are not going to let you see him at first. Trust me, I know how this works. And you cannot go there to the hospital covered in blood because they won't let you in!'

I glanced down at myself. I'd been wearing a cream polo neck and pale blue jeans; there was blood all over them.

'Nicole please, you have to calm down. I promise you they will be doing everything they can for him, but you cannot go like that. Come, come back inside. You need to have a shower, get changed out of those clothes.' He started walking me back towards the château. 'Go now, upstairs, take a shower. Then we will go to the hospital.'

I don't really remember taking a shower; I know my hair was still wet when I came downstairs again, but I had taken ten milligrams of diazepam, even though for the first time ever I gagged when I tried to swallow it. I didn't want to take it in case it made me drop my guard, made me not vigilant enough, not present enough to insist that D'Artagnan didn't die. But I knew I had to, I needed it. The anxiety was already off the scale; who knew what my crazy bastard brain was capable of suggesting if things didn't – well, if he died....?

I held the glass of water with both hands while I drank and swallowed the pill.

I called Françoise on the way to the hospital. As I pressed her number on my phone, it struck me that this wouldn't be the first time she might be about to lose someone close to her. Although

I cried as I told her, I tried very hard to keep a lid on the hysteria. I could hear the shock in her voice; she told me she was leaving right away and would see me at the hospital. I managed to say, 'Please drive carefully, Françoise. Please be careful,' before she hung up.

They wouldn't let me into the A&E ward to see him, insisting politely, and then less politely, that I had to wait in the waiting room and that as soon as they had any news they would let me know. By then the diazepam was kicking in. I could feel the panic was a little dulled, but my eyeballs still felt like they were jumping about in my eye sockets.

Benoit sat next to me, his arm tight around my shoulders, saying soothingly, 'It's all right, Nicole, it's going to be alright. They are excellent here, they are very professional.' But all I wanted to do was snarl at him: 'How do you KNOW it's going to be alright? You didn't see him, he was nearly dead! Maybe he is *already* dead and they're just waiting until I'm calmer before they tell me.' I bit my lip hard, tried to stop everything in my vision vibrating.

Then I saw Françoise running up the ramp towards us, her face taut with fear, and I threw my arms around her as the automatic doors opened. She gave me the tightest hug, and we both started crying, holding onto each other like the last survivors in a war zone.

'How is he? How is he? Have you heard anything?' She released me, held me by my shoulders and looked searchingly into my eyes. I shook my head, sobbed, 'They won't tell me anything, they won't let me see him. I don't know anything. It's been nearly an hour.'

She immediately let go of me, marched up to the receptionist's desk and, after a short but very heated discussion, the nurse on reception got up crossly and went through the swing doors into the ward. After a seemingly interminable wait, she came back out and I heard her say to Françoise, 'He's stable, for the moment.'

And then the world went black, my knees gave way and I collapsed. Fortunately, Benoit caught me, or half-caught me, and I resurfaced, sitting between him and Françoise. She insisted I stay with my head between my knees while she instructed me to

'Breathe, breathe, breathe, he's going to be okay, Nicole. He's going to be okay,' and rubbed my back soothingly.

But I couldn't believe her. Every time my eyes closed, I saw his face, white, drained of life, his lips blue, the arm of the sofa drenched in dark blood, a pool of it glistening on the floor next to the sofa. I kept having to swallow the sickening awareness that it mightn't have been as bad if he'd just come straight into the house when he'd done whatever he'd done to his leg with the bastard chainsaw, and we'd called the ambulance straight away, or I'd driven him straight to the hospital. How long had he been there? When had it happened? How was it possible that Karl had arrived precisely at that moment to potentially fuck up my life all over again? I suddenly hated Karl with a passion I'd never thought possible, a visceral, almost tangible hatred.

I sat between Benoit and Françoise while we waited for more news and they gently quizzed me about what had happened. I started to say, 'I don't know. He was outside cutting up the tree with the chainsaw and then—' but I couldn't go any further because then I'd have to explain why I didn't know what had happened, that I'd only seen what had happened who knew how much later? Which just set the tears off again as the guilt washed through me. Because of me, because of my messy, fucked-up life, the situation had become much worse, and Guy might die as a result.

Françoise held my hand and stroked the back of it, making soothing noises. Benoit started telling me how many people he had known who had removed, or almost removed, this or that digit or limb, or suffered some traumatic injury involving a chainsaw, how they had all survived and were now back out there in the wilds of South-West France, happily juggling live chainsaws while swinging nonchalantly from tall trees, jousting playfully from the back of quadbikes. The thought of which did cause a small bubble of hysterical laugher to rise inside me.

They let me see him after the first blood transfusion and before he was wheeled into surgery to clean and stitch the wound. He was heavily sedated, but I took the tiniest comfort from the fact that his breath was misting the inside of the oxygen mask.

Perhaps, just perhaps, his face wasn't quite as white as it had been when I'd found him.

Then Françoise insisted that we go back to the château; she had been permitted to see him too, and had spoken to the doctor who told her there was nothing more they could tell us that evening. The surgeon would do his best, and Guy would be transferred to the intensive care ward for another transfusion after surgery. If anything changed, they would call; otherwise, we should come back in the morning and perhaps we would be able to see him.

When we got to the château, Françoise went straight to the baroque drinks cabinet in the salon, took a bottle of Benoit's cognac and two crystal tumblers and shepherded me ahead of her into the dining hall. She ignored the large bloodstain on the salon floor and the slightly smudged trail of blood across the creamy flagstones in the dining room, where Benoit had clearly tried to mop up while I had showered earlier.

'Sit, Nicole,' she commanded, and we both sat at the dining table while she poured us each half a glass of cognac.

'Drink! To your health! To his health!' We both took a big gulp. My hands were still shaking, and the liquor burned in the back of my throat, but it felt warm as it went down, and I felt the smallest de-contraction of the muscles in my shoulders.

'Do you think you can eat something?' she asked.

I stared at her. She looked exhausted, her normally pretty face gaunt, her eyes puffy. For a second I wondered what I looked like, and I had a vision of a petrified prehistoric cavewoman with wild, staring eyes and matted hair, which caused another bubble of hysterical laughter to start rising.

'No, not at all, I can't. Please don't make me.' I shook my head. 'I'm so grateful you're here, Françoise. I don't know what I would have done without you. I'm so sorry you have to go through this, too.'

She frowned. 'He's my younger brother, Nicole, this is where I need to be. With you, his wife, that he loves so much.' She took my hand, squeezed it. 'He's going to be alright. You have to believe that.'

'I don't dare to,' I whispered. 'I really want to, but I don't dare. And besides, it's all my fault.' The tears started rolling down my face again.

'Nonsense!' she said and took another sip of cognac, motioning to me to do the same.

'But you don't understand,' I started to say, then choked on the cognac. She waited until I stopped coughing, then went into the kitchen and got a glass of water. 'Where is your Valium, Nicole? Guy told me that you need to take Valium sometimes.'

I nodded numbly, pointed to my handbag slung over one of the chairs.

'Do you have enough for me too?' she asked, reaching for it.

I smiled, felt a tiny bit better that I wasn't the only pathetic one in need of pharmaceutical assistance. 'Knock yourself out. I've got loads.'

So, we both took ten milligrams and sipped our cognac, and she told me stories about their summers in the château as kids. While she was speaking, I resolved not to try to explain any more about what had happened that day because really, what did I want? Absolution from her? How could she give me that?

And that, of course, made me remember that today, for the first time in four years, I had seen Karl again, and I had to take another big gulp of cognac because those ripples should have been tsunamis, given the magnitude of the explosion they had brought about. Two direct missile hits in the same hour, my own personal Armageddon.

I started to feel woozy, but managed (without falling over although it was close) to feed the Muffins, who were by now shouting quite loudly about the poor quality of service in the establishment. And then Françoise and I went upstairs and both passed out, fully clothed, on the bed.

They let me see him in the afternoon the next day, but he was still heavily sedated with morphine and didn't wake up. I held his hand against my lips and willed him with all my might to survive, to get better. Afterwards we waited and waited in the corridor outside the ICU until the duty doctor finally appeared and gave us the lowdown.

Guy had done a significant amount of damage to his outer thigh muscle, but had just missed a fairly major artery; if the wound had been a centimetre further over, that would have meant almost certain death. I clutched at Françoise's arm at that, and the room wobbled, but I made an effort to focus on what the doctor was saying about recovery.

Fortunately, because Guy was quite fit, there hadn't been any organ damage due to the haemorrhaging (as far as they could tell). The surgeon had done the best he could to stitch up the muscle damage; although Guy was going to be in a lot of pain for a while, there was a good chance that, with rest and physical therapy, it would heal and he would regain the use of most – if not all – of his leg.

I made a Herculean effort not to start crying again when he said that, but my eyes were glassy as we thanked him and he hurried off.

When I went in on the third day, D'Artagnan's eyes were open and the oxygen mask was off. He gave the faintest of smiles when he saw me, and I started crying. I leaned over to kiss him as gently as I could.

'*Ma belle Nicole, je t'aime,*' he whispered. He was flying on morphine.

I smiled through the tears, took his hand, touched his forehead, smoothed an eyebrow, whispered back, 'I am so, so angry with you, my darling, darling man. How dare you nearly die?'

He smiled wanly, then his eyes closed again and he slipped back into unconsciousness.

On the fourth day, he was transferred out of intensive care into a private room. The nurse warned Françoise and I not to tire him, that he was still at risk and must rest.

'*Pfffft,*' he said when she left the room. 'I am much better already.' But he was still very pale, very drawn, and his eyes kept closing.

Françoise stayed for a while, telling him quietly that his children and his nieces were thinking about him and asking for news, how worried they had been. They would come and visit when he had recovered a bit more.

I stroked his hand gently while she talked, allowed myself to just look at him, to watch him and let a little ray of hope that perhaps he was going to be okay after all, to shine into my blackened soul. I'd spoken to Emmanuel and Charlotte every day. Although I felt it wasn't my place to say they shouldn't come to see him, I explained that it would be difficult while he was in the ICU, that he would probably appreciate them visiting when he was a bit better. Isabelle called me as soon as she heard and agreed that it was best that he didn't have lots of visitors yet, which put my mind at rest.

Françoise left the room, signalling to me that she was going to wait outside. I stayed there, stroking the back of his hand. He turned his head and fixed me with his beautiful brown eyes. He smiled a small, tired smile. 'How are you, *mon amour*?'

I shook my head slightly, tears welling. 'So, so relieved that you didn't die, my angel. Why didn't you say something? You should not have sat there not saying anything – you could have died. I love you so much, my darling, I can't imagine trying to live without you.'

'I am sorry *mon amour*,' he whispered, 'but I could not say something. It was very important that you talk to your Anglo-Saxon. This need to happen, *mon ange*.'

'Not at the risk of you dying, my darling.' I shook my head, wiped away the tears on my cheeks.

He did the very faintest approximation of a Gallic shrug; his eyelids were heavy.

And as I gazed at him it finally dawned on me; this proud, stubborn, arrogant man really was descended of D'Artagnan: he was a musketeer. He wasn't anything like Karl: supernaturally beautiful but ultimately mercurial, slippery, unable to ever really be held, relied on, trusted. D'Artagnan was everything Karl was not: brave, honourable, solid. He would never leave me. He would even die for me. I could trust him with my life.

D'Artagnan blinked slowly, that languid blink over those soft brown eyes that made me fall just one tiny bit more in love with him each time he did it. 'But I didn't die.' Another tired smile. 'I need to sleep now, Nicole. Will you stay with me?' And then he was out cold again.

I kissed his hand softly, put it down gently on the bed, tiptoed out to see Françoise. She heaved a big sigh of relief and gave me an enormous hug. 'He's going to be okay, Nicole. You don't need to worry anymore.' She stood back, smiling. 'But I wonder, do you think you would be okay if I go home for a few days? I will come back with the girls, probably on Wednesday when he is a bit better. Will you be okay on your own? Will you get a taxi home?'

'I'll be fine.' I hugged her again. 'I can't thank you enough. I think you saved my life, Françoise. I don't know what I would have done if you hadn't been here. I could never have coped. I'm so sorry for being so pathetic—'

'No Nicole, you were not pathetic, you were in shock. I know how it is. Please don't think you must excuse yourself. I will message you when I get back to Bordeaux. Look after my stupid little brother, give him a kiss from me, tell him I will see him in a few days.'

I spent the rest of the afternoon by his bed, holding his hand while he slept, and I also fell asleep, half across the side of the bed. We both woke with a start when the door banged open and the nurse came in to change his drip in the early evening, and told me crossly that I shouldn't still be there; visiting hours had ended two hours ago.

Guy rolled his eyes at me, and I rolled mine back at him, and then I left to find one of the mythical Cognac taxis, which was surprisingly easy as their home base seemed to be the hospital. Who knew?

The next day, a lot more alert but clearly in a lot of pain, Guy was half-sitting up in bed. He gave me a big smile when I walked in and I went straight to him, not stopping to put my bag down. He reached up to wrap his arms around me and I saw a bolt of pain flash across his face.

'Oweeee,' I empathised through clenched teeth as we hugged. 'Is the pain very bad?'

He shook his head. 'No, it's okay. But they have stopped the morphine, now I only have Doliprane in the drip. I just need to be careful.'

I moved back a little and sat on the edge of the bed. 'The doctor said that if you're sensible and you see a physio, the wound should heal up just fine. You were SO lucky, my darling. You *are* so lucky. It's going to be alright. I bloody TOLD you this would happen, didn't I?! Don't you remember? This is exactly what I said would happen! I can't believe you weren't more careful – what the fuck happened?'

He gave a little smile. '*Pfffft*. It was just a little mistake. I didn't pay attention for a minute. I look up, I see a car, I saw it was the Anglo-Saxon.'

My eyes opened wide, horrified. 'Oh my God ... that's just ... oh my God. Do you see my darling, do you see that I'm not good for you? Do you see, bad things happen when I'm—'

He lifted his hand, the one without the drip, put his finger firmly against my mouth. '*Non,* Nicole. I am very happy that this happen. This is not a bad thing. This need to happen. Your Anglo-Saxon, he needed to come to find you. And, *mon amour*, do not forget, it was not you with the chainsaw, it was me. I should have been more careful.'

He lifted one of my hands, kissed the back of it. 'I am fine, *mon ange*. There will be some pain, but I will get better. I am more worried about you, Nicole. I can see you haven't eaten anything for some days now. You are looking very thin, very tired. You need to eat something, *mon amour*. You have to get strong so you can help me when I come home.'

'Yes,' I said absently, still immersed in guilt at indirectly nearly having killed him. 'But that won't be for a while yet.'

'No,' he frowned. 'It will be very soon, maybe tomorrow.'

That sank in, and I stared at him. 'Are you mad? You have a massive wound in your leg that is going to take ages to heal, and you've just had three blood transfusions. I think it might be a while before you can come home.'

'Nonsense. I am bored, Nicole. The food is unbelievable *MERDE*, and the bed is uncomfortable. I want to go home. I want to sleep next to my wife, next to you. *Tu me manques, mon ange.*'

'I miss you too, darling man, but you'll probably have to stay in hospital for a while longer,' I insisted gently, feeling a vicarious twinge of sympathy for the nursing staff at having to look after a bored D'Artagnan, a D'Artagnan in pain.

'*Non,* Nicole. It is normal to go home as soon as possible, then the nurse will come every day to the château and continue to treat the wound.'

It seems this is true. The French health system has a couple of weird little quirks; as soon as you are considered to be stable, out of danger and no longer need to be on a drip, you are dismissed. All further hospital care, the re-dressing of wounds, the daily anti-coagulant and any other injections, are provided by a small army of local, independent nurses, one of whom will come to your house every day and treat you until you have recovered.

It can, however, be a bit tiring for the patient's partner.

But I didn't know all this at the time, so after he'd insisted for the fifth time that I go and ask the nurse – 'Just go, go, Nicole. There he is, that nurse there. He's just outside the room, go now, go and ask him' – I relented and did so. I sounded very hesitant while I asked, fearing the nurse would think I was a bit mad, that I was an uncaring wife demanding that her husband be released from their care long before he was ready.

But the nurse did a Gallic shrug, peered in at Guy through the door for a minute, went back to the nurses' station and looked at his chart. 'Maybe the day after tomorrow,' he said. 'If he continues to improve.'

Which shocked me. I went back into the room and told Guy. 'Why not tomorrow?' he asked crossly.

'Oh my God, Guy! You nearly died five days ago, and you want to go back home tomorrow? You can't even walk!'

'Yes, I can. I have supports.' He meant crutches, but I knew he hadn't used them yet, because I'd arrived a bit earlier than I should have and seen him having a bed bath. From the male nurse. He must have loved that. Perhaps it was why he was so crotchety.

Chapter Nineteen

We brought him home on the Monday, the sixth day after he'd been admitted. Benoit and I steadied him on the crutches after we'd carefully extracted him from the car, walking slowly beside him as he negotiated the stone steps, resting at the bottom of the staircase before the daunting, gargantuan task of reaching the first floor.

By the time we eased him down on the edge of the bed, Guy was white with pain, a cold sweat on his forehead, and he lay back against the pillows I'd stacked with a stifled groan, eyes closed. I had to swallow hard, several times, to stop myself crying. It's horrible to see anyone in so much pain, but it was particularly difficult to see my energetic, bombastic D'Artagnan so destroyed by it.

Françoise, the girls and Conor came on the following Wednesday morning and we had lunch in the bedroom with him. She'd stopped by one of his favourite Thai restaurants in Pessac and they'd prepared an entire three-course meal for six, which I was very grateful for because food was already becoming a problem subject. Guy was astounded that I couldn't even make an omelette.

'*Bah* Nicole, it's really easy! You just have to mix the eggs together with some milk, add some seasoning and cook it on the gas. And then put some mushrooms, and some cheese and maybe some prosciutto into it and, when it's cooked, fold it over. It's easy!'

'I'll try,' I said, in a small voice.

I brought him all of the ingredients scrambled up together on the plate, to which I'd added a sprig of parsley in a feeble attempt to disguise the mess.

He looked at it, looked at me, laughed and shook his head. But he ate it because he was hungry, and I'd bought lovely fresh, warm bread from the boulangerie. The next day I discovered that they also sold bottles of homemade vegetable soup, so I bought several of those which he was also surprisingly enthusiastic about, given the lack of dead animal.

Charlotte came, stayed for the weekend and spent hours playing chess with him (which gave me a bit of free time to continue honing my plans for Phase 2(b) of Project Bonjour 21C!: A Third Bathroom Is Not Excessive. It was also a wonderful relief because one of the qualities Charlotte had inherited from him was a love of food and cooking.

She took over in the kitchen and made him duck *à l'orange* and *dauphinoise* potatoes and buttery green beans, and they spent the whole meal arguing about the best way to cook *bœuf bourguignon*, which was wildly boring for me to listen to.

He spoke to Emmanuel on the phone and fondly discouraged him from making the journey on condition that he come for Christmas instead, with his new Italian girlfriend.

But Charlotte left after the weekend and D'Artagnan became bored. He insisted on coming very gingerly downstairs the following day, clutching the banister with one hand and leaning heavily on my shoulder with the other.

'Are you sure you should be trying to do this now?' I asked for the tenth time as he gritted his teeth and breathed heavily. We were halfway down the stairs.

'Stop asking me that Nicole, *MERDE*!'

We finally got to the bottom of the stairs and I handed him his crutches while he leaned against the wall, a sheen of sweat on his pale forehead.

I bit my lip hard in an attempt not to say 'I told you so' – or rather 'You IDIOT man, I TOLD you, the nurse TOLD you, you're supposed to STAY IN FUCKING BED and not try to go downstairs yet!!' But once he'd got a little more colour in his face, he made his way slowly into the kitchen on the crutches.

I brought a chair from the dining room into the kitchen. He stepped back from perusing the fridge contents and looked at it, then at me. 'What is that for Nicole?'

'In case you get tired, my angel.'

'No, take it away, I won't get tired, it will get in the way.' Crossly, 'And Nicole, we need to go to the shop, to the *marché*. There is no food in the fridge.'

I put the chair back in the dining room, sighed, took a deep breath and went back into the kitchen. 'Guy, darling, it might be a little too soon for shopping trips, don't you think? Given that it took twenty minutes to get down the stairs?'

Disdainful sniff. 'Tomorrow then. Or Wednesday. The *marché* in Cognac is good on Wednesday.'

'Didn't Charlotte say she had cooked some meals for you? She told me she'd left some in a Tupperware in the fridge – chicken casserole, or something?'

'Yes, it is there. But I am bored of that. I had some of that yesterday. Anyway, my leg is sore again. Nicole, can you go and get some more Doliprane for me?'

'You only had a tablet about two hours ago, don't you remember? It's too soon to take more.' Thinking, *Oh God, I really don't know how we are going to get through several weeks, or worse, months of this.*

'Please?' he said, ignoring what I'd just said.

I shrugged, tried not to make the eyeroll too obvious. 'Okay, I guess you can take a bit more every now and then. But really, Guy, the reason why your leg is sore is because you're not supposed to be coming downstairs yet. You're supposed to be resting in bed!'

'You should not believe everything the nurse tells you, Nicole. They are very cautious you know. I need to keep moving, otherwise the muscle will not heal.'

Which was not at all what the nurse, nor the doctor, had said. I went upstairs to get the paracetamol, feeling slightly helpless and slightly tearful. D'Artagnan, incapacitated and in pain, was proving to be extremely difficult to deal with.

Thankfully, his mood improved slightly as he pottered in the kitchen. He put on some music and we had lunch together in the dining hall (him: omelette with smoked salmon and spinach; me: *sans* smoked salmon). And fresh bread and fruit yoghurt to finish, after which he began to look decidedly drained, so I persuaded him (without too much resistance) that perhaps it was time to go upstairs again.

That took another agonisingly slow twenty minutes and quite a lot of swearing about his *putain* leg, the *putain* doctor who had not fixed it properly, and generally the whole *putain* world that clearly had it in for him. Then, thank God, he slept for a bit.

I lay beside him, his arm around me holding me close under the soft merino-wool throw. It was raining, and the room was gloomy in the half-light as I drowsed, waking to see him watching me, stroking my hair away from my temple with his thumb. I smiled sleepily at him. He smiled gently back at me, continuing to stroke my hair. 'Can I say something, Nicole? About your Anglo-Saxon?' he asked quietly.

I sighed, nodded. 'Yeah, sure.'

'*Bah, mon ange...* I think you need to forgive him. You need to talk to him and forgive him. Not for him, but for you. I don't really know what happened, but you are carrying this around in you and you will never be rid of it if you don't forgive him.'

The tears welled up in me as I realised he had heard most, if not all, of the conversation Karl and I had. I decided to tell him all of it, everything, right from the beginning: how insanely in love I had been with Karl; the drugs and the madness; the deception and the pain; the wrecked dreams of a family and a future with him; the terrible sense of loss, betrayal and grief.

I hesitated before I told him about what had happened in Ireland, what I had found out, that terrible, ironic catastrophe. But then I forced myself to form the words, to speak them out loud; the fact that I could have had that child, if I hadn't fallen. Because I knew that if I didn't it would carry on festering in that dark little corner of my soul.

And I told him that, finally, a state of acceptance had prevailed. I could accept what had happened and I was calm again as I stood there in the pale-blue house on the harbour at Cobh, watching the ships and the ferries coming in and going out again.

I cried while I told him, and he cried too. He held me tightly against his side until I'd finished talking and gradually the endless flow of tears began to subside, until I lay quietly against him feeling drained and exhausted.

And also, somehow, cleansed. Saying the words aloud, acknowledging the enormity of the love I'd felt for Karl, and admitting to the agony when he finally broke my heart enabled the tight little knot of anguish that I had been shielding from myself, from Guy, from everyone else for all those years, to unfurl. And a sensation of relief, of peace, washed over me.

I rang Karl a couple of days after that. We didn't speak for very long because I didn't feel there was much more to say; I had no more anger, just a residual sadness. I told him that I forgave him and I heard that he was crying when he said, 'Thank you, Nicky. I can't tell you how much that means to me.'

I told him that I loved the man I had married, I told him I loved Guy, that there was no reason for him to continue to think there was something between us. He was quiet when I said that, after I said that.

After I hung up, I didn't cry. I stared out of the window at the naked poplar trees across the lawn, the late-afternoon winter sun colouring their tips gold. I took a deep breath, let it out again, probed very cautiously at the dense space inside me that used to be seething, tortured and raw, and found that, while it was still tender to the touch, it was now unencumbered, empty.

Then I rang Jules. I told her I had called Karl, that I had forgiven him, that I was over him. It felt so ... incredibly liberating to say the words out loud. It made me feel that I was finally an adult, someone who had control of her life.

I also asked her to give me the name of the therapist she had told me about that a close friend of hers had recommended, a therapist who would do sessions over the phone. I decided that I was going to get a grip on my life, on the panic attacks. I was going to start sorting that crap out.

After I'd said goodbye to Jules, I looked at myself in the hallway mirror at the top of the stairs and I smiled at me. Life was good. I felt calm, clear-headed and – proud. I felt as if I was in control of my life, my destiny; it was a new and very pleasant sensation indeed.

D'Artagnan's leg was healing very gradually and he was still in a lot of pain, but his mood was improving in proportion to his mobility. Both Emmanuel and his girlfriend Christina, and

Charlotte and her boyfriend Felipe, were coming to spend Christmas with us, and the Christmas Eve meal Guy was planning was like something out of *Babette's Feast*.

I had to stop him when he began describing to me in detail the main course he was preparing, which seemed to involve stuffing one dead bird inside another slightly larger dead bird, and then inside an even larger one and so on, like some sort of barbaric, culinary Russian-doll horror story.

One evening just before Christmas, I was upstairs taking a leisurely shower and washing my hair in our beautiful bathroom. I then moved on to Heaven and slathered myself in luxurious Dyptique body lotion before descending, head to toe in cashmere.

Guy seemed happier, almost pain-free that evening as I wandered into the kitchen. Pink Martini was playing loudly on the stereo and the deeply mournful cello chords of 'La Soledad' were just starting as I wandered into the kitchen.

He swept me up in his arms, eyes all dreamy and soft, and sang the whole song to me in his most seductive voice while he half-twirled, half-hobbled me around the kitchen. I had first heard the song in the exhilaratingly breathless, early days of our relationship when he took me to San Sebastian, or Donostia in the Basque language. We were in a lively *pintxos* bar in the thronged old part of the town, both a little drunk, when it started playing; he held me closely against his warm, strong body as he leaned against the bar, crowded with locals and tourists alike, and he translated the Spanish for me line by line, his breath warm against my ear. And then we kissed, drowning in the refrain, all swooping, bruised cello and Pepe Raphael's tormented baritone, and afterwards, when the song and the kiss finally ended, I felt like I had just experienced the most cosmically romantic moment of my entire life, of all life.

It also put an end to his slightly outraged incredulity that I was continuing to refuse to try the many and varied *pintxos,* displayed alluringly (if you like your food unidentifiably colourful) under the glass counter, on the grounds that pretty much none of them were vegetarian.

'But this is why we come to Donostia, Nicole, to eat *pintxos*! This is what it is famous for! How can you not want to try them?

You can at least eat the fish ones, the seafood ones. How can you not try these?!'

'Where, in the word "vegetarian" Guy, are you finding the words "fish" and "seafood"? Vegetarian does actually mean vegetables. You do know this about me – I think we've discussed it before?'

'Yes, but Nicole, I have vegetarian friends, they also eat fish.'

'I think you will find these friends of yours are what is known as "pescatarian". Or otherwise, they are that slightly misleading tribe of vegetarians who insist on describing themselves as vegetarian, and then add "but I do eat fish", which is fine. I'm not judging them, but it's not correct. Either you're vegetarian, or you're not.'

I was conscious while I was saying this of my sneaky little *moules marinières* habit, but given that none of the *pintxos* looked as though they were in any way affiliated with mussels, it didn't seem necessary to confuse him on that point.

Those were the early days of our relationship, and I had not yet learned how, where and when to stand my ground. The taming of D'Artagnan had hardly begun. I had eventually relented and taken a bite of one of his *pintxos* with some sort of fish paste/olive combination on it, but I didn't like it, and there was some epic eye rolling at the face I pulled. I liked the Manchego cheese and the local Idiazabal cheese very much, though, and the *tortilla de patatas* was perfectly palatable (except for the potatoes).

So 'La Soledad' intervened that evening and banished all thoughts of disputes about food. I suppose, after that night, it became 'our' song and every time I hear it, I think of that night in San Sebastien and am floored by how wonderfully, achingly romantic it was, and how intoxicated I was by him.

And, when the song ended that wintry evening in December, he leaned against the granite counter top in the kitchen and we kissed softly and my heart felt light, joyful and filled to overflowing with love for D'Artagnan.

Further info...

If you enjoyed reading 'Taming D'Artagnan', watch out for the second novel in the series of three, 'Deceiving D'Artagnan' due out end February 2023, and please visit my Facebook page at 'Fi Whyms, Author' for further updates.

Many thanks Publish Nation for their invaluable assistance, and to BespokeBookCovers.com for the gorgeous cover!

Printed in Great Britain
by Amazon